DEAD STARS
AND
STONE ARCHES
A COLLECTION OF UTAH HORROR

Dead Stars and Stone Arches:
A Collection of Utah Horror

Copyright © **2022, Timber Ghost Press**
Published by Timber Ghost Press
Printed in the United States of America
Edited by: Beverly Bernard
Cover Art and Design by: Greg Chapman
Interior Design: Firedrake Designs

Print ISBN: 978-1-7365867-9-2
Ebook ISBN: 978-1-7365867-8-5
Library of Congress Control Number: 2022934318

www.TimberGhostPress.com

CONTENTS

Foreword   vii
Betty Rocksteady

THIS ONCE WAS A SEA   1
Lehua Parker

FEEDING A DARK MUSE   15
C.H. Lindsay

EYE OF EUROPA   17
Jonathan Reddoch

IN ABSENTIA LUCIS   19
C.R. Langille

STANDING SILO   35
Cygnus Perry

THE WASATCH HORROR   37
Derek Hutchins

THE TERROR BEGRUDGINED   49
Daniel Cureton

TICK WAY   51
Paul Starkey

SOUR   67
Joshua P. Sorensen

SKIN DEEP—THE CITY OF DEMONS   71
Joseph Hope

AWAY GAME   73
Michael Jess Alexander

LIFE OF A LEPER   85
Steven Dee Kish

DEEP WITHIN   87
Carter Lappin

GUARDIAN 91
Heidi Voss

NEBULOUS STRIKE IN MINN. 95
Nnadi Samuel

DERELICT 99
K. Scott Forman

INSATIATE 107
C.H. Lindsay

HOLY GRAIL 109
William R.D. Wood

SHOOTING STAR 121
Joseph Hope

FOG OF SAND 123
D.J. Moore

WISH BONES 141
Kristi Petersen Schoonover

HABEAS CORPUS: IN WHICH I 151
DEMAND MY FATHER'S BODY
Nnadi Samuel

FLESH AND FEATHERS 153
Nicholas J. Evans

THE MOUNTAIN THRONE 167
Cygnus Perry

ME AND MINE 169
Eric Nirschel

SHADOWBORN 183
C.H. Lindsay

THE LYING SKY 185
Levi Robinson

THE DANCER IN THE CLOUDS 203
Cygnus Perry

THE BEAUTY PARLOUR 205
SJ Townend

THAT SHADOW ON THE WALL   219
Bryan McEntire

THE VOICE IN THE NIGHT   235
Mickie Bolling-Burke

THE LETTER FROM SOMEWHERE   247
Cygnus Perry

SCARLET'S FINAL GIFT   257
JM Cullen

THE ESCALANTE PORTAL   277
Chad A. B. Wilson

SOME DISSEMBLING REQUIRED   295
Donald Evans

OGDEN DAWN   299
Arthur Goodhill

SANDCASTLES   305
Henry Snider

About the Authors   331

FOREWORD

BETTY ROCKSTEADY

Deep down, we know. We try to hide it. We set goals, we cling to routines, we dive deeper into our lives. But we know.

Anything can happen.

Anything.

There is very little we can hope to understand. We believe what science says about the earth and the universe and our place in it. We ground ourselves in reality, or in how it has been explained to us. We trust history to show us the mistakes we've made and we try not to make more, both personal and on a larger level. We reassure ourselves with the things we know. We dismiss the things we don't. Some of us turn to religion and take comfort there.

I do too, mostly, a little bit of each, believing in the cold reassurance of science, or sometimes the wonder and mysticism of religion. But always there is the undercurrent of something else that sneaks in, that leaves me breathless, the way the stars sometimes seem to move in the sky and whisper that there is too much for me to ever hope to understand.

I think we all feel those moments, especially alone. It's easier to dismiss in company, when you have friends and family around to distract from the deepening wonder beneath. But then there's a prophetic dream, or a late night outside when you can feel the twisting of something else behind you, the suggestion of things too large to hope to understand. The look on your lover's face that makes you realize you can never see all the way inside, when you realize they have their own stars swirling in their head, and someone else entirely could lurk beneath their face.

Deep down, we know that anything is possible. We know that the shadows could come closer, the stars could rotate in the skies. We could wake up tomorrow, discard our virtual reality goggles and step into something entirely different. We could never wake up, remain locked in dream logic for eternity, turning, turning, turning forever.

The only thing I know is that I know nothing.

The only thing I know is that it would only take an instant to disprove the concrete reality I think I see. One moment could change everything forever. I could hear insects whispering secrets I thought long forgotten. The earth could open up beneath me, stairs could descend into her depths, and I could turn away from those secrets, pretend I never saw them, spend the rest of my life convincing myself I saw nothing at all.

I can feel it, beneath everything. Reality is fragile. Our sanity? Even more fragile. What would it take for me to believe in something that is now incomprehensible to me? What would it take to convince me?

Our familiar neighborhoods hold secrets behind every door. Every patch of woods hides unseen depths of life and love and death. Even our own heads hold countless secrets. My brain filters out information constantly, hides things from me, focuses on what it wants me to know. What it can allow me to know.

Our lives feel rich and vibrant and full. Or cold and small and scared. Most of us get a taste of both. But regardless, they feel important to us. They feel big. But we are the merest blip of time, the universe blinks and entire generations are forgotten, dust settles, the world moves on.

I believe there are moments in our lives where the spell breaks. Our sureness of the world is challenged. The monsters are real. There is something beneath our feet that rumbles and chews its way through the earth. There is something in the sky that peels back and lets us see swirling meat and guts and something too huge to even notice us destroys us all, in an instant. The moment when we see the horrors are real, our precarious sanity is exposed, and everything changes. Forever.

There are very real monsters to tackle. We are in the midst of a pandemic that's killed tens of thousands as it ripples through the globe. Before that, wars fought by people with more money and power than most of us can ever dream of, countless casualties for motivations we as individuals can never fully understand. Already, our lives are one of the smallest things in the universe. Does that make them less precious, or more?

And outside of our neighborhood concerns, our country's concerns, our planetary concerns, what else is there? The scope of time in the universe suggests that humans are only the merest blip on her face. What is our true purpose?

Is it all chance?

What else might be out there?

Cosmic horror explores some of these themes. It opens our eyes to what may lie beyond the veil. It explores ancient curses, Gods older than human society who barely notice us, secret societies with occult missions and the entities they serve.

But really, it explores us, humans both as a species and as individuals, and how we cope with things that are too big to hold in our minds. With so much outside of us controlling our lives, we must explore ourselves, we must live in those moments that open us up to so much more, and explore the universe, and our place within it.

Timber Ghost Press has carefully chosen this variety of cosmic horror fiction and poetry to explore these themes, while maintaining a connection to Utah. *Dead Stars and Stone Arches* invites you to dive into the Great Salt Lake to witness the ancient mysteries that lay beneath its waters, to explore the occult depths of its pine forests, to allow the sand dunes to wash over you, and as the grains of sand gradually erode your flesh, to discover the strange secrets carved into your bones.

THIS ONCE WAS A SEA
LEHUA PARKER

From the safety of her rented SUV, Leticia Greenbaum watched rain fall in sheets, obscuring the sign over the main doors of a big industrial building painted in shades of deep-sea green. Squinting, she could just make out the logo for Salt of the Earth Inc., and the words Field Operations Center, Gilgamesh, Utah.

This must be the right place, she thought, throwing it into park and cutting the engine. *What a shithole. Nothing but sage brush for miles.*

A senior account manager with Bountiful Insurance, it had been more than a minute since she'd last done an onsite appraisal. Back in Seattle, most of her time was spent wining and dining big corporate clients and signing off spreadsheets, but this claim was too big to leave to junior adjusters.

Damn Janice. This is her account. She should've been the one to drive to BFE Utah. What a baby. Appendectomies are no big deal.

Leticia unplugged her phone from the console and slipped it into her briefcase. *Whatever. Just get through it. Take a few statements, snap some photos, and put it all in the rearview.*

Easy-peasy. She checked her Fitbit and scowled. *Too much sitting. But if I hurry, I can make the last flight and get more steps in at the airport.*

Fiddling with the keys, Leticia was looking down when something struck her window. She looked up. Sasquatch waved. She shrieked, the sound rising like a chainsaw through a brick wall.

Sasquatch jumped back. "Whoa, there! Sorry, ma'am. Didn't mean to startle you. I'm Barry, Barry Giles. You the adjuster?" Barry was six foot six in stocking feet with a barrel chest and beard that rivaled Santa's. When he was sure she wasn't going to pull a gun, he shifted his golf umbrella to his other hand and leaned forward, peering through the SUV's window.

Not Sasquatch, but maybe his cousin.

Leticia swallowed her heart back into her chest and nodded.

"Oh, good. You found us." Barry hefted his umbrella. "It's raining." *No shit, Sherlock.* "Thought I'd come get you."

Yeah, not getting that close to you, buddy. Nice try. "Thanks, but I'm fine." Leticia pulled the door handle. The dome light flashed on.

"You sure? It's coming down cats and dogs—"

"Yes." She tried to ease the door open.

Barry raised the umbrella higher. "It's no trouble, ma'am."

"Could you back up a little? The door—"

"Oh, sure. Careful, it's—" Leticia swung her leg out, stepped down, and sank, cold sludge filling her Miu Miu loafers. "—muddy."

"What the actual—"

"Yeah," Barry sighed. "Parking lot's six inches deep. Look, you got boots or something? Hip waders, maybe?"

Rain ran from the edge of the umbrella down the collar of her shirt. "No."

"They told you this was a flood claim, right?"

"I—"

Barry shook his head. "You can't walk in those. Just slip them off and leave them. We'll find you something else inside."

Standing in the lobby and dripping on the cement floor, Leticia began questioning her life choices. Icy red clay oozed between her toes, her oyster-colored nail polish looking like rotting teeth in a charnel-house mouth. Her pants were soaked and muddy to the knee, and her hair hung in wet tangles, smearing her glasses.

"Found 'em." Barry came back with a pair of irrigation boots, a Tyvek suit, and a couple of shop rags. "Best I could do." Leticia took a shop rag and blotted her hair. He held out the boots. "They'll be big, but better than barefoot. I tucked a pair of socks in them." Leticia blinked, her eyes wide through her streaked and spotted glasses, her mascara bleeding like a bruise. Barry looked away. "Don't worry," he said. "They're clean."

Leticia set her briefcase on the reception desk and took the clothes. "Where is everybody?"

Barry shrugged. "Corporate sent them all home. Salt's not worth anything wet."

"You're claiming total loss?"

"Millions of years ago, this was an inland sea. Cut off from the ocean, the water dried up and left rich deposits of pure salt just below the surface. We're a shaft operation— rooms and pillars, the deepest less than 300 feet. Our mining operation is a matter of scooping and loading trucks. All the salt gets sent to our packing facility in Price —easiest thing in the world." He eyed her ruined power suit. "They really didn't tell you how bad it was?

"I'm not from the Utah office. I'm from Seattle."

"Oh, good. So you know about rain." Leticia looked at him, nonplussed. Barry cleared his throat. "Like I said, I'm Barry, the Operations Supervisor. I didn't catch your name."

"Leticia Greenbaum, Senior Account Manager."

"Well, Letty—"

"Leticia."

Barry paused, then nodded. "If you'd like, you can change in my office, Ms. Greenbaum. I'll wait in the back. The main entrance to the mine is through there."

She picked up her briefcase. "There's paperwork. Forms and interviews—"

"Of course, and we'll get right to them. But there's something you need to see first."

"Barry, I know what flooding looks like. This ain't my first rodeo."

He bit his lip, careful not to catch her eye or look at her muddy bare feet. "Didn't think it was," he said, shaking his woolly mammoth head. "But nothing I say will make sense unless you see it first." He turned and pointed. "Office is that way, first door to the left." The overhead lights flickered. "Power's iffy. The lines are unstable. I left you a lit lantern on my desk. Bring it when you come back. You won't need your briefcase where we're going. You can leave it on my desk."

"I need photos."

"Up to you, then."

As she turned to head to his office, the big picture window in the lobby flexed; the cement beneath her feet trembled.

"Whoa! That was a big 'un," said Barry.

Leticia smiled. "Not really. I've felt worse." Like two

furry caterpillars, Barry's eyebrows raised. "Dad was in the Air Force," she added.

"Sonic boom?" Barry asked. "You think that was a sonic boom?"

She lifted her chin and looked down her nose. "Of course. I grew up around them. They're no big deal."

"Nope," said Barry. "Not a sonic boom. That's coming from the ground beneath us, not the sky." Barry paused. "Feel that one? That one's just a little baby."

If she hadn't been paying attention, she would have missed the slight sway beneath her feet, like standing with your toes on the end of the dock on a warm spring day. "What—?"

Barry shrugged. "Things shift in a salt mine."

"Even before the flood?"

Barry cocked his head as if listening to something far away. "They're more frequent now. Water's filling spaces it hasn't in aeons. Things bubble up." He stepped back, rubbing his face and smoothing his beard. "You're shivering. I can see the goosebumps from here. Why don't you get changed? Sooner begun, sooner done." He spun on his heel and headed deeper into the building. "Don't forget the lantern," he called. "We're going to need it."

Alone in Barry's office, Laticia rolled her eyes. *All he needs is a framed photo of the company picnic.* On the wall next to his desk were his geology diploma from the University of Southern Utah and a framed certificate of mining safety training. On the bookcase behind his desk were rows of heavy three-ring binders lightly coated with dust and a photo of the Giles family on vacation, three strapping boys and an uncomfortably tall girl at the beach. But what really caught her eye was the crystal ball paperweight glistening in the lamplight. There was something in the middle bigger than her fist. She picked it up.

Heavy. She rolled it between her palms. *Smooth. Polished.* She peered closer. *WTF? Is that a bug?* She counted. *Eight legs and two lobster claws. Not a bug. Some kind of crab, maybe? And what are those things coming out of its head? Antennae? Mandibles?* She tipped it into her other hand to see it from another angle. She held it closer to the lantern. *It looks like a flea mated with a king crab. What's that on its belly? Some kind of octopus sucker?* She shuddered, remembering how her father lit a match to burn leeches off her legs the summer her cousin pushed her into the pond.

Soulless. Eyeless. A monster. Who keeps a monster on his desk? She dropped it back on the pile of papers.

As she turned away, shadows flickered and danced in the crystal. *Did it twitch? Was the right claw now higher than the left?* Leticia closed her eyes. *Stop. Just stop it,* she thought. *You're letting Sasquatch and the creepy mine get to you.* The hair stood on the back of her neck. She slapped at it. *It's just water dripping. Nothing's crawling down your spine. You're freaking out over nothing.*

She glanced at her watch and made a promise to herself. *It doesn't matter how late it gets. I'm not staying around here. I'll drive to Vegas to catch a flight if I have to.*

Leticia slipped off her wet pants, wiping the mud off her feet as best she could. She slid into the jumpsuit, zipped it up, and rolled the sleeves to her elbows and the hem to her ankles. Big wads of rough cloth bunched around her body, rustling like a tarp in the wind whenever she moved.

As much as she tried to ignore it, she kept glancing at the paperweight.

It's probably a fancy prop from a movie like Jurassic Park *or some D&D gamer crap. What a surprise. Sasquatch is a twelve-year-old nerd living in a salt mine in the desert.* She pulled on the boots, three sizes too big. *All I need is a red clown nose. What a shitshow.*

She looked at her beautiful alligator briefcase and shook her head. *I'll just take my phone and snap a few photos. Barry can email me the claim forms later. I'm not staying one second longer than I have to.*

Another thought crossed her mind. *I'm going to have to fly home in a Tyvek suit and irrigation boots.*

Screw it. There's always a Walmart. Nobody will look twice if I walk in like this. No matter what, you're never the weirdest person in a Walmart.

When Leticia waddled up to the entrance to the mine, phone in one hand, lantern in the other, Barry held out a hardhat. She just looked at him. "Regulations," he said, taking the lantern.

Leticia jammed the hardhat on her head. Too big; it wobbled. Barry held the lantern high as she tried to adjust the fit. It was useless. To keep the brim from covering her eyes or knocking her glasses down her nose, she had to keep her head tipped up.

Perfect, she thought, *just perfect. I'm ready for the cover of* Vogue. *Hillbilly-desert Chic.* Barry shifted his weight, swaying a bit as another wave buckled beneath them.

Leticia glared. *He's enjoying this. Making the city girl feel small.*

Barry said, "Did you see the thing on my desk?"

Leticia narrowed her eyes. "The picture of your family on vacation? Cute kids."

"Not the photo. The thing next to the lantern. It was round." He jiggled the lantern as if to jog her memory.

Nope. Not going to feed the fanboy. Leticia pursed her lips and shook her head.

Barry said, "It was in a clear salt ball sitting on a pile of papers."

"Like a paperweight?"

"Yeah, that's it." His eyes sparkled.

"No, I didn't notice anything like that." Like butter wouldn't melt in her mouth.

"Oh. Well." Barry frowned. "I really hoped you would."

"I'm not into gaming," she said.

He perked up. "So you did see it."

Throw him a bone. Get this show on the road. "I might've. What was in it?"

"We don't know."

"What?"

Barry rubbed the back of his neck. "We find them sometimes in the salt. Most are like the one on my desk, encased in a flawless salt crystal. They're perfectly round and usually the size of a quarter. The guys saved that one for me because it's so big."

"How…thoughtful."

"I'm not explaining this well," said Barry. "Look. We used to sell them for a couple of bucks in the gift shop."

"You have a gift shop?"

"Behind reception. For school kids and tour groups. People like big machines."

Leticia adjusted her glasses. "Who doesn't?" she said, like someone who really doesn't.

"It's a goodwill thing. We give them a little bag of salt at the end. We don't charge admission, but we do use the proceeds from the gift shop to support the local Sub for Santa. Me and some of the guys do the local Christmas Eve deliveries. It's fun."

"Of course," Leticia said, swallowing a yawn.

He held up a hand. "We're getting off track. None of this is important."

She tipped hardhat off her glasses, saying, "It's your story. I'm just here for the ride."

"Here's the thing." Barry swayed as another shockwave rolled by. Leticia let it pass through her. It was surprising what you got used to.

Barry said, "About a month ago, I got an email from a grad student from USU's School of Paleontology. His nephew'd showed him one of our salt-bug balls, and he wanted to come see the mine. He thought the salt-bugs were related to trilobites—or were at least that old. But the lower levels had already started to flood, so I put him off and just sent him a couple of samples. We continued to email and text. I sent him some photos. He was curious why the salt-bugs balls weren't squished like trilobites or fish fossils. He thought they were...I dunno, too *plump*. He was running tests. Yesterday I got another text. The salt-bugs are not related to trilobites or crabs. They're even older."

Leticia opened her mouth, but before she could say a word, another not-sonic boom rumbled, sending ripples through puddles like a crocodile's wake through the bayou. "Are we safe here, Barry?" she asked. "All this shaking and booming makes me anxious. I feel like it's all going to collapse."

Barry adjusted his grip on the lantern. "Don't worry. The mine won't collapse, even if it fully floods. The supports are designed for this. *Over*-designed if you ask me. You should know—it's one of the riders on the insurance policy."

The ground rumbled again, sending shockwaves through her toes to rattle her too loose helmet down over her eyes. "You sure about that?" she asked, pushing it back.

"Yeah. The ground's already saturated. It's been raining for forty days and forty nights in the mountains north of here."

"Forty days? That's—"

"Biblical?"

Leticia grimaced. "I was going to say *a lot*."

"I forgot you're from Seattle. Maybe it's not so unusual for you."

"Barry, I'm trying to make a flight."

"Let's get to it, then. This way." At the small side gate to the mine's cavernous entrance, he paused, looking back at her. "You're insured, right?"

"Hilarious, Barry. Now open the damned gate."

He unlocked the gate, swinging it wide, and walked to an electric panel. "Leave it open," he said as he threw the main light switch. The high bay fixtures overhead flashed once, twice, then sizzled. He slapped at the panel, flipping breakers. "Son of a bitch!"

"Barry?"

"Yeah, that's what I was afraid of. Here, let me—" Barry reached over and turned on the headlamp in her hardhat. The warm yellow glow hit Barry squarely in the chest. "That's better. Follow me. Watch your step. It angles down from here."

At the entrance, the first thing Leticia noticed was the smell—salty, briney, like kelp beds at low tide along the shores of Puget Sound. She tipped her hardhat back, the light shining more on the ceiling than the walkway and followed Barry into the gloom.

Barry walked out on a platform and stood by a railing. He motioned her closer. "This is the observation deck. From here you can see all the way down into the center of the mine, about 100 feet to the floor. From there we have a few main shafts that go deeper. A conveyor belt runs along the right. Normally, we back the trucks in over there."

"Oh my God," she whispered. "The water is level with the platform." She took out her phone and snapped a few pictures, the red and white walls twinkling in the flash.

"Yeah. It's a giant pool. Let me light it for perspective." From his pocket Barry pulled out a flashlight tied to a thin rope. "Waterproof," he said as he turned it on and chucked it into the water like a fishing line. The light spiraled down, bouncing crazily as it pushed past pink clouds of semi-dissolved salt. Leticia leaned over, snapping as the light drifted down, down, down.

"This can't be from rain," she said. "Noah's flood wouldn't account for all this water."

Barry shook his head. "I don't think so either. Ever heard of Howard Reservoir?"

"No."

"It's about two miles upstream from us. The state owns it. Forty years ago, guy by the name of Philips got a lease and started, well, *diverting* local tributaries."

"That's illegal," Leticia said.

"Yeah, but who's looking? We're out in the desert. Philips created campgrounds, boat ramps, the works. Brought tourist and tax dollars in. Good for the local economy. Nobody's asking questions."

"Typical," she said. "But…"

"But he used embarkment dams. Soil's not right for that."

"You suspect the reservoir's leaking?"

Barry scoffed. "I know it is. Channeling under bedrock and through salt pockets. This is where it's collecting."

"That's great!" Leticia said. Barry leaned back. "I mean for your claim. If the state owns the land but wasn't making sure improvements were up to code, they're liable. We'll look into that. States have deep pockets. That's good news."

Barry sighed. "Litigation takes years. I don't think we have that long."

Another tremor rippled across the water. The light in the pool winked out.

In her Tyvek suit, Leticia stood taller. "There are federal aid programs. Low interest loans. Salt dries; it's not completely ruined when it gets wet, not like silk or wheat. This is just a pause, Barry, not the end of the world."

"From your lips to God's ears, Letty," said Barry. "But all this water isn't what I wanted to show you." Barry swung the lantern to the left. Encased in the salt wall was the same creature as on his desk, but this one the size of a horse.

Leticia gasped.

"This is Oscar. He's the biggest salt-bug we found, but he wasn't encased like the little ones. Kids on fieldtrips used to dare one another to lick him. The crew called him their good luck charm." Another boom echoed through the cavern; this time waves splashed over the edge of the deck, salting her boots and stinging her nose.

"There's more. The text from the grad student said the salt-bugs were eggs. He thinks Oscar's a juvenile."

"A juvenile? That means—"

"We don't know what that means. But these creatures aren't like trilobites or crabs. They're closer to cicadas."

In the flickering lamplight, Oscar twitched.

Another boom. Chunks of salt rained down from the ceiling.

Boom, boom, boom.

Stillness.

Barry turned to Leticia. "What do you know about cicadas?"

BOOM.

Splash.

They turned. From the middle of the caldron rose a red beach ball stuck to the top of a yellow flagpole. It split open, the green cat-eye pupil locking on the lantern held high. Around it the water roiled, hissing like cicadas rising in a storm.

Leticia dropped her phone, shattering glass into a million pieces. Barry stepped between her and the leviathan, his Sasquatch body bold as waves crashed around his knees. "Run!" he screamed, pushing her toward the gate. She turned and fled, high-stepping in the too big boots, the toes catching and tripping. Lying on her back in cold, red earth, she watched the creature emerge from the brine, *boom, boom, boom,* one eye stalk, two eye stalks, a claw, and a terrible beaked mouth undulating in the center.

The last thing she smelled was salt.

FEEDING A DARK MUSE

C.H. LINDSAY

By night he comes, as darkling Muse,
to feed the mind with twisted dreams
and urge the artist recreate
the images his dreams will taint.

Then day by day, he sees her paint
the twisted nightmares he evokes.
He revels in her growing art
and hungers for her to be his.

He fuels her passion through her work,
a craving only he can sate.
For focused passion's what he craves:
the energy that comes from craft.

Her soul that's now inured he binds
and takes her back to Sheol's lair
to feed his need for human lust,
and make her his eternal slave.

EYE OF EUROPA
JONATHAN REDDOCH

We built cities massive and constructed marvels great. Flags unfurled in triumph across the stars. And in our hubris, we achieved dominion over the many spheres of our galaxy.

But lo! We dared too greatly.

For eye hath not yet beheld what terror lurks in the heart of the furthest reach of the solar system. Europa is no mere moon which floats yonder. It is a cellular element of the sleeping colossus which comprises all things, both living and dead. For eons untold, it has slumbered, hidden under rock and stone and ice and fire.

On tiny Europa, we disturbed it.

And in our disruption, eye number one opened, shaking and crumbling the human world built up around it. Pillars of steel and sapphire collapsed like castles in the sand.

This optical eruption was followed by eye two on Io. Soon, eyes greater in number than the sands of the sea opened across celestial time and space.

The universe is awakened, and it sees.
The pestilence of man revealed.

IN ABSENTIA LUCIS

C.R. LANGILLE

UTAH TERRITORIES, 1862

E velyn Horn stared at the small campfire. The way the embers popped and sent tiny glowing stars floating into the night sky had always mesmerized her. It sent her back to when her father would take Evelyn and her sister, Sylvie, out on camping trips. He would spin yarns about knights in castles going on quests. She never understood why the princesses couldn't just take care of things themselves though. If Evelyn had spent her life waiting for a knight in shining armor, she'd still be fighting for scraps in the streets, or worse.

Evelyn wished her father were here now and that she was merely camping. However, wishes and hopes were about as useful as a golden knife—pretty, but not practical. She brushed a stray strand of red hair from her face and glanced across the fire to her companion, Raymond.

He wore his typical crooked smile, but the way he looked into the flames told her his mind was somewhere else. If she were a betting woman, and she was, she would wager his thoughts were on Buford O'Henry. She couldn't blame him. If someone had shot down her brother in cold blood, it would be difficult to focus on anything else.

Evelyn scooted closer to Raymond to steal some of his warmth and to break him from his reverie. "Do you think we'll find him soon?"

Raymond shrugged. "I think so. If not, we'll have to head back to Fairfield for supplies."

Evelyn shuddered at the thought. The last place she wanted to go was back to that godforsaken town. She could still see the darkness billowing out from the one-eyed brothel madam's skull like some sort of inky snake. And Lord above, that voice…

Do you seek the truth?

She had to play the role of knight and save Raymond from the one-eyed woman and her associate, a deranged colonel with a wooden hand. Instead of relaxing in a nice hotel in the city, Raymond had wasted no time in continuing his search for O'Henry. Evelyn didn't want to see him hurt or dead, so instead of heading back to Chicago, she followed him out into the mountains of Utah. To say she was exhausted would be an understatement.

Raymond had saved her many times before, and if it weren't for him, she would be living a different life completely. He had pulled her from the darkness at a young age, helped set her straight. She loved him, and he loved her. There had been a time, a time before O'Henry, that they were to be wed.

Evelyn pulled her coat tighter around her chest. "Well then, let's hope I am correct. If I am, we should intersect with O'Henry and his gang tomorrow."

Raymond turned that crooked smile toward her and nodded.

The distinct click of a pistol hammer being pulled back sounded from the trees.

"Or maybe you'll find him sooner than that," came a gruff voice.

Evelyn reached for her pistol.

"I wouldn't do that," said another voice, this one from behind her.

Something hard poked the back of her head.

Raymond stood and clenched his fists. "O'Henry, you loathsome piece of—"

A large man stepped from the shadows and smacked Raymond with the butt of his pistol. He was tall and rotund, with a scraggly beard the color of dead pines and eyes the color of the winter sky. His mouth curled into a lunatic grin.

"O'Henry," Evelyn said.

"Ms. Horn, I presume? Heard a pretty little redhead by your name was tailing me."

Raymond groaned and sat upright. He rubbed the back of his head and his hand came away bloody. The man behind Evelyn walked a wide circle until he stood next to O'Henry. He was skinnier with angular features and about ten days' worth of blonde stubble on his chin. He shot Evelyn a gap-toothed smile and licked his lips.

"Ma'am," the man said and tipped his hat.

"This here is Pete the Stick. You already know who I am. Question is, who sent you?" O'Henry's eyes reflected the fire's light and gave him a devilish complexion.

Raymond spat on O'Henry's boot. O'Henry shook his head and raised his pistol back to smack Raymond once again, but Evelyn blurted out, "Pinkertons."

Instead of hitting him again, O'Henry squatted down to look Raymond in the eyes. "See there, she has some manners. A bitch speaks when spoken to. Next time you give me any lip…" O'Henry put the barrel of the gun on Raymond's forehead. "…I'll paint these trees with your brains."

O'Henry grunted as he stood. He walked over to a fallen tree and sat down. He kept his pistol on his lap, and Pete the Stick kept his gun trained on the both of them. O'Henry pulled a pipe from his coat pocket, packed it with some tobacco, and lit it with a burning stick from the fire.

"Well now, Pete, would you look at that? I heard old Pinkerton was hiring girls to do a man's job. Didn't believe it. But lo and behold, we got one of the Pinks right here in our presence. What do you think about that?"

Pete snickered and licked his lips again. Evelyn got the feeling that, left to his own devices, Pete would be doing some unsavory things. She shifted away from him and hugged her chest.

"Are they all as pretty as you?" O'Henry asked.

Evelyn refused to answer.

"Should we deal with them proper, Boss?" Pete asked.

O'Henry took a puff on his pipe and blew a ring of smoke into the air. He scratched at his beard, making a show of the whole process. "No. Bring them with us. I think we can find a use for these two ticks."

O'Henry and Pete disarmed them both. Pete took her Colt Police revolver and stuck it in his belt. He also grabbed Raymond's pistol, and even the little gut-gun she had hidden away in her boot. However, they hadn't taken her bladed hairpin.

Pete used a length of rope and secured their hands first, then tied them together at the waist with about four feet of rope between them. Then, with Pete leading their horses and O'Henry trailing behind, they made their way through the scrub oak and pinyon pines.

Evelyn looked up into the night sky and found the pole

star. They were heading north by northwest and higher up into the mountains. O'Henry kept quiet during the journey. He constantly looked over his shoulder and peered into the trees. At one point, Pete started to say something, and O'Henry quickly shushed the man. "You don't want to end up like Bill, do you?"

Whatever had happened to Bill was enough to keep Pete quiet, and Evelyn figured it was best to follow suit. O'Henry didn't seem like a man who was easily rattled, so whatever spooked him in these woods was something to worry about.

They continued up the mountain for about another 45 minutes before coming to a steep game trail. There were four horses hobbled in a nearby glade. O'Henry instructed Pete to do the same to their mounts.

While Pete was busy, O'Henry walked over and lit his pipe again. He kept his voice low. "Probably wondering what's going on, eh? I would be too. But don't you worry your fiery little head about it. You'll find out soon enough."

With that, he wandered over to a large roan in the field and dug some torches out of the saddlebags.

Raymond mumbled something under his breath. She turned to look at him and found he was pale and staring at the ground.

"Raymond, are you okay?" she whispered.

He looked up at her, his eyes unable to focus on any one spot. "What?"

"Are you feeling okay?"

He started to say something but turned to the side and threw up on a lichen-covered rock.

O'Henry shuffled over, looking all around. "You keep quiet now, you hear? Make too much noise and I'll slit your throat and leave you in the woods."

"He's hurt. I think you hit him too hard," Evelyn said. "He needs to see a doc."

O'Henry smiled. "I don't think it's going to be a problem for much longer. Pete! Let's get going."

Pete secured a line of rope to Evelyn and took the lead. O'Henry once again brought up the rear with Raymond in between. They started up the game trail.

The trail was rough, full of roots and loose rock. Many times, the scrub oak made it near impossible to push through. However, Pete appeared to know where he was headed and picked his way through the brush with relative ease. Evelyn could have made it through easier if she hadn't been tied up, but she managed. Raymond was a different story altogether. His legs were wobbly, and he threw up two more times along the way. Evelyn did the best she could to help him.

The trail crested the top of the mountain and ended at the mouth of a cave. Ancient petroglyphs covered the red rocks that stood guard of the entrance. They were similar in style and detail to those Evelyn had seen before, during her travels; however, the subject matter was most strange. The petroglyphs depicted animals moving away from a mountain. Warriors with spears and bows fought a large creature. Having seen petroglyphs before, odd creatures and scary figures weren't that uncommon. However, this one was circular with several wavy lines coming from its body. Inside the creature's body was a star-shaped symbol.

"God damn it, where are they?" O'Henry asked.

"Don't know, Boss. Think they ran off?"

O'Henry took his hat off and scratched his head. "No. Their horses were still down there. Those fools probably went into the cave."

"What is this place?" Evelyn asked.

O'Henry turned on her. The smile was gone from his

face. "This is where the darkness speaks. This is where we seek the truth."

Do you seek the truth?

"You best just give up on this, O'Henry, your bosses are dead," Raymond said. His speech was slurred, but he looked like he was feeling a bit better.

"So you killed the one-eyed bitch, eh?" O'Henry replied.

"Yeah, and the fellow with the wooden hand, Col. Green, back in Fairfield."

O'Henry chuckled. "Well, seems like you did us a favor then! Means we don't have to split the treasure down here with those spooky sonsofbitches."

Pete laughed along with O'Henry, and they lit their torches. Pete drew his pistol and entered first. O'Henry had his signature smile on again and motioned for Evelyn and Raymond to go on in by waving his gun at them. "After you."

It was noticeably cooler inside, but not just the regular chill that comes with being underground. This was different. Evelyn's breath formed small clouds in front of her face. The darkness ate the torches' light as well, leaving them with a dim glow. Aside from the chill, there was something else. As if something watched her from the darkness.

"Come on, let's get moving. If those idiots went too far, who knows what might have happened," O'Henry said.

The cave angled down, deep into the earth. They traveled slowly and went through two more torches along the way. At one point, there came a low moan from deeper down in the tunnel, almost like the wind was blowing through the trees. However, there wasn't a wind. The air was stagnant and clammy. It made Evelyn's hairs stand on end.

Up ahead, Pete stopped. "Hey, Boss! You'll wanna see this. I think I found them."

O'Henry grumbled as he pushed his way past Evelyn and Raymond. With both of them distracted, Evelyn reached up and pulled the bladed hairpin from her hair. She put her lips next to Raymond's ear and whispered. "Hold this and don't move."

He nodded. She placed the hairpin in his hands and then began to work her bindings across the bladed edge. It was thick rope and difficult to cut through, especially with Raymond trying to hold it steady while she worked at it in the dark. Finally, they cut her free and the rope slipped loose. Evelyn quickly took the knife from Raymond and began to work on his bindings. She was halfway through when O'Henry came lumbering back up the tunnel.

"Quit your kissing in the dark and get your behinds down here," he said.

Evelyn had to stop. She hid the knife in the palm of her hand and nudged Raymond forward. She kept her wrists together and hoped that O'Henry and Pete wouldn't notice the rope was gone.

As she closed in on O'Henry, an awful stench made her nose wrinkle. It was a smell she'd only experienced a couple of times in her life, and it made her gag. Insides made outside, the scent of blood and fecal matter.

The source of the foul odor became apparent as she rounded the corner. Laying on the floor were the two henchmen O'Henry had been looking for. One's gut was ripped open, and his innards spilled out upon the rocks. Something had torn out his eyes as well. The other was in pieces and strewn about the cavern. Blood covered the walls and floor and even dripped from the ceiling.

"What game are you playing at, O'Henry? Who else is down here?" Raymond asked.

O'Henry turned towards Raymond. "You think this is a game? Far from it. I'm searching for something down here, but it appears something is awake and hungry. That's where you two come into play."

Evelyn blanched. He meant to use them as bait.

O'Henry pushed Raymond and Evelyn in front of him. "Get moving. Pete! Let these two lovebirds take the lead in case we come across anything nasty."

She almost slipped in the gore and had to hold her breath as she made her way through the nightmarish scene. With her back to O'Henry and Pete, she started in on the rope that was tied between her and Raymond. She cut through the final strand and then tugged on Raymond's end to get him to stop.

Pete came walking up behind them and pointed his pistol. "Get moving!"

Evelyn spun around and knocked his arm out of the way. Pete fired, lighting the tunnel up with a bright flash and thunderous boom that rang something horrible in Evelyn's ears, but the shot went wide. She lunged forward and put the knife in Pete's throat. Pete's eyes went wide with shock. He dropped his torch, and he reached up to his neck. Evelyn withdrew the blade and stabbed him two more times in the lungs.

O'Henry drew his pistol, but his boot slipped in the pile of guts. His shot missed.

She grabbed her pistol from Pete's belt with her free hand and shot at O'Henry, using Pete's body as a shield. His body went limp and threw her shot off the mark. The bullet only clipped O'Henry's shoulder. He let out a pained growl and retreated around the corner of the tunnel. Evelyn dropped Pete's dead body and grabbed his gun before returning to Raymond.

"Come on! We got to move!"

Raymond didn't say anything. She turned her attention from O'Henry's direction towards Raymond and found him on the ground. His hands were still bound, but he was doing his best to press against his stomach. Blood soaked through his shirt and jacket and was spreading fast.

"Raymond!"

Evelyn knelt next to him. She quickly cut the rest of his rope and moved his hands so she could see how bad it was. Blood poured from the wound. She had to slow the bleeding. Evelyn pulled a handkerchief from her coat and wadded it up. "Here, press on it with this."

Raymond didn't take it. He looked up at her with a glassy gaze. She knew what Death's mask looked like.

"Damn it! Damn it!" Evelyn muttered. "Raymond, I…" Everything she wanted to say sounded empty.

"Sounds like I got your loverboy!" O'Henry shouted. He peeked around the corner and shot. The bullet hit near Evelyn's head and sprayed her with rocky debris. She screamed and returned fire, but O'Henry had slunk behind cover.

Raymond looked past her. He reached up as if he were grasping for something. "It's dark in here, Eve. So dark."

Evelyn grabbed his hands and pulled them back to his stomach. "You have to keep pressure on this, or you're going to bleed out."

He'd already lost a lot of blood. Even in the dying flame of the torch, she could tell he was pale.

Boots scuffed the stones behind her. She turned and fired another shot, and O'Henry let out a yelp before diving behind the rocks again.

When she looked back to Raymond, his eyes were sharp again and trained on her. "I love you."

Tears welled up in Evelyn's eyes. She wiped them away. "And you're a fool for it."

Raymond smiled. The smile faded from his face, replaced with a relaxed look. A dead man's look.

"Raymond?" Evelyn shook him, but he didn't move.

There was laughter, but it came from deeper down the tunnel. The laughter bounced off the walls and rocks.

Rage boiled deep in Evelyn's guts. She gripped the butt of her pistol until her knuckles hurt. Everything she had done to save him. Everything she had endured to get back to him. All dashed to nothing in a matter of moments. All because of O'Henry!

O'Henry revealed himself from around the corner, but this time, Evelyn was ready. As soon as he appeared, Evelyn squeezed the trigger.

There were no distractions.

There were no impediments.

This time, her bullet flew straight and clipped O'Henry in the face.

He let out a howl and fell to the ground kicking and screaming. Evelyn walked over. Blood gushed from the man's face as he looked up at her with hate-filled eyes. He tried to say something, but it came out as a gurgle, as her shot had destroyed most of his jaw.

The laughter from the tunnel got louder. Whatever it was, was getting closer.

O'Henry stopped his blabbering and peered past Evelyn. He let out a blood-choked sound that could have been a scream. O'Henry reached for his pistol, but Evelyn kicked it down the tunnel. He tried to crawl away, but Evelyn stuck her knife into his thigh. He let out a loud cry and clutched his leg. She ripped the knife out.

"No. You ain't going nowhere." Her accent had slipped through, but she didn't care none. "It appears something's awake and hungry. That's where you come into play." She threw his words back at him.

O'Henry's eyes went wide as the realization sunk in. Evelyn returned to Raymond.

The laughter turned to a giggle then morphed into a wail that was a cross between a cougar howl and a hurt child. It sent shivers through Evelyn's body.

The torch was almost burned out, but through the dim firelight, some of the shadows moved.

The ropey shapes slithered like snakes.

She stuck her pistol in her holster then did her best to drag Raymond back up the tunnel. She spat on O'Henry as she passed, but he didn't notice. He was too busy watching the cave. Waiting for *it* to arrive.

Evelyn dragged Raymond about thirty yards. Her legs burned, and she couldn't find a good grip no matter where she grabbed. Given time, she could get him out; however, time was a luxury she couldn't afford, not with whatever was in the tunnels coming for them. Evelyn let out a frustrated growl and sat on the rock floor. She thought about the night before he had begun his chase after O'Henry. She shouldn't have let him go after the man, should have made him stay with her, but how could she stop him? He promised he would be back soon. Then he wasn't. She couldn't let him go again. It was her time to be the knight and save him one last time.

Not willing to give up, she stood, grabbed him under the arms, and began to drag him further along. After a dozen steps, she tripped on a rock and fell backward.

Back down the tunnel, O'Henry began to wail. In the shadows that danced along the rock wall, Evelyn saw O'Henry trying to fight off… *something.* Evelyn didn't know how to describe it other than a shadowy octopus or a tumbleweed with a ravenous mind of its own.

The inhuman laughter picked up again, and O'Henry's cries of pain echoed through the cave. Then they stopped. The sounds of tearing and snapping took its place.

Evelyn pulled Raymond's dead body up into an embrace. There was no way she could get him out of there and survive.

"I'm so sorry."

"It's okay, Eve. I've seen the truth. It is lovely."

Her heart skipped a beat, and Evelyn dropped him. She scrambled backward until her back hit the rock. He had been dead. She knew it.

"Raymond?"

He sat up. She hadn't been able to bring a torch with her, but some of the light still spilled down the tunnel. Raymond's face was twisted into a large, rictus grin. His eyes, Lord his eyes! They were black pits.

He stood and took a step toward Evelyn, moving like a drunkard who had just stepped off a ship. He extended his hand. "Follow me, and I'll show you the truth."

Evelyn couldn't speak. She shook her head violently. The smile never faltered from Raymond's face, but the eyes grew even darker.

"Shed the lies and embrace the darkness with me. Embrace the truth."

Evelyn finally found the will to stand. She rose and moved away from him. Raymond cocked his to the side and then spun lazily on his heel. He almost skipped down the tunnel, back toward O'Henry, back toward *it*.

Soon the cavern filled with the combined laughter of Raymond and that thing.

Evelyn wasted no time. She turned tail and blindly made her way back up the tunnel. It was slow going without light. Each footstep was exploratory, and she kept her hand along the wall as a guide.

Soon, the sound of something wet slapping across the

rocks came from behind her. Then, Raymond's voice. He sang a song, one he used to sing to her when the night was cold and they stared at the stars. But this version was wrong. It was discordant and without mirth.

Beautiful star in heav'n so bright,
Softly falls thy silv'ry light,
As thou movest from Earth afar
Star of the evening
Beautiful star

Evelyn moved faster.

Her knees were bloodied, and her fingertips were raw, but she dared not stop. They were gaining on her. Then, from the darkness, was light. Up ahead, the first rays of sunlight pierced the darkness of the cave. Evelyn ran toward the entrance.

"Eve."

She stumbled to a stop and whipped around, gun in hand. Raymond stood there in the dark tunnel, swaying back and forth. He shot her a cold, unforgiving smile. His skin was glasslike, veins bulged, and black under his now thin skin.

Behind him, tendrils of shadow slithered and writhed. A large mass, darker than a coal mine, rose. From within the mass burned a ruby energy, pulsing like a heartbeat.

Star of the evening
Beautiful star

The red star from the petroglyphs. O'Henry's treasure.

Before she knew what she was doing, she took a few steps back down the cave, toward Raymond, and toward *it.*

Raymond opened his mouth and words spilled out. Thousands of voices screamed in unison. Within that cacophony, Evelyn picked out Raymond's voice.

"Come join us, Eve. Come and see the truth."

Evelyn stopped her advance. The thing's tendrils

reached for her, moving slow and deliberate. If they touched her, it would all be over. Tears streamed down her face and she aimed her pistol with a shaky hand.

"I'm sorry," she said.

The pistol barked, and the bullet struck Raymond in the head. He stumbled backward but didn't fall. He continued to look at her with those baleful eyes of shadow and smile.

The sun's rays warmed her back and crept further into the cave. As it neared Raymond, the creature wrapped its tendrils around his body before pulling him back into the darkness.

Evelyn found herself at the bottom of the game trail next to the horses. She didn't remember making the hike down or how long she had sat on the cold ground. The sun was high in the sky, and she wondered how it was midday already.

The horses eyed her warily. Evelyn didn't blame them. She was covered in blood, some her own, some not, and she was filthy.

Evelyn took a moment to gather her wits, then she got to work getting the horses ready. She wanted to be as far away from the cave as she could when the light gave way to darkness.

There were things in the dark.

Things that wanted her.

STANDING SILO

CYGNUS PERRY

The road turns by the silo
Its onyx paneling vanishes
with the fading rays of sun
All that stays is the steady
cobalt beacon perched on top
It is the eye of the obelisk
that stalks the stray travelers
under its star and stare
It harbors a spirit of
discontent caught out of space
Its hands creep down Its sides,
through shadow-cloaked fields,
seeking solitary wildlife
to feed its growing star

THE WASATCH HORROR
DEREK HUTCHINS

My name is Enos Finch, and this may be the last thing I ever write on God's green Earth. The reprehensible narrative I wish to convey began last Wednesday, when I woke to find all twelve of my chickens, or what remained of them, slaughtered. Their bones and feathers were strewn about my backyard in bloody clusters, and I found a hole the size of a golf cart torn through the chicken wire that surrounded their enclosure. My initial theory was that a cougar was the culprit, as I live at the base of the Wasatch mountains in Northern Utah, and to my knowledge, there was no other predator in the area that could cause such damage.

The damage was done, however, and after I had repaired the fence as best I could, and buried the scraps that remained of my feathered friends, I sat on my back porch, gazing up at the cascading curvature of the cyclopean mountains, and keeping my eyes open for any sign of life, pondering what potential menace lurked just beyond my line of sight. There had been buzz among my neighbors in recent weeks of similar disturbances to gardens and farms in the region, as well as a few claimed sightings of supposed beasts which were foreign to the area. Don Hadley down the road claims he saw a dog-man or were-beast, as he called it, as he was driving home the other night. It just stood on its hind legs in the middle of the road and looked at him before scurrying off into the brush. Of course, anyone who knows Don knows that his stories aren't worth the price of the hole-ridden overalls he's worn for the past twenty years, but I saw the fear in the man's eyes as he recounted his tale, and I believe he saw something that spooked him.

As for myself, I'm a rational being, and like to think that I exist on a higher plane than many of my neighbors, who stoop to claiming the newest conspiracy theories and superstitious fables with religious fanaticism. But I am a seeker of tall tales and arcane lore. In my discussion with the descendants of the Ute Indians, I learned of their legends of the darkness that spread from these very mountains on which I now live, and the horrors and nightmarish abominations which stalked that accursed ground. My interests in the occult led me to studying the *Lex Tenebrarum*, the infamous grimoire which was discovered only a few years ago. The Salt Lake City Library holds one of the few copies that were reproduced, and I spent several days in which I did not eat studying the strange text, which contained a reference to one Elbozra, spider spawn from the stars who legend says dwells deep under the Wasatch mountains and has dwelled there since before man was. At the time, I dismissed the reference as foolish blather, but now I know better.

I am not one to let an act of treachery go unavenged, and I went out and bought eight chickens which I planned to use as bait to lure in my enemy. As I returned home, I discovered that my sister in law, Sarah Young, a professor of biology at Colorado State, was visiting, and I told her and my wife of the events of the morning. Sarah agreed with my theory that it was probably a cougar or perhaps even a roaming bear. After getting the chickens settled, I called my old mission companion, Hyrum Pratt, who knows a thing or two about hunting, and requested his advice on my situation.

Instead of advising me over the phone, he immediately drove over to my place, his truck loaded with traps and an arsenal of guns, some of which I don't even think were legal. Pratt slapped a six pack of energy drinks on the table and proclaimed in his usual bombastic way, "Cancel your plans for the evening, Finch. We're about to have us a stake out."

Wrapped in a layered thermal jacket, Pratt and I sat on the back porch with no lights, our eyes watching for any sign of movement around the coop. He had a rifle resting across his lap, one hand situated over the trigger, the other supporting the barrel. I was merely a spectator, but seeing as it was my property and my problem, I felt compelled to stay and keep him company. Hours we sat without any sign of movement, until darkness had swallowed us, wrapping us in its thick cloak with songs of welcome. Then, finally, slinking its way down the steep incline, half hidden behind the dry brush and sparsely growing foliage, was a pair of luminous yellow eyes gleaming in the night. I almost made an auditory exclamation but caught myself, remembering that silence was our ally, and slowly nudged Pratt with my arm, motioning out into the void.

Slowly, Pratt raised his rifle, keeping his eye on the creeping beast until he had a good shot, and fired. The creature jolted and took off. Pratt swore and took a few steps after him before turning back to me. "The hunt is afoot," he declared with contagious conviction, and before

I could protest, he gripped my coat with beefy hands and dragged me into the house behind him.

I didn't want to go hunting, but I did want to protect my investment, and seeing as I had started this whole thing, I felt it was my duty to see it through. We returned inside and quickly packed our supplies, mainly water and food (Pratt also loaded himself up with ammunition). I escaped a deep interrogation from my wife, mainly with the aid of Sarah, who was so interested in what kind of creature we were chasing that she asked if she could accompany us. I looked to Pratt, who had become the default leader of our hasty expedition. He growled his approval, but only at the request that she didn't complain or slow us down.

Within the next few minutes, the three of us headed off into the mountains, unaware of the horrors that awaited us. Sarah and I followed Pratt as his scrutinous eyes scanned the ground for prints, not totally sure of how he was able to see in the utter darkness, but he swore that he could. Sarah and I kept our own eyes searching the darkened hills for any sign of movement or any glimmer of reflected light. We continued to climb the steep and often precarious rocky mountainside, a journey made ever more arduous and dangerous in the black of night. I don't know how long we followed Pratt through those haunted hills and eldritch valleys, but we soon lost sight of my house as we followed our intrepid leader into the chasm of the unknown.

The hills we traversed were known for their treachery, and many hikers and nearby civilians had become lost in those mountains, never to be seen again. Most recently was Josh Fairbanks, who lived only just down the road, a teenager who decided to go mountain biking alone. I recalled the bleak faces of his family in the months following his disappearance as I gazed out at the steepled beacons of the temple-filled basin and shining lights in the homes of families safe in their beds. At a certain point, long past the witching hour, when the world was silent as the grave and not even the late-night crowd passed along the distant freeway, Pratt turned to us, and we could tell from the look in his eye that he was not about to present good news.

"I lost him," Pratt growled, his eyes downcast with the embarrassment of failure and having dragged us along with him on a futile trek. "Maybe we could set some traps around your coop."

I was about to voice my consent when a terrifying howl erupted through the night, cutting straight to my heart. Whatever it was, villainous spirit or foul monstrosity, it was not far from where we now stood.

Sarah grabbed my arm and forced me to look behind us. A wolf-like creature stood there, watching us in the pre-dawn gloom. Its face and snout were that of a wolf or dog, but the torso was elongated, too thick to be a wolf, causing me to second guess my initial view. Its legs were scrawny, and as we looked at it, the beast stood on its two hind legs and let out another soul-splitting howl.

The bullet from Pratt's rifle tore through the wolfman's throat, and the creature collapsed to the ground. I turned on my headlamp to get a better look at the creature. The thing's fur was mangy and patchy, clearly diseased, and by all appearances sickly looking. However, my amateur observations are of no consequence, as Sarah was the expert and kneeled to get a closer look at the still rising chest of the dying beast. Her expression was one of utter bewilderment and complete fascination.

"Have you ever seen anything like that?" I asked.

"No... This is not an animal I've seen before. How

interesting." She took a few pictures before she stopped, eager to point out a new discovery. "Look. Look here. What do you see?"

I looked closely and saw small white worms writhing beneath the fur of the creature. There must have been thousands of them, all over its body. "Worms," I stated, with disgust.

"It looks like a wolf," Pratt grunted.

"Wolves don't stand on two legs," I said, flashing him a worried glance.

"It's not a wolf," Sarah confirmed. "At least not one I've ever seen. Besides, wolves aren't local to this region. Boys, not only have you managed to protect your chickens, but I think you may have discovered something new. We won't know until we bring this thing in and study it."

There was talk of what we should call the creature, as he who discovers a new species should get to name it. But before we could settle on a decision (my suggestion was the Wasatch Wolf, but Pratt wanted to name it after himself), Pratt silenced all discussion with a loud *Shh*! He pointed, and following his arm, I saw that several more of the wolf-man's brethren had snuck up behind us and were sitting only a few feet away, observing us with lurid curiosity. They had us surrounded!

For a moment, all was still, then one of the creatures growled, and Pratt fired off another round, no doubt hoping to scare them off, but this only seemed to anger them further. The wolves launched themselves at Pratt in an organized attack. He screamed and fought like a madman to escape from the wolf horde as they descended upon him and sank their fangs into the arms he had held in front of his face to protect himself. Stunned, I could only watch in horror and know that I was next. Sarah jumped into action, flinging rocks at the monsters with deadly accuracy, trying to drive them off. Following her lead, I found a large branch and began to beat the foul denizens of the hills away, until at last they deserted their attack and fled into the dark, whimpering as they went.

Under the limited light, we scrutinized Pratt's condition. Miraculously, there were few puncture wounds, limited to his forearms and one on his right leg. He would live. Sarah set to work, using the limited supplies at her disposal to bandage his wounds, wrapping them tightly with cloth to staunch the bleeding. As she did, I thought I saw white worms slithering in the open wounds, but my gaze was broken when Pratt grabbed me roughly by the collar.

"Finch, I need you to do something for me. I need you to follow those bastards and kill as many of them as you can."

Before I could protest, he thrust his rifle at me and fished for his box of ammo in his pack, but I protested anyway. "I'm not a hunter. I haven't even shot a gun since I was a teenager—"

He would have none of it. "I got bit for you; you do this for me. You owe me that. At least try."

I swallowed my pride and looked to Sarah. "Can you get him back?"

She threw an accusatory look my way. "Are you kidding me? This is a terrible idea. What if they attack again?"

"Then he'll be ready," Pratt responded for me. "Come back at dawn. Not a minute before."

How could I refuse my friend's request? He could have died helping me. Was I willing to do the same for him? Against my better judgment, I took his gun, ammunition, and my pack of supplies, and bidding Pratt and Sarah adieu, set off into the hills to seek my revenge.

As I was not a seasoned hunter like Pratt, I kept my

headlamp on and continued my journey up, in the direction I saw the creatures flee, until I arrived at the crest of
the hill. I sat down on a rock until I could determine what
to do next. Dawn would come in a few hours. How would
I spend my time, as I had no idea what I was doing?

By fortune or fate, it was at that moment that my eyes
fell upon a set of paw prints in the dirt. There weren't
many of them, but there were enough that I was able to
determine which direction they were heading. I stayed that
route until I arrived at a grouping of towering rocks on a
downward slope. After closer inspection, hidden behind a
bush, there was an opening not more than three feet wide,
into the mountain.

A cave.

And within that cave, glowing eyes peered up at me.

Yes, the same creatures I had been hunting made their
nest in this foul pit, and it was my unfortunate duty to
pursue them. However, by the time I had raised my rifle,
the dogs had already fled out of my sight, necessitating my
venture into their den. I could have ended my journey
there, waited for sunrise, and lied to Pratt about my unsuc-
cessful hunt, but my integrity would not let me. I had made
a promise. A promise, that as you will soon understand, led
to my downfall.

My headlamp provided enough light for me to see a
few feet in front of me, enough to glimpse the seemingly
endless descent I was facing, as the space around me grew,
so I was able to stand comfortably as I continued my trek
toward the belly of the earth.

Down, down, down I went. Time was meaningless
down there under the earth's skin, and I prayed that the
batteries in my lamp would not die, for I would surely
follow. Before long, I began to notice that the walls and
floor seemed to be moving. At first I thought it was a trick

of my mind or the lighting, but the shifting continued, and I knelt to get a closer look, only to discover with absolute revulsion that every surface of the cave appeared to be covered with the same wriggling white worms that had seemed to be populating the wolfman's flesh.

Horrified beyond belief, I almost turned back then, and if not for the sudden barking I heard ahead of me in the darkness, I might have abandoned my quest. I soldiered on, reminded of my purpose, and it was not long before I met my next obstruction. Gradually, I began to detect spiderwebs above me in the fathomless abyss. They seemed to drape down, growing thicker and more plentiful as I went, until they were all but blocking the path ahead of me. I brushed what I could out of the way, but it was never enough, and wisps of webbing clung to my arms, torso, and head. It was only then that I realized that the same worms that covered the floor were also strung up in the webs! I felt them inching along the back of my neck, and images of them swarming me, crawling through my hair and down my spine, plagued my mind, causing me to spin and jerk and claw, trying to scrape and pull every bit of web off me, only to find that the more I moved, the more webs clung to me. I tripped and fell, my hands sinking into puddles of stagnant water inhabited by more worms. I was beyond sanity. My only thoughts were of escape, but as I looked up, all other thoughts were struck from my mind as I beheld the thing that will haunt my nightmares forevermore.

A great beast was strung up in the webbing. It had the head and torso of a man, with numberless spindly arms protruding from its back. The thing had no legs, but had a bulbous mass of flesh, an enormous sac that drooped from its midsection. Two or three times my size at least, the sight before me was beyond my comprehension, and I knew that

I was looking upon Elbozra, the spider god from the stars, slumbering in her eternal lair.

The dogs clustered beneath it in a ring, whimpering and pleading, apparently unafraid of the abysmal abomination that slept above their heads until their master shifted in her webbing, and I realized that she was waking up!

I knew I had to escape, but I was so close to my goal. The dogs were in my range! I quickly aimed and fired off several rounds, and I watched as two of the wolfmen fell and writhed in the dirt, but my efforts only sped up the waking of the sleeping god above. Numberless eyes speckled over her head opened at once and instantly found me. In that moment, my mind was no longer my own. I was seized by some incomprehensible power and shown things that I dare not write, and I doubt I could even if I tried—things that would drive a lesser man insane, as they almost did me. Suffice it to say that I saw the cosmos spanning out before me in infinitesimal glory and splendor, and felt my spirit curdle within me as I witnessed the wraith-haunted pit from which the spider god crawled, dreadfully aware of my inconsequence.

When the visions ceased, I opened my eyes and found myself lying in a sloped field overlooking my home. The rifle was nowhere to be found. As soon as I had the strength, I descended the hill, and when I stepped into my home, my wife, with tears staining her face, told me of the horrible events that occurred in my absence.

When Sarah brought Pratt back to the house, he was in bad shape. The bleeding had stopped, but he was acting aggressive and refused to be taken to a hospital. That's when they noticed other changes as well, like the thick, coarse hair sprouting from his arm around his wounds, and the strange way his teeth seemed to be lengthening. When

Sarah grabbed Pratt to try and restrain him, he tore away from her and took off into the night.

I asked them which direction he went and mumbled some excuse, as if I was going to go look for him, but I have not traveled far, just out of view of my house, where I now sit and write this final letter.

I have put the pieces together in my mind, and the truth is altogether too horrible for me to accept, yet my heart will not let me forget what I now know. It's the worms, you see... They are the connection I did not understand. They sprang from Elbozra herself, infecting her human hosts and turning them into her dog fiend servants. I don't have to search for Pratt because I know where he's gone, called to her side to serve her as one of her slaves, to complete his horrible transformation. The disappearances, the strange occurrences, it all fits so well now.

I write this message on my phone, yet I lack the heart to send it off, but I will leave my phone where it will be found. To whomever finds it, I ask that you return it to my wife. Sabrina, I love you, and I wish that things could be different. I wish that I had never entered that blasted cavern, but none of this I can change. All I can do is protect you from what I know I will become. For the reason I know I will not return home is the same reason I know where Pratt has gone—*because I can feel the worms crawling through me!*

THE TERROR BEGRUDGINED

DANIEL CURETON

Uninvited,
it seems,
finds its way around the gates.

To be in the terrored home.
There is no door closed for the
Uninvited.

Shadows and space,
dark foreboding in its place,
finds its way around the gates.

Mystic take—
Of the give and rake—of the
Uninvited.

Terror bringer
of the shamed past—making sins anew,
finds its way around the gates.

Flee before the presence
of a guest begrudged, seen—
Uninvited—
find its way around the gates.

TICK WAY

PAUL STARKEY

"Of course Utah is named after the Utes. I mean it's obvious, right?" Cal took a drag on the spliff, then handed it her way.

Shaylee shook her head. "I'm good."

He nodded. "One of us needs a clear head, eh?" He laughed, took another drag.

Shaylee had always thought it was myth that your toes could curl, but she felt them now, inside her sneakers, forming little fists.

"Utes. Utah." His eyes were wide in disbelief, like a man who'd only just made the connection.

Shaylee was fearful that her toes might actually break if this lunkhead didn't shut up.

It was bullshit anyway; you didn't need to be one quarter núuchi-u to know that. Yuttahih was an Apache word, the Spaniards pronounced it 'Yuta' and well, there you go.

Shaylee wasn't going to correct him. He didn't strike her as the kind of guy who took well to a woman showing him the error of his ways. Not for the first time today, she wondered what the hell she was doing, sluffing school to spend the day with this guy.

She knew. He was cute, he had a car, and she'd been bored. Too much studying at BYU. She needed a break; she'd just picked the wrong distraction. Yes, he was cute, but however pretty those blue eyes of his were, the clear lack of much going on behind them muted the overall effect.

And sure, he had a car, only the Taurus was older than it looked, and much like Cal, a decent exterior masked a substandard interior. The suspension was rough, the engine coughed and wheezed like her fifth grade teacher Mr. Jensen—a fifty a day man who'd died before she reached seventh grade—and the inside was filthy and stunk of stale weed.

She wouldn't have minded if he'd taken her someplace interesting. As much as she loved Iceberg milkshakes, it wasn't exactly a classy location for a date, but he'd driven them out to Orem all the same.

And now the sun was waning, he was clearly moving to the next phase of his plan, driving them to a secluded makeout location.

"Where we heading?"

Please don't say Squaw Peak, please don't say Squaw Peak…

He grinned. "Somewhere real quiet."

God he was a jerk. She should have known. Anyone who wore a University of Utah Utes football shirt in Provo was a dick, but she was horny, and the shame of it was that she still wanted him. At least if they were screwing, he'd hopefully stop talking.

She rolled her eyes. "Let me guess, Squaw Peak." God how she hated that word.

He didn't know she was a quarter núuchi-u, probably didn't even know she was a local, or at least had been. The family moved from Provo to Boulder five years ago when she was fourteen. She'd always planned on coming back. She might not stay, but it was good to see Provo again, to see the mountains and the great Salt Lake.

He shook his head. "Squaw Peak ain't quiet. I don't get off on people watching, you dig?"

She closed her eyes. *I'm really gonna regret this in the morning.*

"Then where?"

Another shit-eating grin.

You'd better be worth it, Cal.

"Tell me or you can just take me back to my dorm."

He carried on grinning, certain in his own mind at least that she was bluffing. "Tick Way."

She felt very cold all of a sudden. Tick Way, a stupid anglicised translation of an old Ute word. Tickunarraway.

It meant simply '*Hungry*'.

"We shouldn't go there."

He laughed. "Shit, you don't buy those old legends, right?" he drawled. "It's just bullshit; the Indians made it up to scare people off."

Shaylee knew better. She still remembered Gramma Chipeta's stories when Mom and Dad left them alone. Gramma never talked about the old ways when Mom and Dad were around. Mom especially didn't like it. She loved her mother and wasn't ashamed that she lived with them, but for her part, she wanted no part of that side of her heritage.

For Shaylee it'd been different. She'd loved hearing the stories. Maybe that was part of why she'd come back to Utah, to reconnect with her roots.

She remembered Gramma talking about the hungry place many times. She said bad things had always happened there, that her people had avoided the area for centuries, that even the dumbest brave knew better than to get within a mile of that spot, especially at night.

The sun was almost down.

She forced a smile. "Isn't it miles away?" She gestured outside. "Lots of turnoffs, secluded country lanes." She put a hand on his thigh. "Why waste time driving when we could be doing something else?" She let her hand run up his thigh, began stroking his crotch.

"Oh yeah, that's good." He smirked. "But I've always wanted to do it at Tick Way."

She made to move her hand, but he took one hand off the wheel and held her fingers to his groin. The car slewed slightly as he compensated.

"Shit! You wanna crash?"

"No, I want to screw, and I want to screw at Tick Way." He lifted his hand from hers tentatively. "If I put my hand back on the wheel, are you gonna keep yours there?"

She sighed. "Yes." Christ, this day was proving more trouble than it was worth.

"My kinda girl."

Shaylee thought about opening the door and jumping out, but while they weren't going fast—thanks to the weed rather than Cal's natural inclination, she suspected—they were going fast enough that she'd risk a broken bone if she did.

New plan, maybe if she kept working his crotch he wouldn't be interested in her anymore. Not exactly how she'd wanted tonight to go, but beggars couldn't be choosers.

"Don't ever go there, Muatagoci," Gramma said, repeating the warning every few months in case Shaylee had forgotten, using the special nickname reserved only for when they were alone, because she said Shaylee was her moon. "Don't go there," she chided, wagging a gnarled finger. "Especially not after dark."

Of course, Shaylee had been there. She and a few friends had driven out there, or rather been driven out there by an older boy with a truck. It had been a dare, not long before Shaylee's family announced they were heading to Colorado.

Nothing had happened. In fact, it'd been a huge letdown. The place wasn't even particularly pretty. It was just a clearing at the end of a dirt track with an okay view, but the kind of view you could get from a dozen other places that were easier to get to, and why would you bother when you could get an even better vista further up, when you could actually see Provo lit up like a Christmas tree?

That had been in daylight though, and right now, Shaylee was painfully aware of the dusk settling upon them like a funeral shroud.

She kept kneading Cal's groin. He kept groaning. More than once, the car swerved a little, and Shaylee considered how embarrassing it'd be to be killed while holding tight to a guy's dick.

But she also remembered Gramma Chipeta's stories about Tickunarraway, about how long before the white man came to their land, the peoples of the núuchi-u had avoided this place for centuries. She remembered tales of those—usually young white men—foolish enough to visit the place, either by accident or as a dare, how every few years someone would go missing, and how it would quickly become apparent that they'd been on their way to Tick Way.

No trace of them was ever found.

No trace of girlfriends either.

"I'm not his goddamn girlfriend," she muttered.

"What's up?" he said, dreamily looking her way.

She gave him a squeeze. "Eyes on the road, Caleb."

He snorted. "Shit that's what my mom calls me." He did as instructed though.

Shaylee's hand was starting to grow numb; what did it take to get this guy off?

"Here we go!" he yelled suddenly, swerving off the main road and into darkness.

Shaylee yelped.

Cal laughed. "Relax. I've done this a dozen times, the gap in the trees is plenty wide enough.

Her heart was still pounding, however. She really didn't trust Caleb as far as she could throw him.

Maybe this would be okay though? He'd been here before, and Momma always said Gramma Chipeta was full of shit. Take the tale of a giant monster slumbering at the bottom of the Great Salt Lake for instance.

Something about Tickunarraway though, when she talked about this place her voice was different, the cadence, even the way she held herself. When talking about the great lake beast she'd always look furtive, as if she couldn't quite bring herself to look Shaylee in the eye.

When she talked about Tickunarraway though, she barely blinked, and the fear in her voice sounded true.

"You really been here before?"

"Yeah, don't sweat it. Four, five times. To be honest, it ain't great, but it is quiet. That old Indian spook story keeps people away."

It was then she realised that when he'd slewed off the road, she'd taken her hand away from his crotch. She didn't put it back. Instead, she flexed her fingers and rubbed at the wrist.

She could barely see anything. Outside of the head-lights, the only light was a slender beam that seemed to hover overhead, the dribbles of waning sunlight that made it through the canopy of trees. Looking to her right, all she could see were shadows that she presumed were trees, though as her eyes adjusted, the shapes didn't become more treelike. Instead, she couldn't shake the feeling that a line of figures was proving an honour guard for them on their way to...

"Here we go, Shay!"

She'd told him three or four times that no one called her Shay except her dad. She just hoped he wouldn't keep using it once they got down to business.

Looking ahead, the trail opened up as the trees thinned.

Cal killed his headlights. She was about to yell, but the words caught in her throat.

Ahead the sky was dark, not totally black though—dark blues like brand new jeans before you wore the colour away, the deep purple of royal robes. And dotting this velvet blanket were stars, thousands of them, *millions* of them, the sky so clear that she wondered if she was seeing every star in the sky.

The sky engulfed her, made her feel tiny. A million stars, millions of lightyears away, with a million other worlds orbiting them. She'd felt like this before, of course, lain out on a blanket on a summer night, staring up at the sky a hundred times or more, but she didn't think the sky had ever looked this big.

And she thought something else. Lying on that blanket, the sky had looked empty. She'd had no problem contemplating the vast distances separating each point of light, no difficulty in comprehending that most of the universe was nothing but empty space. Growing up in Utah, this was easy to do.

Tonight though, the sky they were driving towards didn't feel empty; it felt crowded. Suddenly, the stars didn't seem far apart. They looked so close to one another, as if a hand from one might reach out and grasp a hand from its neighbour as easily as she might now take Cal's fingers in hers.

She couldn't shake the feeling that the universe teemed with life. And right now she felt like most of those intelligences were focused on her, gazing through her like she was made of glass, like she was so fragile a sharp jolt might shatter her.

"I want to go home," she whispered.

Cal laughed. "But we're here."

She looked ahead. The track threatened to disappear into nothingness, the car was slowing as Cal applied the brakes, but it didn't seem to be slowing fast enough. She had visions of them driving off the edge, the car tumbling down the mountainside, the car slowly compacting around them like they were bugs in an empty beer can.

She reached out and grabbed Cal's arm.

"That's more like it, babe," he said.

The car stopped.

Shaylee felt embarrassed. She'd let Gramma Chipeta's stupid stories wind her up, let herself get scared on a simple drive to a lonely makeout spot.

She tried to pull away from Cal, but he grabbed her and kissed her before she could.

She tasted marijuana on his breath, but it wasn't unpleasant, and he was a good kisser. She'd learned that after Iceberg, when his breath had tasted of fry sauce, not weed.

Shaylee forgot about her worries and leaned into the kiss, let her hand drift back to his groin, even as one of his hands slipped under her t-shirt.

And then suddenly he was gone, and there was a cool breeze whipping into the car.

She opened her eyes.

The driver's door was wide open. Caleb was standing outside.

"C'mon," he said. "I've got some blankets in the trunk, and we can start a fire." At this he started flicking the Zippo he now held in his right hand. "Just need some twigs and stuff."

Shaylee hugged herself. This really wasn't what she'd envisaged when they'd hooked up.

Cold air tickled her bare skin. She tugged her t-shirt down. "Damn it, Cal, get back inside."

But he was gone. She heard the trunk open then close, and then he was back again, holding some rough-looking blankets.

"What are they, horse blankets?"

"No," he said indignantly. He sniffed each blanket in turn as if to convince himself. "You coming?"

She shook her head.

"You'll be sorry," he sang.

"So will you be when I steal your car and leave you stranded."

Cal grunted. "Good luck with that; the keys are in my pocket." A sly look came over his face. "Come get them!" And then he was gone.

Shaylee reached over and tugged the door closed. She looked through the windshield. Cal was laying the blankets down on the ground, midway between the car and the cliff edge. Or at least he was trying to. Each time he put one down, a gust of wind caught an edge and flipped it, threatening to send it sailing into the night.

Shaylee shook her head. When God was handing out cute, he may have been at the head of the queue, but brains on the other hand…

In the end, he held tight to both blankets and moved to

the edge of the clearing. Shaylee watched him go, half convinced that she'd see him vanish at any moment. She wondered how easy it would be to hotwire a car if he did just disappear, and laughed at the thought. Never mind the supernatural, there was more chance a gust of wind would catch one of those blankets and drag him over the edge.

He was back now, awkwardly holding the blankets, some twigs, and a couple of rocks.

This time he put rocks on the blankets to hold them down.

This is what it must have been like, she thought, hooking up in the Stone Age. Never mind a guy with a car, just give me a Cro-Magnon with his own cave and the ability to make fire.

Talking of which, Cal was now arranging the twigs, creating a teepee-like structure far too close to the blankets. When he started flicking the lighter again, Shaylee knew she was going to have to get out and go help him before he inadvertently set fire to the damn rugs.

Figuring the night couldn't get any worse, she clambered out of the car.

She hung herself over the open door. "For fuck's sake, Cal, do you want to set fire to…"

The sentence drifted off into the night. Shaylee couldn't finish it; she was too busy shivering. A gust of icy air, *arctic air*, washed over her. The kind of cold it wouldn't be for months yet. The kind of cold where you stayed indoors, snuggled under the blanket with Netflix on your iPad and a mug of hot chocolate and marshmallows sitting by your bedside.

Worse than the cold was the direction it had come from and the duration it had lasted. It had heralded from behind her, and it had lasted for just a few seconds. This was odd because before it washed over her, the breeze had been light and was coming at her head on, and once the cold snap had passed, the breeze remained, still coming at her, not from behind her.

A thought bounced around her head like a pinball, a thought she very much didn't want to have, but every time she tried to ignore it, it smashed its way to the front of her prefrontal lobe once more.

It had felt like someone standing behind her had exhaled.

The cold may have passed, but she was still trembling. Reason told her to just turn around and prove there was nothing there, but the voice of Gramma Chipeta was telling her to stay completely still, completely silent, telling her that the Tickunarraway might choose to ignore her.

"What did you say?" yelled Caleb.

Shaylee's eyes widened. She wanted to tell him to shut up, but if she did that, she'd be telling Tickunarraway where she was.

"Shay?" he shouted again.

And then she knew that if something had been hovering behind her, it was behind her no more, because Cal yelped, and even in the dimness, she could see him shivering.

"Fuck, it just got cold."

Shaylee couldn't stay silent. "Run!" she shouted. "Get back in the car!"

Cal ignored her. He kicked one of the rocks away and snatched up a blanket, wrapping it around himself. "Come on Shay, come get warm." And then he laughed.

Shaylee didn't laugh.

She felt it then.

Not cold.

Pressure. As if something heavy and invisible was bearing down on her, as if she wasn't standing on the side of a mountain but was instead at the bottom of the ocean, with fathoms and fathoms of cold dark water threatening to crush her.

She sensed something above her, and this time she looked, raising her head defiantly.

Oh my God, the stars!

There were so many of them, but it wasn't just that the number seemed to have increased, it was how close they were, as if they had leaned down from the heavens to place themselves within easy reach of this stupid nineteen-year-old girl who right now was really regretting not jumping out of the car earlier.

It was like the sky was full of fireflies, and she somehow knew that if she were to reach up she would touch something that burned with a fire colder than the depths of hell.

"Shay?"

He sounded scared now, as if he'd finally realised something was wrong.

Fearful that the sky full of stars would collapse upon her head, Shaylee still looked away. Looked towards Cal.

For a moment, she didn't know what she was looking at. He stood there, still tugging the blanket close around himself, but the earth around him was moving. For a moment, it was like he was an insect caught in a Venus flytrap as the earth formed petals that moved as if to engulf him.

And then she realised that the earth wasn't doing that, it wasn't rising of its own accord, it was being pulled from above. And so was Cal.

She watched him lift into the air. It was like a magic trick on TV, like a special effect worthy of a Marvel movie.

He was several feet off the ground before he even seemed to notice. When he finally did, he screamed, but

Shaylee heard no sound, not a single noise. It was as if the night itself was swallowing all sound.

Higher and higher he went, those petals of earth still with him, dirt falling like rain.

She saw something drop, wafting in the wind like a giant bat.

The blanket.

He must have been half a dozen yards off the ground now, still screaming. He looked beyond fear; he looked in agony. His hands were clasped to his head, and she wondered if he was feeling the same pressure she felt? If he did, she knew it must be so much worse. If she was at the bottom of the ocean, then she could only guess at how deep he felt he was.

And then it was as if a silent firework had exploded in the night sky, and he was gone, vaporised in a cloud of red dust that continued to hang there like an illusion.

She waited for it to drop, for what remained of his flesh and blood to fall like rain.

It didn't. It hovered there a moment longer and then it simply disappeared.

Finally, she heard a noise. A sucking noise that was gone almost as soon as it began.

Shaylee had heard that noise before, earlier today when Caleb had been slurping his milkshake through a straw.

Noise returned to the night. There wasn't much of it—the whisper of the breeze, the sound of Mormon crickets in the trees. Soft sounds, light sounds, yet after that impossible silence, it was like suddenly finding herself in Times Square, and she clasped her hands to her ears until she could acclimatise.

Minutes passed. She took her hands away from her ears.

The intense cold had gone. The pressure had gone. The stars seemed back in their rightful places in the heavens. Still, she didn't dare move.

Eventually, her legs began to ache, and she knew she had to do something. She had no keys for the car, so her choice was simple: walk back to the road with only the flashlight on her phone for company, or try and find his keys.

She left the car door open and tentatively walked out to the spot where Caleb had stood not so long ago, where Caleb had existed not so long ago. She shone her light on the ground, still expecting to see blood soaking the dirt, but no, the sand looked clean. Dry.

The little teepee of twigs had collapsed, and a single blanket still flapped in the breeze, anchored to the earth by a rock.

In the distance, she watched as the other blanket, the one Cal had wrapped around himself, flew off the edge of the cliff and into the darkness.

She went back to looking at the ground.

Something glittered in the light.

She dropped to grab it but left it where it was when she realised it was Cal's Zippo.

She swung the light left and right, and was about to give up when she found the keys lying there in the dirt.

She picked them up, pausing just before she touched them, fearful that Tickunarraway would choose that moment to reach out and take her too, that he was still hungry, that he had not been satiated by Caleb.

The keys felt warm.

She ran back to the car, locked the doors, and started the engine. It suddenly struck her that if the keys had been in Cal's pocket, then how had they escaped whatever fate had befallen him?

As she swung the car in a slow arc to face it back towards the road home, a thought struck her. Someone had been looking out for her. She looked up at the night sky.

"Thank you, Gramma Chipeta," she whispered, a smile on her lips, tears in her eyes. "Thank you."

She put the car in drive and headed away from Tick Way as fast as she dared.

She had no idea what she was going to tell the police about Caleb, but she had plenty of time to come up with something.

It was a shame though.

He'd been really cute.

SOUR

JOSHUA P. SORENSEN

"The ground is sour!"

I looked up from my tablet. There he stood, in defiance of court order and "No Trespassing" signs. He claimed to be a shaman, protesting the Krueger Mine since its inception. Always with talk of the land being sour, cursed, and not for humans.

I keyed my radio. "Could I get security over at the mine entrance?"

It only took a couple minutes. Security hauled his ass away, and I continued my reviews of the day's progress. Today would be the day that we proved the naysayers wrong. Everyone said we wouldn't find commercially viable veins of iron in the Uinta Mountains. The corporation's geologists had disagreed.

After multiple tiny deposits, we had finally found a promising vein, right where the corporation's geologists had said to look. At least, we thought we had.

A stubborn granite wall blocked our progress. It resisted blasting. The rock didn't shatter. It had to be chipped out bit by bit. Several workers quit due to the grueling conditions with little apparent progress. More miners probably would have quit if there wasn't a recession in this part of Utah.

I brought this up to my superiors; but the bosses at the corporation insisted that we keep working at that specific point in the mountain. They even sent out a team of geologists, strange, pasty-skinned fellows, unlike any geologist I had ever met. That team all agreed that a rich deposit lay just beyond this strangely flat wall of solid grey stone.

Slowly, the work continued, the granite breaking off in huge vertical columns. Every chunk bringing us closer to our goal.

Magnetic sensors ticked off the proximity to a magnetite vein just beyond this next layer of stone. I double checked the estimates on my tablet and headed into the mine.

The descent into the Earth was cathartic. A transition from light to dark; a journey from chill mountain breeze to the stifling, warm stillness of the depths. The ventilation system and strings of electric lighting did little to break the creeping feeling of thousands of tons of stone just above my head. But, after years of supervising mining projects across the World, that change felt like coming home.

At the end of the tunnel, I ran into the foreman, Joe Hunter. Four other miners operated impact drills. Roger Thompson, Tom Bascom, and the Oakes twins all worked on the granite surface.

With sufficient work, a column of stone could be pried from the overall mass. Currently, they had three of them on the verge of releasing.

There was a crack and a grinding sound as the first shifted and fell away from the wall, revealing a cavity behind the granite surface. Illumination from the head-lamps did little to penetrate the darkness.

With a snap, the second block plunged to the earth. Excitement tickled my insides. We were finally breaching this obstacle.

The last of the cyclopean pillars broke free, slamming into the ground. Dust filled the tunnel, obscuring everything. Beams from headlamps only exacerbated the obfuscation, turning the billowing clouds into blankets of white.

Out of the darkness came a glimmer. Pale yellow light poured out of the cavity revealed by the collapsing postpile. Like molten gold it slid out and across the ground. A tangy odor assaulted my nose, a continuingly shifting aroma akin to warm apple pie roasting on brimstone. Shrill noises echoed through the shaft as the superheated liquid oozed across the floor, cracking and fissuring the stone as it went.

And then came the voices. Whispered cries of agony and fear. So soft, so quiet, so deafening in their madness. The utterances emanated from the glow like pulsing beams of light.

I looked at Joe Hunter. His eyes wide in terror, he had removed his hardhat, and his lips quivered.

The glowing fluid spilled towards us in laughing ripples. It flowed across Thompson's boots and up his body. He screamed in wild shrieks as it engulfed him, his entire body glowing like an angel in a cheap B-movie. He crumpled onto the ground, the bright deluge sweeping over and around his corpse.

Tom Bascom slammed himself into the wall, clutching and grabbing in a vain attempt to climb. He suddenly stopped. His body keeled over and was motionless. Daryl and Mike Oakes both ran up the tunnel towards the shaft entrance; that was the last I ever saw of them.

The stream of yellow ambience continued to surge forth through the darkness. It sputtered and bubbled across the fallen stones. Puddling together, it slithered towards me and Joe. I grabbed Joe's jumpsuit and tugged.

"Joe, come on, we need to get out of here!"

Joe just murmured unintelligibly, his eyes fixed on the oncoming mass, his feet immobile. The voices in my head crescendoed without increasing volume. Vertigo overcame my senses. Then, mercifully, I drifted from consciousness.

I don't remember much after that. I'm told that I carried Joe out of the smoking wreck of the mineshaft. He remains as catatonic as he was in that hell unleashed on Earth. Of course, there were police inquiries and lawsuits; but Well-Combes Industries had ceased to exist. There were no records that it had ever existed at all save for a logo on pay stubs and signs outside the mine.

But the doctors say that someone has been paying my medical bills. Those can't be cheap — regular counseling, a drug regimen that would kill a horse, and residential care. At least, that's what they call it. I call it imprisonment.

My memories are a jumble. Hypnosis doesn't help. I'm even forgetting events from before. But we released something in that mine. We let it go and we didn't put it back. I try to warn them, but no one listens, no one believes me, and I can't fight past the brain fog to explain.

One thing, I remember clearly.

"The ground is sour!"

SKIN DEEP—THE CITY OF DEMONS

JOSEPH HOPE

Under the skin
there are rooms big enough.
Corridors that connect
to endless streets.

A world: torn apart & together.
Cell rooms for every crime.

There is music
baritonal, a barrack of suffering,
a depot of brand-less memories.
Lies—enough.

Like the palace of a greedy Greek god,
there is a large square where a black cat
is pawing at the wall of curiosity.

Under the skin, there are enough demons
to overrun a city.
It never ends. The standing.
The bending. The hurricane
legs dashing about at random.
There is noise, enough
to black out your thoughts.

One machine cuts into two.
There is a machine that grinds men's souls,
cutting them like logs at intervals.

It never ends.
The becoming. The involuntary
transformation from a larva to a beast.
There is enough darkness
to blackout the sun.

AWAY GAME

MICHAEL JESS ALEXANDER

T race tucked his foot underneath himself, propped his chin in his palm, and gazed at the barren hills beyond the baseball field. Through the glare of the afternoon sun, he surveyed the landscape for something more interesting than his younger brother's Little League baseball game. Running his eyes along the grey hills, his search morphed into a game of directing an imaginary digital sprite over the terrain. He halted and glanced back to a low spot in the sky.

I swear that spot went purple. Like a glitching pixel.

In a frenzied burst of creativity, he conjured in his mind such explanations as secret government cloaking technology or being trapped in a virtual simulation, but reality, like an encroaching storm, ruined such fancies. Trace had only imagined the purple spot, and with a slight frown, he realized that daydreams were not enough to keep his boredom at bay.

A hand slapped his back.

"Your brother's on deck," Uncle Camden said, smiling.

Rory, Trace's brother, stood outside the dugout,

tapping the sides of his cleats with his bat. He was loose and confident, Trace thought.

God, I wish I were home.

An eruption of cheers jolted Trace to attention. The batter had hit the ball into left field and was already rounding first base by the time Trace realized the reason for the excitement.

Despite the crowd's enthusiasm, Trace observed mere routine. Inspired by the warmth of the sun on his back, he began to imagine those on the field succumbing to a great heat, melting like crayons forgotten inside a car during the summer.

"This is new," a man's voice said, sounding as though he were speaking directly into Trace's ear.

Trace glanced around. The voice hadn't belonged to Uncle Camden, and the only other person sitting close to Trace was a petite, middle-aged woman.

The pitcher wound up and lobbed the ball.

"Let's realize this fantasy," the voice said.

A pained shriek sounded from home plate. The batter dropped his bat, and his trembling hands drifted to his side, outlining the baseball embedded in his torso.

Everyone on the field joined in a chorus of panicked wails. Parents bolted from the stands and dashed to their children. This included Uncle Camden, who hurried in the direction of Rory.

Trace's stomach bottomed out, and despite the summer heat, he shivered.

Through a grimace, Rory observed his arms. Trace's eyes widened at the sight of his brother's forearms bowing like thick lengths of taffy.

I don't want this!

An especially loud scream drew Trace's attention to first base. The first baseman's father held his son as the boy's mother, who was responsible for the scream, watched her child yield to gravity and drape in her husband's arms.

Why are you making this happen?

"I'm not. You are," the voice replied.

Returning his gaze to his brother, Trace watched as Rory's arms flopped to his sides like limp tentacles. Uncle Camden approached Rory but stood before him, seemingly unsure of what to do. Rory moaned again, the increasing laxity of his throat and vocal cords shifting the sound into a gurgle. Uncle Camden knelt down and cradled his nephew. He held firm even as the boy's head began to droop over his arm.

I'm not doing this!

"You are," the voice said.

Trace surveyed the field. Desperate adults tended to misshapen lumps of flesh that flopped out of baseball attire. At the front of the away team's dugout, the third base coach, who had gripped the chain-link fencing for support, bulged through the chinks while the players inside bawled. And out in right field, a lonely blob convulsed.

Clenching his fists, Trace closed his eyes and took a deep breath. He imagined everything as normal—as it had been moments ago.

"Clever boy," Stothgaul said.

The young Earthling did not respond.

Through vermilion eyes, Stothgaul scrutinized the youth on the screen before him. The boy's resourcefulness brought a grin to Stothgaul's face. In his experience, most Earth subjects empowered by the Actualizer become overwhelmed after their first significant realization. He recalled the woman who went into shock after her husband exploded. The woman had been upset over her husband's imprudent purchase of a vehicle. *A four-wheeler*, Stothgaul remembered. She had thought of her and her husband's debt "blowing up." And then she, with this expression in mind and with adequate focus for realization, had imagined her husband following suit. Which he did.

Stothgaul marveled at the screens in front of him. He had yet to outgrow the novelty of watching reality reset.

A HAND SLAPPED Trace's back. He opened his eyes and found his uncle to his left.

"Your brother's on deck," Uncle Camden said, exactly as he had before.

Looking to Rory, Trace discovered his brother tapping the sides of his cleats, preparing to go to bat.

Turning to his uncle, Trace pleaded with his eyes.

"What's wrong, buddy?" Uncle Camden asked.

"He won't believe you. He'll think you're insane," the voice said.

"Uncle Camden… " Trace whimpered.

"What is it?"

"Something weird is happening."

"Oh?" Uncle Camden glanced around.

"There's a voice…"

Uncle Camden furrowed his brow, and Trace felt his nauseousness return.

"I'll show you," Trace stammered.

"This will be interesting," the voice said.

Closing his eyes, Trace imagined everyone at the field, besides himself and his uncle, as frozen in place and asleep.

Opening them, he found everyone besides his uncle with their eyes shut, fixed in mid-movement.

Uncle Camden sprung from his seat as if a tarantula had fallen in his lap. He scanned the bleachers and the field, his mouth agape. He set his gaze on the petite, middle-aged woman, who sat rigid with her hands in the midst of a clap. He brought his hand to her shoulder. She remained suspended. He patted her, but she stayed firm, not yielding to the impact of his hand.

Forcing himself to speak, Trace murmured, "The voice is—"

"Just," Uncle Camden cut Trace off, "give me a second." He sat back down and rubbed his hand over his mouth, staring at the bench in front of him.

The two sat in silence.

STOTHGAUL WATCHED the young Earthling browse the stopped humans.

"It's like a museum," Stothgaul suggested.

Leave me alone! the boy thought, his words announced over the control room's sound system.

Stothgaul laughed. *You subjects are fortunate*, he thought. *I've prevented you from suffering the fate of that prodigal Earthling.* He patted the console before him, smiling. After the snafu with the exploding husband, Stothgaul had deliberated and determined the current limits for the Actualizer, which he had communicated to the device himself. These prevented a user from manipulating beings beyond the point of restoration. A fresh source of pride, Stothgaul thought of the rare approving nod he received from the boss for this development. As the boss was apt to remind him, it was best to reuse these subjects in multiple trials.

BREAKING THE STILLNESS, Uncle Camden asked, "A voice?"

In shaky, sometimes breathless words, and ignoring the voice's interjections as best he could, Trace walked his uncle through what had occurred since the voice first spoke. He shared that those on the field had begun to melt but spared his uncle more specific details. The thought of his brother warping and deflating in his uncle's arms brought a tremble to Trace's lower lip. He added, "It happened to Rory, too."

Uncle Camden looked to Rory's fixed form. "We need to get away from here," he said. He turned to Trace. "Here's what I want you to do. But wait for me to finish before you begin to imagine it."

"But," Trace whimpered, "what about the voice?"

"I'm not sure," Uncle Camden said, "We'll go to my house and figure out what to do next."

The quiet suddenly felt oppressive to Trace.

Uncle Camden's expression softened. "It's going to be okay. I promise."

Trace nodded.

"I'd like you to imagine Orrin." Uncle Camden pointed toward the dugout. "He's in there, on the left. I'd like you to picture him on deck in your brother's place. And move your brother to the back of the Jeep, but don't wake him yet. Then after we walk to the Jeep, you can wake everyone and imagine them playing like normal, but without your brother." He continued to look Trace in the eye. "You understand?"

"Yeah," Trace said, nodding.

"I like this plan," the voice said.

Please! Leave us alone!

Trace filled his lungs and clenched his eyes shut. Opening them, he found Orrin on deck with a bat in his hand, frozen in the same stance his brother had been in. Glimpsing the Jeep, he located his brother, propped in the back seat.

Making their way to the Jeep, Trace and his uncle walked as if a careless step might wake those around them.

They arrived at the vehicle. Trace climbed into the passenger seat while Uncle Camden got behind the steering wheel. In tandem, they glanced back at Rory.

"Can you make him think I spoke to his coach and said we had to leave because of an emergency at my job?" Uncle Camden asked.

"I can try."

"Okay, wake him and resume the game."

Trace closed his eyes. He opened them and looked at his brother.

"What?" Rory snapped.

"Nothing," Trace murmured.

"You could melt him again, you know," the voice suggested.

Ignoring the voice, Trace held a hand over his eyes and peered through the windshield. Like usual, the players exhibited varying degrees of determination while the spectators exhibited varying degrees of interest.

The Jeep growled to life. Uncle Camden backed out of their parking spot and drove along the dirt road that led to the paved street of a neighborhood. The gentle rumble of the gravel gave Trace a small measure of relief.

"You'd better not go too fast," the voice said.

Trace flashed a worried look at his uncle.

"The voice says—"

Trace thrust into the dashboard as the Jeep came to a violent stop. He felt Uncle Camden's hand on his shoulder.

"Are you okay?"

"Yeah," Trace groaned as he rubbed his forearm.

"Are you okay, Rory?" Uncle Camden asked.

"I'm all right," Rory said, crawling back onto his seat.

"What in the world?" Uncle Camden said, his face a mask of distress.

"What's going on?" Rory cried.

The Jeep had crashed into nothing.

"We've gained enough information from these trials," the voice announced.

Please let us go.

"But where would you go to?"

The space in front of the crashed Jeep distorted, spreading outward like a rash. Simultaneous distortions erupted in the sky, replacing blue with shades of green. Beyond the Jeep, Trace now beheld a foreign landscape, replete with lush, unfamiliar flora and strange structures, such as massive metal obelisks and illuminated spheres. Yards away, towering humanoids with pinkish skin and large, triangular heads lumbered toward the Jeep.

"Until next time, young Earthling."

Consciousness abandoned Trace.

SUDDENLY AWARE, Trace found himself standing in an unfamiliar room. Displays and control panels lined the walls, the neon glow of which illuminated the otherwise dim room. Before a control panel, two of the imposing humanoids, one seated and one standing, made guttural clicking noises at each other.

Wanting to bolt from these beings, Trace realized he couldn't move. In his periphery, he saw his uncle and brother, also immobile.

The standing being stepped to Trace and knelt to meet his eyes. While roughly humanoid in form, the being had salmon-colored skin and reddish-orange eyes with horizontal pupils. A cluster of bony ridges emphasized the triangular shape of its head. These ridges, each row more prominent than the one preceding it, comprised a mass that suggested a hybrid of antlers and a peacock's train.

The being glanced to the one still sitting and uttered more clicks. It thrust its hand into a tunic pocket and produced a small, rectangular device, which it then prodded with its finger.

"Stothgaul," the kneeling being said, a regular human female voice sounding from the device as the being continued to click, "is quite impressed with you, young Earthling." She gestured to the sitting being. "He tells me you were more inventive in your use of the Actualizer than the average specimen."

A smile crept across Stothgaul's face. Trace doubted its benevolence.

"In fact, he has suggested—since our testing is finished and you are no longer needed—that we return you to Earth." The female being grinned, stood, and turned to Stothgaul. "Now that the trial phase is complete, I'm ready to practice with the Actualizer. Transport me to the replicated environment. And," she said with a knowing smile, "remove the limits."

The female being disintegrated into nothing. One of the screens before Trace turned on, displaying the baseball field. The female being reappeared on the screen, standing near the pitcher's mound, facing the outfield. Lined up before her in four rows stood the spectators and players, frozen like before. The being pointed her arm to a man in the front row and gestured toward first base. The man floated like a rag doll to this spot.

Indicating that he had been awakened, the man darted his head around, noticed the being, and screamed.

In the direction of the man, the being brought her hands together as though she were crushing an aluminum can. The man imploded out of existence.

DEPUTY BRODY SWITCHED on the overhead lights and grabbed a novel from the passenger seat. The cover of this novel depicted a hearty band of dwarfs trekking across a majestic landscape.

Through the windshield, he eyed the fluttering police tape that hung from the sides of the bleachers and blocked the entrances to the field.

Nope, he thought, *not going to think about what happened to those people*. He flipped the book open.

A grumble emanated from his stomach, and with a sigh, the deputy sat the novel back down. He leaned over to a brown bag on the passenger side floor, rifled through it, and brought out a candy bar. He sat back and hollered, flinging the candy bar from his hand.

Pulling back the blinker lever, he threw light on a yellow Jeep that hadn't been there a moment earlier.

Leaving the low beams on, the deputy exited his truck and walked toward the Jeep. Inside the vehicle, a man and two teenage boys watched as he approached.

That's Camden Allen! the deputy realized.

He stepped to the driver's side and knocked on the window. Camden rolled it down. Lit by the truck's headlights, Camden and the boys' shell-shocked expressions gave the air of a coerced interrogation.

"Camden?" the deputy asked, moderating his tone. "Where did you come from? Where are the others?"

Camden clenched his eyes and cradled his face in his hands.

"Camden?"

"I don't know," he said. Forcing a shaky breath, he added, "I don't remember!"

Deputy Brody, eyeing Camden Allen and Allen's nephews, felt unusually vulnerable beneath the open night sky.

LIFE OF A LEPER

STEVEN DEE KISH

I'm a disease; my family told me my mental illness is too much for them to bear.

Forced to live in a forever quarantine to stop the poison seeping out of my depressed mind.

Rejected by loved ones, I seek a quiet place and eventually metamorphose into a social leper.

My safe place becomes a cabin tucked away in the Deep Creek Mountains.

I shed my old human skin and try to become one with nature.

My fingers turn into claws, as I need them to survive in the barren land.

Hikers and hunters call me a beast, Bigfoot, or Skinwalker.

Love could turn me back to the human I once knew.

The only love I receive is a friendly lick from the offspring of Old Ephraim.

I am afraid!

Not because of the creatures that lurk in the mountains.

Oh no! I am afraid that I will turn the claws on myself.

Suicide thoughts rattle around in my mind like the rattlesnake outside my cabin.

Feeling my heartbeat in my neck.

I can imagine myself ripping the carotid artery and bathing in my blood.

Death is too merciful for me; the Devil wants me to suffer and endure.

Madness is settling in and finding a comfortable place in my brain.

Trying to find a reason to live and justify my existence becomes a chore.

Living in a state of perpetual conflict, praying for a different mind.

Hoping the disease of depression leaves my body.

Acceptance is buried in the depths of my mind. Is acceptance viable?

Nightmares become routine; there is no peaceful REM sleep for me.

Dreaming of waking up on the Great Salt Lake with waves of shame sinking my boat.

Struggling to find my way back home without any oars.

Legs dangle in the salty water with the mythical Water Babies pulling me under.

The nightmare fades…

The ringing from my vintage twin-bell alarm clock enters my consciousness.

Eyes open and fix on the wooden slats on the ceiling of my cabin.

Tears run down my dirty woodsman face, and I start the day… living the life of a leper.

DEEP WITHIN

CARTER LAPPIN

The copper mine stretches out beneath my feet, deep as I can imagine and even deeper yet. Its maw yawns grotesquely, revealing sharp teeth scattered irregularly across the cavernous space. They say it's the deepest pit dug by human hands in the country, and I believe it. All around me, sound echoes—tools clanging off of stone walls, men's voices calling to each other indistinctly, a distant rumble of moving earth. But there's no one here but me. They're ghosts, all of them, the echoes of themselves trapped deep within the unyielding walls.

The air tastes like metal. No—like blood, coppery and warm in my mouth.

The far edges of the mine are uneven and packed with soft dirt, ready to slide down into oblivion at the slightest provocation. I pick slowly over the ground, feet noiseless. A small rock, no bigger than a pebble, is dislodged at the encouragement of my shoe and goes tumbling down, down, down, into the cavern. If it ever hits the bottom, I don't hear it.

I sit down, so close to the edge that my knees jut out

over it, suspended above the void. I press a hand into the soil and find that it's grittier than I had expected. I pick up a handful and let it sift through my fingers, falling into the pit below. My palm is left near-white with the grainy dirt that's left over. I lick it, leaving a glistening stripe of spit across my palm. Salt. The ground tastes like salt.

I try to call out, but nothing comes out of my mouth, not even the strained rasp of my throat. A moment later, a sound is bounced back from the depths of the pit. A scream. It sounds like my voice. It sounds desperate. I don't try to speak again.

A hand on my shoulder. It's heavy, heavier than a hand should be. It would be easy enough to turn my head to look at it, but I don't. I don't look at the hand, and I certainly don't look at the person it's attached to. I feel a huff of warm air on the back of my neck and on the curve of my ear.

Without looking, I put my hand on top of the one on my shoulder. In comparison to the other, my hand is miniature, like a doll's. In Morse code, I tap it out. *Who - Are - You*. I still can't bring myself to speak out loud.

The air is warm despite the lateness of the hour. The moon shines bright overhead. Its light caresses my skin then drips, slowly, toward the bottom of the mine, where it's suddenly and unceremoniously devoured by the darkness. It's jet-black down there, but every so often, I think I might see something moving among the pitch.

The hand taps back. *I - Am - You*.

Finally, finally, I turn to look. There's no one there. The night is warm.

There was a landslide here, a few years ago. Thousands of tons of dirt and soil were dislodged, tumbling down the sides of the mine and gathering at the bottom. When it fell, it sounded like an avalanche. By a stroke of luck, nobody was killed, not even injured. The bottom of the pit had swallowed both the loose dirt and the ground-shaking sound.

I tap it out on my own knee. *Who - Am - I.* I wait, but this time I get no response.

The rumbling of a landslide sounds like thunder in the night, roiling and clashing in the gray-dark sky. I can still hear the sounds echoing in my ears. It's not happening anymore—just the ghost of it, like all the others, but I hear it anyway, slow and regular, like blood rushing in my head. Phantom voices are all around me, too, but when I put my hands over my ears, those disappear, while the roaring of the landslide does not.

The clouds above look gray and sickly; polluted. The moon is bright. Its white light claws through the haze, decimating anything in its path. Anything but the darkness at the bottom of the pit.

That—that stays as it always has been, implacable and unmovable and impenetrable. The moon tries, shoving and straining against the slate, but in the end, it retreats, tired and defeated. The darkness is unaffected. Something is definitely moving down there. The shapes are indistinct, but I find they're somehow familiar.

I drop another pebble downwards. This one is devoured by the darkness much earlier than the last one was. After what seems like a lifetime, I think I might hear it hit the bottom. The sound echoes strangely, as though it's coming from somewhere else entirely, and is louder than it should be, like I've dropped a boulder instead of a rock no larger than a penny.

The sound is familiar, and this time when I drop another, I'm sure. Morse code. It's funny. I can't remember where I learned it.

Come - And - See. The rock taps out against the side of

the pit as it tumbles down, down, down, and is consumed by the dark. The air tastes like blood—no, like metal, like copper dug desperately from the ground with my bare hands, still dirty and unrefined.

Who - Am - I. I tap against my knee again, softly, like I'm afraid someone might hear it. *Who - Are - You.*

Come - And - See. Says the mine again, this time without the need for falling rocks. The thunder in my ears is getting louder and louder.

I can still hear the ghosts, the men calling to each other and the tools against the side of the mine and the rattle of the elevator as it takes people deeper and deeper into the heart of the mine. The wraiths have taken on a different pitch from before, though. They sound almost frightened. Desperate. My own voice is among them somewhere. I don't dare attempt to pick it out from the rabble.

The pit in front of me stretches out, dark and almost inviting. The moon shines brightly on my face, so bright it almost burns my skin. It's a hot night. I move, still sitting, so that one of my feet dangles over the edge, untethered over oblivion.

Come - And - See. A hand, heavy and warm on my shoulder. I don't dare turn to look at it. I hesitate. *Come - And - See.*

The night is hot. The mine stretches out in front of me. The air tastes like blood and copper and salty tears. The moon shines desperately. *Come - And - See.* It's dark. There's a hand on my shoulder. It's dark.

GUARDIAN
HEIDI VOSS

ost guardian angels don't have as many legs or eyes as me, but this has not stopped me from keeping careful watch over my charge, Emma Dalisay. When she was young, I shielded her from accidents on her skateboard and kept her from wandering from her parents in shopping centers. Now that she's grown, she frequently rides public transit. I follow her onto the train, curl my many legs and body segments around her seat, and probe the crowd for problematic strangers. If hands brush too close to her backpack or hungry eyes linger on her for too long, I stare at the offender. They can't see me, but their stomachs will turn, their hands will shake, and a sour taste will fill their mouths until they turn their attention elsewhere.

She can't see me, but I think she is aware of my presence. Once, when I was injured in a fight with an overpass goblin, she asked a friend to drive her to the grocery store instead of taking the light rail. She wouldn't accept any guests in her home that night and only left the next day when I could accompany her to work.

Today she's on her way home from something called "stitch and bitch." She dozes on a seat near the window clutching a bag of yarn, knitting needles, and a half-finished project.

An imp boards at the next station. Imps disguised as humans are fairly common on commutes, but I keep an eye on him just in case. As the train creeps on and other passengers exit, the imp moves closer. I stiffen, preparing to lunge at him if he draws too close.

He wears a navy blue suit and the skin of a blonde man. He takes a seat across from Emma. "You've already claimed this spirit? I was hoping for a good meal tonight."

I flex and unflex a set of forelegs. "This woman is my charge, not my dinner. I'm her guardian angel."

The imp laughs so hard he clutches his stomach. "A guardian angel? You?"

Sitting a bit taller, I arch three of my six eyebrows. "I have protected her since she was a child."

The imp's eyes shine in the fluorescent light of the train car. "Do you realize how large your body can become? How much more powerful you would be with even a few human hearts in your stomach? You could swallow this train whole."

I press my mandibles together. "Angels protect people, not eat them."

He shakes his head. "Does she know about you?" He nods toward Emma.

My cheeks flush. "She is semi-aware a spirit guides her."

The imp leans closer, clasping his hands under his chin. "Does she *know* about you? What do you think she'd say if she knew something that looked like you was following her every move?"

Heat warms my upper body sections. Sweat pricks my

black exoskeleton. "She would be pleased to know she's under such careful watch, even if I don't look like the other angels."

He stands and approaches Emma. "Let's test that, shall we?" He flicks her forehead and Emma blinks her eyes open.

She starts at the sight of the imp standing over her. She withdraws a knitting needle from her bag. "Do you need something?"

"This guy says he's your guardian angel." He tilts his head toward me.

I curl my upper and lower body together in an effort to look smaller. Her eyes widen at the sight of me. I bury my face in my forelegs.

A hesitant touch grasps one of my back legs near her seat. I peek an eye open.

She gazes up at me with polished amber eyes. "Were you the one who set off the car alarm when that weirdo followed me home?"

I swallow and nod. "He made eye contact with you at the ticket machine and thought it was meant as an invitation."

Emma whips her head back to the imp. "That sounds like a guardian angel to me." My heart stops. Is she really okay with the way I look? She isn't frightened?

The imp steps back, gritting his teeth.

She brandishes her knitting needle at the imp like a baton. "Guardian angel, would you please take care of this man? He's disturbing my ride home."

I uncoil my long body and reach forward with my forelegs. "With pleasure."

Nebulous Strike in Minn.

Nnadi Samuel

Six months into prepartum trauma,
    I occupied the alley,
       tummy-red & indecent with
    blood clotting fiercely like
iridescent fog on a Sunday, as I irony
    my way into a female talk
       with my godmother. Her
    passion for poetry, squeezed
from tonight's sharp want, to cause a
    small miracle of breeze and
nebulous strike in Minnesota—
       whose landscape toughens
    with maple wood snow
    ridden by
the thickest
       pang of dust: monsoon flatu-
    lence. a gas breaking on my
    elephant feet.
I kegel in the warmth, memorizing

the old baobab plant potted by
my foster
father, whose mortgage
        exceeds a headcount & by all
    means, indebts we—his descen-
    dants and
all our afterbears. Loan, beyond esti-
    mate sits nameless as a scattered
    blood
right we inherit with caution.
        the curse we put a face to, as
    banks flag down our surname.
    Right here,
taking my godmother
        to the moon and back with a
    love poem, I tongue distance—
    the length of
a metaphor.
        her uplifting to the chorus,
    desperate for a rising. The way
    the fetus
inside me attains weightlessness,
        manly afloat in baritone pulse.
    the vibe that brings life to
    rectum.
Tell me about birth, my traveling,
    my approach to language in
    concealed
weightlessness
of a lost flesh: days I cribbed in my
    godmother's hut. red clay,
printing it's brutal remarks on my
    turned back. my feet,

        sashaying the railing my foster
      father fixed decades
back, in the timely fashion
of a stone coffin—durable in its
      wearing out. from the audible
      distance
of a co-wife, the shout fills me with
      monsoon, ruptured breath.
a daggered flatulence,
        released in the harmful
      custom of a birthing. dust,
      reeling
the way the fetus folds, clenching its
      shapeless fist while I stabilize my
eager, worn-out breath to suit the
      calmness of township:
        my Iowa dreams, exaggerated
      everywhere across the border
holding those who raised me. I
      dragged my skin like an animal,
throughout three cardinal points
      —'til my
        luck went South. A wanderer,
      unsettled by the inner works of
      clime.
unable to language in clearly
      distilled allomorph.
        I'm torn apart by grammar.
      the manner of its safe delivery,
      stuck
between my thighs.
Woman, if not anything, a terror
      gadget, surviving pills & the messy

contractions, to forge a replica from
        her fallen relic.
Woman, if not anything
            uncontained as the whirlwind.
    a neat violence, stretched
    across a
young navel withstanding all harms
        thrown at it:
the tactics of warfare.

DERELICT

K. SCOTT FORMAN

T he wall was made of stone, three feet tall at its highest point. It ran for about one-hundred feet end to end and was alone. It had been longer once. Employees of the state built it many decades ago, but it could have been centuries—before the darkness came, before the spores and hordes of living dead. After, time really didn't have meaning. It was a war between the living dead and what would become the dying dead.

The wall became a decoration along a walking path. It guarded against amnesia.

"You used to walk on this path for fun, for exercise?"

Tess turned and looked at her little brother. She was the oldest, he the youngest, and the only two that had survived of their siblings. There had been six; four and their mother had died early on, the spores had taken care of that.

"Yeah, weird, huh?"

Dylan just shook his head.

They reached the familiar wall. It held back contaminated soil, the growth of poisonous plants, and possibly what was left of a derelict sewage treatment plant. It was a battle, and the wall was losing.

"What's that smell?"

Derelict was probably the wrong word.

"Raw sewage, rotting corpses, decaying plants, stagnant water," said Tess.

"The treatment plant must be in full operation."

"I don't think that was its purpose."

The small boy looked up at his sister, as if she had the answer to every question. She smiled and kept walking. He tried to wait her out. She anticipated his question and gave in to conversation.

"The plant treated raw sewage, so it wouldn't stink, of course. It also reclaimed the water used in flushing toilets for other uses."

The boy laughed. His sister's eyes brightened for an instant, but the haunted glaze that mirrored her skin and bones overpowered the momentary hope. Her features retreated into the strength that camouflaged despair.

"I remember flushing toilets," said Dylan.

Tess smiled again and kept walking. She had to keep walking.

"Do you think what we're looking for could be out there, out there at the old plant I mean?"

"I doubt it."

"Do you think there's anything to eat?"

She did not respond. Every conversation ended with food.

An hour later, the next town came into view. It looked like their own town: black, burned, empty. Tess had been sixteen when the asteroid or the meteorite or whatever it was hit the earth. The scientists were never sure. Some believed, after the sickness started, that it had been a preemptive attack by aliens. If that were the case, the aliens never showed up to claim victory.

The object had struck near the tri-border area of Afghanistan, Iran, and Turkmenistan, between two cities Tess had never heard of, Herat and Mary. Everything for several hundred miles around the impact zone was annihilated. The dust cloud that the impact created blocked the sun for months. Then the sickness started.

"Are we almost there, Tess?"

"Yeah, just over the train tracks and we'll be there."

She looked. The train tracks were bare. The glow of silver had long vanished, the light too dim to see the brown of rust. What would it be like to see a train again, a real train, running on the tracks, carrying food or clothing or medicine or new cars? She remembered waiting for a train to pass at a crossing. She had been in the front seat, her mother driving, and they had made a game out of counting the passing freight cars. She remembered her brothers and sisters…

…and then the sickness.

The screams and moans had been the worst, and then the change. They became something that was no longer human, something that fed on lust, murder, and human flesh. She tried to forget the wailing of women for their husbands and children, the screams of those being eaten, and the whimpering of those who had been raped or sodomized or worse, a fate worse than death that passed the sickness on. Then came the mass eradication and quarantines put in place by the government: she could feel the flames, the acrid smoke in her throat, and the smells of things worse than even the sickness.

"Tess, do you ever get scared?"

The question was unexpected, the answer not clear in her own mind. She looked at her brother. She would have been terrified if she had been in his place, but he seemed to take it all in stride.

"Not as much as I used to be."

She was twenty now, Dylan almost eleven.

"Is that because you're bigger?"

"Maybe."

She let the single word hang, trying to connect the dots for a real answer. Dylan would need a good answer, an answer that would quell his fears and bring peace to his sleep.

"I think because most of the things that could harm me are dead."

"Because you killed them."

Her laugh brought an ease to the boy's face. She had not erased all his fears, but enough that he could make it for at least another week or two, if only—

"I wish Mom could be here."

Tess felt the stinging in her nose and the tears threaten. She kept walking, her back to her brother. Their mother had been taken by the government, only her ashes returned.

"Do you miss her?"

She stopped, turned, and tried to speak. The tears spoke for her.

"I'm sorry."

"Don't be," she said. "We loved her, and we miss her."

She paused, but only for a second.

"We've got Dad and Rufus."

"Rufus would have enjoyed a walk, and maybe even the sewage plant."

Tess continued walking. She raised her voice so Dylan could hear her.

"Catch up, slowpoke. We might have time to see Mom's grave."

"Rufus would have liked that too."

"Someone had to stay back and guard the camp."

"You mean guard Dad," said Dylan.

Tess stopped and tuned back to her brother.

"What do you mean?"

"I know I'm just a kid, but I'm not stupid, Tess."

She measured him. He was half her age, but he had grown more on the inside in three years than she had in the first sixteen years of her life. He was already old and wise. What would he be like when, if…? She pushed the thought from her mind and continued.

"So, what is it you think you know?"

"Really?"

Dylan rolled his eyes and sighed. He looked over her shoulder.

"Really," said Tess. "I don't want you getting any crazy ideas."

"He's already becoming one of them, one of the infected, Tess, and you know it. I've seen the black lines spider-webbing from the corners of his eyes into his hair, the black dots on the back of his hands, and then there's the smell."

Tess wanted to argue, but she couldn't lie. Dylan was a better observer than she had given him credit for, although it wasn't hard to see the signs of the sickness. He would know if she tried telling him a story, tried to make it seem everything was okay.

A story: that's what their father had tried to tell her, but he wasn't very good at it, or at hiding things. She had confronted him, called him out. That had not been a pleasant day. It was a week before he would talk to her, and then only to apologize and acknowledge she had been right. He had retreated into himself. He couldn't accept the fact or embrace what he would have to do.

Colin had tried to talk to him. There had been more than words exchanged. Colin was gone. Why did Colin leave her?

"We could leave, Tess, before Dad changes. We could go find Colin."

"I know," she said.

Dylan surprised her. He was a thinker, but there was more. The doctors had thought he might be on the autism spectrum, but then the strike, the endless night, the constant winter, and—

"You're going to kill him, aren't you?"

"What? What did you say?"

"You heard me," said Dylan.

Her father had agreed that if he or she or Dylan became infected they would have to destroy them. The infection had to be stopped. Her father had told her he would kill her and burn her body if he had to, and he expected her to do the same, the same to him, Dylan, and then her boyfriend, Colin. Death didn't matter, life did: kill or be killed. When the time came, when he started to show signs, fear changed the agreement, at least from her father's point of view, but she knew she would have to follow through.

"Was Colin infected? Did Dad infect him? Is that why he left?"

Dylan was staring at her, his eyes telegraphing emotions, knowledge, understanding.

"No. No, I don't think so. I don't know why he left."

She turned and started walking again. She was thinking about what Dylan had said. You're going to kill him, aren't you?

The answer was simple. Dylan was right. She would do it to protect them. She would do it to relieve the suffering, to be merciful, to protect herself. She was the only one—

"When are you going to do it?"

She stopped again and looked at her brother. How could she do it?

"Very soon, I suppose."

The tears came again, and she closed her eyes. She felt her brother's hand on her arm and pulled away but then stopped and looked at him.

"I'm sorry Tess, sorry about Dad, and about Colin. When did he leave?

She felt the same hot tears building, the same needles stinging her nose.

"Last night."

"They argued, didn't they?"

She nodded. She looked into his eyes. It was unfair. This was not a world for children, and these things, this anger, this love, the emotions, not for a boy, a boy without a mother or father. It wasn't fair to her either. What sister would have to do—

"I don't know. I don't think so. I don't know."

She took the rifle from her shoulder, stripped off the day pack, and looked for somewhere to sit down.

"Let's take a rest. I think I have something to eat in here somewhere."

"I'm not hungry."

She stopped what she was doing and focused on Dylan. He was always hungry. He could feel her attention and withdrew more into his logical mind.

"We have two problems: father is infected and must be dealt with, and Colin is possibly infected, and if he is, will probably return and try to kill us."

He walked over and sat down on a rock.

"We don't want to waste ammunition. Have you considered smothering or drowning father? Maybe poison?"

Why not just bash his brains in while he slept or slit his throat, she thought, but that would expose too much blood, too much risk. She had thought of so many things, but almost all of them, save poison, would be risky. Then one day, she decided thinking about it had been a waste of time and energy.

"I don't think about it, I just—"

She stopped herself. Thinking, doing, it all hurt her soul, especially what she still had to do before returning to their camp.

"We could find a poison, put it into his food," said Dylan.

"That's why we came to Centerville."

"I thought we came to see Mom's grave."

"That too," said Tess.

He knew she was lying. He always knew.

They walked over the old bridge that crossed the railroad tracks and the old Interstate. There was water in the low spots, and they could hear frogs croaking. She remembered throwing rocks into the ponds to quiet the frogs. She avoided throwing rocks in water now, especially standing water. The frogs would retaliate. The spores had done weird things to more than humans.

They reached the halfway point on the bridge. The frogs were louder, the water deeper. Dylan walked to the edge and looked down. She followed.

"I know why we really came here, Tess, and it's okay, I understand."

"What are you talking about?"

"I know I'm infected. I just wish—"

She placed the pistol behind his ear and pulled the trigger in one fluid motion.

Then she really cried.

INSATIATE

C.H. LINDSAY

Hunger claws inside
soulless Nightwalkers
desperately craving
a semblance of life.

HOLY GRAIL
WILLIAM R.D. WOOD

**RED PINNACLE RED PINNACLE RED PINNACLE
DO NOT DUPLICATE DO NOT DUPLICATE**

251809ZMAR21 (March 25, 2021 1109 MST)
Executive Summary
Dugway Proving Ground

****

SUBJECT: "Black Knight" object

Operation Holy Grail 020800ZDEC99
[December 02, 1999 08:00 GMT]

MISSION SUMMARY: Dispatch AV-71 Archangel flight
from DPG to acquire and return Black Knight object from
low earth orbit (LEO).

AV-71 Archangel: Payload capable orbital stealth craft. Crew of two. One pilot and one mission specialist. Assigned Lt. Commander Jason Elder, USN, pilot, and Lt. Colonel Allesandra Juarez, USMC, mission specialist – geology, astrophysics, and biomathematics.

Black Knight Object: See Historic Summary

Callsign Legend:
Bridgemaster: Dugway Proving Ground
– AF attachment DeepSatCon
Concorde: AV-71 Archangel aircraft
Enchanter: Lt. Colonel Allesandra Juarez, USMC
Lancelot: Lt. Commander Jason Elder, USN
Rabbit: Black Knight object

TIMELINE EXCERPT ONE (1):
Operation Holy Grail 020800ZDEC99

[December 02, 1999 08:00 GMT]
Night Launch DPG, UT.

[December 02, 1999 08:06 GMT]
Orbital insertion complete.

[December 02, 1999 12:18 GMT]
RCS (Reaction Control System) thruster corrections complete. Rendezvous with Rabbit in three orbits.

[December 02, 1999 16:52 GMT]
Bridgemaster logs RF (Radio Frequency) burst from Rabbit in the gamma ray region. Duration 3.08 seconds. Signal not detected by Concorde, which is located in planetary shadow.

[December 02, 1999 17:00 GMT]
Lancelot: …well, if you hadn't been such a stick in the mud—
Enchanter: Screw you, flyboy. They were your parents.
Bridgemaster: Concorde, Bridgemaster. Status report.
Lancelot: Bridgemaster, Concorde. Approaching Rabbit. Altitude 258 kilometers. Velocity 28,120 kph. Time to rendezvous nine minutes. Initiating roll and brake maneuver. All systems green.
Bridgemaster: Roger that. Do you have visual?
Enchanter: Negative, Bridgemaster. Camera feed only. Still too far away. Getting some unusual RF chatter. Radar image of 4.1 square meters.
Bridgemaster: Ground imaging still showing only 2 meters. Verify calibration.
Enchanter: Calibration is fivers.
Bridgemaster: Payload bay accommodation is still viable.
Enchanter: Roger that. Pending mass analysis. Wouldn't want to spill the soup. Cradles are all adjustable to five meters. Waiting for visual. Will advi—

Supplemental Information A:
Wikipedia entry from 2019 before removal in 2021: "The Black Knight satellite conspiracy theory claims that there is a spacecraft in near polar orbit of the Earth that is of extraterrestrial origin and that NASA is engaged in a coverup regarding its existence and origin."

TIMELINE EXCERPT TWO (2):
Operation Holy Grail 020800ZDEC99

[December 02, 1999 17:11 GMT]

Lancelot: Whoa! Massive lightshow, Bridgemaster. Blue sparks dancing along the nose of the Concorde. Instruments blinked out on us for a second. Systems back in the green.

Enchanter: I think we passed through a high tesla electromagnetic field. Guassometer pegged, so I don't have an exact field strength but, well, my nose is bleeding.

Lancelot: What? Juarez, are you okay?

Bridgemaster: Observe protocol, Concorde.

Enchanter: Roger that.

Bridgemaster: And I'm fine, Lancelot.

Lancelot: Nosebleeds and an upset tummy. Really? Eight gees to get into orbit and now you get a nosebleed? Glad I didn't take you bungee jumping.

Bridgemaster: Lancelot.

Lancelot: Roger that. Rabbit rendezvous six minutes.

Enchanter: Bridgemaster, are you showing a change in Rabbit size?

Bridgemaster: Negative. Holding at two meters.

Enchanter: On board is now indicating 23 meters.

Lancelot: What? That's bigger than we are. Let me… confirmed. Radar Indicating 23.11 meters. Camera visual consistent with onboard radar. Details are sharper.

Enchanter: Flat black in some areas, glossy in others. Lots of angular layers by appearance. Like shale or mica. Roughly cylindrical.

Lancelot: Closing. Altitude 259 kilometers. Velocity 27,900 kph. Final—holy shit. Massive arcs flashing along Concorde's skin. Instruments are all over the place. Rebooting main—shit, shit, shit—

Bridgemaster: Protocol, Concorde.

Lancelot: Eyes adjusting. Polarizing NODS kicked in just in t—my god, that thing is huge. Braking, matching velocity, dipping for parallel view on dorsals. Cameras rolling, guys and girls. Holy mother. I can see it outside the cockpit windows. Must be… radar is saying 611 meters, reticules confirm. How is that even possible? The closer we got the bigger it got—and, Enchanter, before you say anything, I know that's how getting closer works. Enchanter? Juarez?

Bridgemaster: Status, Enchant—

Lancelot: Standby, her face, shit, it's covered in blood—

Supplemental Information B:

Lt. Colonel Juarez and Lt. Commander Elder were formally counseled on multiple occasions regarding fraternization between July 1998 and December 1999, LTC Juarez on two occasions and LCDR Elder on three. LTC Juarez denied serious involvement with LCDR Elder on both occasions. Prior to Operation Holy Grail, LCDR Elder was called before Admiral Myron Carstairs and admitted that a relationship may have existed. ADM Carstairs informed LCDR Elder that if he failed to dissolve any "possible" relationship, a letter of reprimand would be placed in his service record. LCDR Elder replied, "And?" to which ADM Carstairs added that a similar letter would be placed in LTC Juarez's file. LCDR Elder agreed to terminate their relationship on their return from Operation Holy Grail, already scheduled for the following morning. In the interest of esprit de corps, ADM Carstairs granted LCDR Elder one week following the Operation to meet the requirement.

TIMELINE EXCERPT THREE (3):
Operation Holy Grail 020800ZDEC99

[December 02, 1999 18:05 GMT]
Lancelot: Bridgemaster, Enchanter is conscious and claims to be feeling fine. BP is low, heart rate elevated.

Enchanter: Well within mission parameters and not unexpected under the current circumstances, Bridgemaster. I'm sure Lancelot's little heart is racing too.

Lancelot: On station. Rabbit is a big one. Some sort of stealth technology in play.

Enchanter: Agreed. Chance of a natural phenomenon extremely remote. Layered electromagnetic envelope of some kind. RF activity is almost zero, only a portion of our own noise being reflected back.

Bridgemaster: Roger. Abandon Mission A: Object Retrieval. Commence Mission B: Sample Retrieval.

Lancelot: Confirmed. Explains a lot that's happened over the years. Unfortunately asks a whole hell of lot more questions.

Bridgemaster: Maintain protocol.

Lancelot: Blah-ger that.

Enchanter: Lancelot… Lance… Jace, I'm not feeling—

[Three second burst of static over channel followed by loss of signal]

Supplemental Information C:
Black Knight Object - Historic Summary

1899: Radio frequency sources detected during Nikola Tesla's experiments.

1928: Tesla's RF sources confirmed by Jorgen Hans in Norway.

1954: USAF detected (2) artificial satellites in orbit around the earth three years before Sputnik.

1960: Time reported USN detection of a dark object in orbit around the earth.

1963: Gordon Cooper reported an unexplained object in orbit.

1973: Scottish author Duncan Lunan announced his findings that the signals detected by Jorgen Hals originated from a 13,000 year-old satellite around the moon.

1974: Dynawing X-11M dispatched to investigate. Unable to rendezvous. Closest approach: 25 kilometers.

1979: Skylab crashes. Proximity of Black Knight: 850 linear kilometers.

1986: Challenger Disaster. Proximity of Black Knight object. Directly overhead, 225 kilometers.

1994: Mir reports apparent collision with small object. Proximity of Black Knight: 10 linear kilometers.

1997: Mir reports onboard fire. Proximity of Black Knight: 917 linear kilometers.

1998: STS-88 photographs Black Knight and dismisses as space debris, possible thermal blanket from earlier in their mission. Proximity of Black Knight: 50 linear kilometers.

1999: Operation Holy Grail. Proximity to Black Knight object: Direct contact.

TIMELINE EXCERPT FOUR (4):
Operation Holy Grail 020800ZDEC99

[December 03, 1999 21:33 GMT]
Bridgemaster: Repeat, Concorde, please respond. Lancelot, please respond. Enchanter, please respond. Lost your telemetry for over a day, but now we show both of your transponders back on Concorde. Please respond. Concorde—

Lancelot: Shh. I think it's listening.

Bridgemaster: Lancelot, we thought we'd lost you. Is Enchanter with you?

Lancelot: Not so loud! Did you hear me? It's fucking listening.

Bridgemaster: Maintain protocol, Concorde. Just tell us what happened.

Lancelot: Fuck protocol. Who is this? Who am… what's going on?

Bridgemaster: Lancelot, we're picking up telemetry from Enchanter. Is she okay?

Lancelot: What? Enchanter? No, Sandy is not with me. Who is this? Oh, shit, it's listening. It's fucking listening.

Bridgemaster: [muted] Yes, sir. I understand. [normal volume] Hey, Jason. Sounds bad up there. My name's Ramone. I'm gonna help you get through this. Does that sound okay?

Lancelot: Ramone? Okay, yeah… okay. I tried. I tried to save her, man. It, uh, it pulled us in. Big organic looking… this chamber. Sandy was fascinated. Gonna be famous, she said. First contact. Oh, my god. Big open chamber dotted with stalagmites only pointed to the center, except a few bigger ones. Like flowstone or some shit. Been to Grand Caverns in Weyer's Cave, Ramone? Ramone?

Bridgemaster: Sorry, Jason. Pretty crazy over here, you know? And, no, can't say I have.

Lancelot: Beautiful little place. You'd like it.

Bridgemaster: Look, Jason. We're showing telemetry for Allesandra—Sandy, I mean. What's her status?

Lancelot: Sandy? Status? Her fucking status? Fuck that and fuck your 'we're gonna work through this' bullshit. I'm initiating Mission C: Blow It The Fuck Up.

Bridgemaster: Negative, negative. Lancelot, Jason, listen to me. We see you're arming emergency protocols. We need you to stop. Stand down.

Lancelot: It's organic, she said. Organic! You know why you're reading telemetry from Sandy? Because it spit out her fucking helmet!

Bridgemaster: Stand down, Commander.

Lancelot: I'm deploying the package. Payload doors

active. No joy. Reinitiate. Houston, you've got a remote
lockout activated.

Bridgemaster: Confirmed. Stand down, sir. Please.

Lancelot: Give me control, god damnit.

Bridgemaster: Standby, Lancelot. Red Pinnacle is active.
We will advise ASAP.

Lancelot: You can go fuck yourselves. I'll carry it over
manually.

Bridgemaster: Strap in, sir. We're initiating de-orbit
burn in five… four…

Lancelot: Organic! You know what the most organic part
of it was, Ramone? All the fucking teeth!

Supplemental Information D:

Analysis of photos and laser spectrographs indicate metal-
lurgy inconsistent with current theories of solar system
formation. Unexpected metallic properties associated with
carbon and germanium. Multiple complex alloy and
synthetic compounds detected. See detailed report
XXV7719/19.

Ongoing Detection Efforts:

2000: Black Knight Object not detected, disappeared from
radar.

2003: Mark XXX Advanced Detection System online.
Black Knight Object not detected.

2004: Mark XXXI Advanced Detection System online.
Black Knight Object not detected.

2007: Joint Commission Big Eyes System online. Black
Knight Object not detected.

2010: Orbital Expansion Module Series 10 online. Black
Knight Object not detected.

2012: LOVeCRAFT Platforms launched. Black Knight
Object not detected.

2021: See Developments

Latest Developments:
250912ZMAR21 (March 25, 2021 0212 MST)

1. Medical Assessment of LCDR Jason Elder: Lt. Commander Elder suffered severe head trauma from failed restraint system during deorbit. Limited full recovery expected with prosthetic accommodation. Head trauma resulted in fractured memory of operation Holy Grail. In addition, severe PTSD compounding from loss of longtime colleague Lt. Colonel Allesandra Juarez. LCDR Elder promoted to honorary rank of Commander (CDR) and separated from active service. His family were awarded full rights and benefits commensurate with honorable discharge. CDR Elder has since resided in veterans psychological rehab center in Antioch, NY, with supervised visitation only.

2. The New York Times – March 21, 2021
Two Hundred Dead
CDC Atlanta – The plague of spontaneous nosebleeds and nausea sweeping the northeast on Friday were not the cause of solar activity as originally explained, but the result of a deep space gamma burst. Scientists assured a skeptical public the event was once in a million years only hours before a second wave, a hundred times more severe, struck Reykjavik killing 195 and injuring twelve thousand.

3. This morning, March 25, 2021, at 0005 MST (250705ZMAR21) The Black Knight Object was detected in Low Earth Orbit. Altitude 231 kilometers. Velocity 27,960 kph. Thirteen-degree westward progression per orbit.

4. Five minutes later, a second object was detected. Since, twenty-seven additional objects have appeared at various altitudes and velocities.

Recommendations:

1. Immediate media saturation, all modes and methods.
2. Dispatch remote comms team to "Lancelot" facility.
3. As able, review notes from CDR Jason Elder.
4. Deploy all assets.
5. Set Condition Scorched Earth.

****

DO NOT DUPLICATE DO NOT DUPLICATE
RED PINNACLE RED PINNACLE RED PINNACLE

SHOOTING STAR
JOSEPH HOPE

A shooting star is a message from the universe
            someone is searching for us,
shooting stars down,

fiery stones,
emptiness, eternity—
Our souls howl at the moon
from their little cells

somewhere in the middle
of the Atlantic ocean.

we two-eyed, web-less species,
sitting at the sun's backyard, thirty million

light years from emptiness
            ugliness.

They ask their telescope
how far to the next possible life?
Let's shoot down another star.

Some civilizations like us are tired of their
loneliness.

FOG OF SAND

D.J. MOORE

Canst thou bind the chains of the Pleiades or loose the belt of Orion?
—Job 38:31

Seeing the fog approach, I hunched my coat over my mouth. I didn't know if it was urban smog, wildfire smoke, or a dust storm. Whatever it was, I didn't want to breathe it in. Dust storms were particularly bad. Ever since the Great Salt Lake dried up, every stirring of the wind sent another fog of dust our way—a fine mist of salt and sand small enough to get into your lungs. As a result, everybody these days had a cough that wouldn't go away. And it's not like we weren't warned: the same thing happened to Owens Lake in California a hundred years before, making history the ultimate Cassandra.

The dust storms didn't just wreck your respiratory system. They also salted the earth in every direction. Far enough to reach into other states, in some cases. All that water diverted from the Bear River to feed thirsty crops, and now all that crop land was useless. I guess the Great

Salt Lake finally got her revenge, killing the land that dehy-drated her to death.

Everybody had finally stopped watering their lawns by this point. Except for the crappy apartment complex I lived in, apparently. The owner must have thought the lawn made the place look classy, distracting residents from the cockroaches and general squalor. Even though the lawn was covered by a layer of sand. Lawns in the desert: what a joke.

As I rounded the corner to the main entrance, I saw someone had left a dirty old mattress leaning against the wall. There was a dark stain on it that might have been blood. Yeah, this place was real classy.

I trudged up the steps to the second floor. There was a full-length mirror at the end of the hallway. Another touch of class, I guess. When I first moved here, I kind of liked the mirror being there. I could use it to see if anyone was following me. But I must not be as popular as I thought: I was always alone in that reflection.

Lately, I've been avoiding the mirror. The last thing I wanted to see at the end of a hard day was my own sad mug. So I didn't see her at first. I made it all the way down the hall trying to puzzle out what pattern was supposed to be inside the red squares of carpet at my feet. I even began fighting with my lock, the one that always had trouble opening, even though I had the right key. I had to jam my key in forcefully and at just the right angle to get it to go in all the way. If my stupid landlord paid to replace the locks instead of constantly replacing the dying lawn outside, I wouldn't be having this problem.

I looked up at my reflection in exasperation, just to share my frustration with someone. And that's when I saw her. Standing behind me. The woman with the perfect hourglass figure. I could almost see the grains of sand ticking away, reminding me of how short life was. She had a bald head and tattoos running down her arms that looked like cobwebs. Instead of flies, random objects like cars and guns had been trapped by an unseen spider.

Her reflection made eye contact with mine. "Be careful when you stare into the mirror, lest the mirror stares back into you," she said, mangling the famous Nietzsche quote.

I turned around to look at her face to face. The only thing I could think to say in reply didn't make any sense, but I said it anyhow. "Whoever fights against locks should see to it that he doesn't become a lock himself."

She smiled. "Need some help with that? Here." She held out her hand. Stupidly, I gave her my key. "When a lock becomes stubborn, all you need is the right lube." She produced a tiny can of WD-40 from her purse and put some on my key. "See how it glides in now?" She put the key in the lock. Sure enough, it slid right in, easy as you please. She turned my key and the lock made a satisfying click.

"Thank you, ma'am," I said. "Are you the new custodian?"

"No. I'm just passing through. Sharing the good news." She held out a pamphlet. On the cover, there was a dark obelisk thrusting up from the desert. "Interested in learning more?"

I wasn't. Not in her freaky UFO cult, anyway. I was, however, interested in learning more about her. "Sure," I said.

I opened the door, invited her in. And she showed me her spider.

THE WHOLE ENCOUNTER was so bizarre, by morning, I wondered if I'd dreamt the whole thing. But, no. There was the pamphlet with the obelisk crumpled up on the floor. I looked at it more closely. The obelisk had hieroglyphs on it and pictures of people. Men with long beards and tall hats. Soldiers displaying weapons. Men and women carrying sheaves of grain, sacks of gold, and ornate vases. Winged lions with human heads.

She'd given me the sales pitch last night. Ancient gods. Worldwide cataclysm. The utopia that awaited everyone who believed the right things. I smiled politely and nodded, but I didn't pay much attention.

"Tell me," I said, when it seemed she was done. "What kind of woman carries WD-40 in her purse?"

"Well, you never know when you might need to unstick a lock, or quiet a squeaky gate, or remove a troublesome bumper sticker."

"I didn't realize it could do so many things."

"I've got duct tape too." She produced a roll from her purse. "To keep anything that shouldn't move from moving."

"Got anything else in there?"

She gave me a significant look. "I usually save this for level 2s, but since you've gotten through the first lesson so quickly, I suppose I can give you a sneak peek." She reached into her purse and pulled out an oval mirror with Velcro straps. It looked like a rearview mirror that you'd attach to a bicycle handlebar. "Here, I'll show you."

She led me to the bathroom and flicked on the lights. She turned me around so my back was to the bathroom mirror, then she handed me the bicycle mirror. "Look into the reflection," she said. "What do you see?"

"I see my face in the first reflection. The back of my head in the second. Then, my face again in the third."

"Infinite dimensions," she said, her eyes lit up with excitement. I could tell she wanted me to be equally excited. But I wasn't. To me, it was just what happened when two mirrors faced each other.

"They're not really infinite. I can only see three reflections deep." I angled the mirror a bit. "Four maybe. This would work better with two full-length mirrors."

"We have that at headquarters," she said. "But you can see it here too if you look closely. Look. Really look."

I obliged her and looked into the mirror again. There was me and the back of my head and then me again. Wait. That was weird. When I scratched my nose, I swore my third reflection did the same half a second later. I arched an eyebrow. Again, my reflection operated on a delay.

"You see now, don't you?" she asked.

"How does it work?"

She snatched the mirror from me. "You're not level 2 yet."

My gaze followed the mirror back to her and her tattoos. Underneath her neck, there was an hourglass and next to that, a mask.

"Well, if you won't tell me about the mirror, will you at least tell me about your tattoos? Why is everything covered in spider webs?"

"Because of the spider!"

She lifted her shirt, revealing a giant spider on her abdomen. It looked terrifying.

Sand had gotten into my apartment again. It always did whenever there was a big enough dust storm. There was even sand on the floor when I first moved in here. It didn't matter that I put duct tape around all the windows, covered up any cracks I found in the walls, and scraped off my shoes before entering. Sand always found its way in.

My father used to tell me that if I didn't go to sleep on time, the Sandman would get me. If there really is a Sandman, he must be the ruler of this age. Salting the earth. Creeping into everyone's houses. Getting into everyone's lungs.

What happened with the mirror could have been my imagination, but it was intriguing enough that I wanted to learn more about the cult. They called themselves Sibitti. The pamphlet was for level 1s, so it didn't contain much information. I guess I had to join to learn more.

Curious if anyone had done a Scientology-like exposé, I turned to my phone. The cult was still new enough that most of the information about it came from the cult itself. Maybe I could be the one to write the first exposé. Maybe I'd even make enough money to quit my crappy job. Yeah, maybe.

The cult's website didn't contain much more information than the pamphlet did. Reading over it, it seemed like something called *The Song of Erra* was their holy text. I googled that next. *The Song* was a fragmentary Assyrian text found on tablets dating to around 1000 BC. I found a few quotes from it online, and even an academic page with scans of the original tablets, but I couldn't find a complete English translation anywhere. They say you can find anything on the Internet, but I've found that obscure stuff like this is often missing.

I found an old translation of *The Song* available for sale online, but it cost hundreds of dollars. Must be out of print. And there was no eBook available. My local library didn't have a copy, but the university did. I could request an interlibrary loan, but that would take a few days. I decided to head up to the university library after work so I could read the book that day. It might not have much to do with the modern cult, but it was worth a look.

When I got to the library, I saw it hadn't escaped the pervasive sand that was all over Salt Lake City (or as many of the locals now called it, Dust Bowl City). I felt bad that my entrance meant more sand got in, although I did spend more time than most shaking the dust and salt from my clothes in the entryway. I was surprised to see the university library didn't charge any money to use their drinking fountains, although the line was longer than I was currently willing to wait.

Since I had so much trouble finding a copy online, I thought *The Song of Erra* might be located in special collections and I'd need to request assistance to find it, but it was just on the shelf like a regular book. When I found it, I was surprised by how slim it was. It was just about sixty pages, and half of that was the translator's introduction. I could probably read this in one sitting. I wouldn't even need to check it out.

I found a table and sat down with the book. This section of the library was empty. I felt like I was the only person on this floor, although I'd seen others milling around just a moment ago. My quiet footsteps sounded loud in comparison to the pervading silence. Each time I turned a page, it was a rustling of leaves in a wind storm. Each of my coughs was an explosion.

According to *The Song*, the Sibitti were a group of seven gods. "The fierce weapons of Erra." They have a lion-like aspect and burn like fire. They can raze a mountain to the ground with their weapons and can blow the moon out of its orbit with their powerful breath.

The Song overall was an inventory of destruction. Only fragments of it remain, but basically, the Sibitti urge Erra

to destroy mankind for being too noisy. He boasts about
how strong he is and lays out his plans for destruction,
threatening to rival the destruction wrought by Marduk's
worldwide flood. He then carries out his plans. At the end,
he admits he went too far, killing both good and bad alike.
He promises to return his surviving worshippers to their
former glory and help them defeat their enemies.

What did this have to do with the modern Sibitti cult?
Was this their version of the Book of Revelation? When
the world didn't end like they were expecting, what would
they do? Disband and go back to their normal lives? Transition into a mainstream religion that taught the end of the
world was always just about to happen? It was probably
harmless. But then again, there were a handful of cults
that went the way of Jonestown.

Riding the bus back home, I swear I saw the spider
chick. The bus was stopped at President's Circle. Someone
had slapped a red bumper sticker with white letters onto
the stop sign so it looked like the sign read "Stop Sibitti."
After waiting for a few students to cross the street, the bus
started to go again. That's when I saw the spider chick. I
didn't get a very good look since the bus was moving away,
but it looked like she was using WD-40 to remove the
sticker from the sign.

THAT NIGHT, I dreamt of a man wearing a yellow mask.
There was a bird with a lion's head perched on his shoulder. He reached up to remove the mask, a gesture that
filled me with utter dread. To my relief, there was another
mask underneath the first one. Then, I realized the man
wasn't with me in person. He was on TV. The TV was

covered with spider webs. The man was about to remove his second mask when the spider webs became too thick to see through. In fact, my entire apartment was covered with cobwebs, and I was stuck to the couch. I couldn't see the spider, but I sensed it creeping up behind me. It was huge.

I was awakened by a knock on my door. No one ever knocked on my door. I threw on some clothes and answered. It was the spider chick. There was a tattoo on her shoulder I hadn't noticed before. A baby carriage enshrouded with webs. Seeing her again caused me to remember her name.

"Anissa? What are you doing here?"

She smiled. "You told me to come back on Saturday to give you the second lesson. Today's Saturday."

"Of course. But how did you get into the building?"

"I have my ways."

I invited her in, but she said she had to take me to headquarters for the second lesson. Like an idiot, I followed her to her truck. A plain white pickup. Was it hers, or did it belong to the organization? It didn't have a lived-in feel to it. Too clean. Not even that much sand on the floor. But it wasn't new. It was an older model with rusted-out wheel wells.

I asked her about Sibitti on the drive over, but she said I'd have to wait until we got there to learn more. I wanted to ask if I'd seen her at President's Circle yesterday but chickened out. She was playing a CD on the speakers. The music mainly consisted of a plucked lyre accompanied by rattling percussion and chanting in some foreign language, perhaps ancient Assyrian, or some modern person's idea of what ancient Assyrian sounded like.

While we were stopped at a red light, I looked into the rearview mirror. I saw a white pickup parked behind us, and another behind that one. I thought it a remarkable coincidence until I noticed the driver was a bald woman and the passenger looked just like me. It was the mirror trick again, except this time there was only the one mirror.

The truck behind us suddenly jerked forward. I tensed up, preparing to be rear-ended, but Anissa jerked forward a split second later and we continued our drive. Our reflections followed us the rest of the way, mirroring our actions a half-second before we did them. Mirror-Anissa flicked on the turn signal right before she did. My reflection raised a hand to cover a cough before I needed to do the same. It was eerie. What was going on?

When we arrived, I immediately knew which building was headquarters due to the obelisk out front. It was the same obelisk pictured on the pamphlet. I had thought the picture was from ancient ruins in Mesopotamia, not taken right here on the outskirts of Dust Bowl City. Sand had gathered around the foot of the obelisk, which made it look more authentic. I thought idly that the Joseph Smith Sphinx in Gilgal Garden and the Summum Pyramid by I-15 must also look more ancient, now that they're surrounded by sand as well.

Other than the obelisk out front, it appeared to be a normal building. It could have been a church house for nearly any denomination. The other houses in the neighborhood were regular single-family residences. There were even kids playing in the front yard, digging in the sand with shovels. I suppose the entire city had become their sandbox now.

We got out of the truck and approached the main entrance. A gust of wind blew dust and salt into our faces, but at least it wasn't a full-blown fog of sand. Before we reached the door, it opened, seemingly on its own. A man with a long beard stood in the doorway wearing a long, tan coat. He looked exactly the way my childhood self had pictured the Sandman.

"Come inside," he said in a scratchy voice. His wrinkled face was a dry riverbed weathered by the passage of countless gales. "I'm Brother Shamash. Welcome to level 2." He reached out, so I shook his hand. He had leather skin and a firm grip.

"How many levels are there?" I asked.

"Ha!" He let out a harsh laugh, almost a shout. "There's infinite levels."

"Infinite," Anissa echoed reverently, clearly in love with the word.

The door closed behind us. An acolyte began sweeping up the sand that had followed us in. I noticed several other people milling about, crossing from one room of the house to another.

The front room appeared larger than it was due to full-length mirrors facing each other on opposite walls. I saw myself and the others repeated endlessly. The ceiling was covered with stars. I recognized the constellation of Orion. At the far end of the room, there was a statue of an ancient king or god seated upon a throne. He had a long beard, a tall hat, and a lion-headed scepter.

"What are those?" I asked, indicating five weathered stone tablets hung on the wall behind the statue.

"*The Song of Erra*," Anissa said.

"But *The Song of Erra* is fragmentary," I objected. "These tablets are complete."

"Indeed." Brother Shamash paused to cough. "Only level 2s are granted access to the complete text. What do you know of *The Song*? The parts of it you've read?"

"It's about destruction," I said. "A worldwide flood."

"There's more to it than that. In time, you'll appreciate the full glory of Erra."

"How can you speak of Erra so reverently?" I asked. "He kills both good and bad alike. His worshippers and his detractors. Why would you worship a god like that?"

"Because we aren't part of the herd," Brother Shamash said. "We are more than just worshippers. We are the Sibitti. The Dingir-imin-bi. Erra's fierce weapons!" There was a savage light in his eyes that frightened me. If the members of this cult thought of themselves as weapons, they might be dangerous after all. Then again, mainstream religions also sang hymns about being soldiers marching into war without ever doing anything violent. They still might be harmless.

"But there's only seven Sibitti," I objected. "I've seen more than seven people in this house."

"Look up," Brother Shamash instructed. "Do you know the name of the constellation in the center of the ceiling?" I confessed I did not. "Today it's called the Pleiades, the seven sisters. But in ancient times, it was known as the Sibitti. When viewed with the naked eye, there appear to be only seven stars, but there are actually hundreds of them! Over a thousand! And you can be one of us!"

"After I advance through infinite levels?"

"Ha!" His laugh sparked another cough. "There's only seven levels you need to get through in this life. The rest await you after death. You've already made it to level 2 and most don't get that far. Do you wish to continue your journey?"

If I was going to write an exposé of this cult, I'd have to stay in it and advance as far as possible. Plus, I couldn't explain the weird things I'd been seeing in mirrors lately. While Brother Shamash did make me uneasy, I didn't feel like I was in any imminent danger.

"What do I do?" I asked.

"Look into the mirrors." He extended his arm toward one of the walls.

So I looked. I was expecting it to be like before: to see my mirror-self move in an out-of-sync way. Instead, my reflection remained the same. So I looked at the reflections of the others. Brother Shamash. Anissa. A couple acolytes I hadn't been introduced to standing in the back. None of their reflections were out of sync either.

I turned my attention to the statue. The bearded face wasn't looking at me but seemed to be judging me just the same. The stone figure seemed to be carved from the same rock as its throne. The arms of the god connected to the arms of the chair. Feet connected to the base. The body attached to the backrest. Just one solid piece of rock. The only thing that really stuck out was the lion-headed scepter.

As I watched, the lion turned its eyes towards me and snarled.

I jumped back despite myself. "The lion. The lion!" was all I managed to say.

Brother Shamash clapped a firm hand onto my shoulder. "You've seen the truth. That statue is more than just a statue. It's Erra himself."

I SPENT MORE and more time at the temple, getting to know the other members and advancing through the levels. I learned how to use the mirror in a telescope to see further than should be possible. I could see the surfaces of planets, the civilizations that once inhabited them, and all the future civilizations that would one day come to be.

Humans, I realized, were just one civilization out of

countless others. We were insignificant on a cosmic scale. I'd long ago resigned myself to the fact that when I died, no one would remember me beyond close family and friends. But now I knew that it was more than that. All humans, all artists and scientists, political and religious leaders, generals and celebrities: all of us will be forgotten.

I could handle my own personal insignificance. But knowing that Shakespeare will disappear from the memory of the universe? That filled me with such despair, I almost wanted to become one of the Sibitti. Erra, at least, was immortal. Any who served him would surely be remembered long after the human race itself was utterly forgotten.

But no. Even if I ultimately proved to be insignificant in the grand sweep of history, I still had to live with myself in the here and now. The past is a memory. The future, a dream. Only the present truly exists. I had to do what was right in this moment, no matter the consequences.

So I formed a plan. And just in case my plan failed, I wrote out my exposé, everything I knew about the Sibitti, and published it on my blog. Even if I died, everything I had learned would live on and someone else could continue what I had started.

I waited until night and took the last bus out to the Sibitti Temple. The bus didn't go directly to the temple, of course, but it got me close enough that I could walk the rest of the way. I broke open the front door with a crowbar. I was loud enough that I may have alerted some people in the neighborhood, but as long as nobody interrupted me in the next few minutes, I'd have enough time.

The Sibitti considered the statue of Erra to be Erra himself. Maybe it was. After everything I'd seen, I couldn't rule anything out. Either way, the statue was key. If I damaged it—broke off the scepter, chipped off its nose or a toe—then Erra's power over the cult would be broken. If I had time, I'd reduce the entire thing to rubble. The human race would still go extinct someday, but at least it wouldn't happen on my watch.

I'll admit, as I approached the statue, I hesitated. I'd never been right next to it before. Being this close filled me with a sense of awe and admiration. The sense of power was palpable. But I persisted. I lifted the crowbar and swung.

Something stopped me. I tried to continue my swing, but I met with resistance. Someone wrested the crowbar from my hands. Brother Shamash.

"How did you know?" I asked stupidly.

"I'm level 7," he rasped. "I could see that you would do this from the moment we met. Did you think you could lock Erra out of our plane? You can no more do that than bind the chains of the Pleiades!"

Anissa appeared from the shadows and pulled a roll of duct tape from her purse.

"What are you going to do?" I asked, looking between the two of them.

"We're going to take you to the next level," Brother Shamash said. "Now put your hands behind your back." When I hesitated, he said, "Don't make me use this," and leveled the crowbar at my face.

I did what he said. Anissa wrapped me up in duct tape like I was a fly in a web. Brother Shamash continued speaking.

"I was once like you. I once thought it was possible to save humanity. But don't you see? It's already happened! You're too late. You were too late before you were even born. The world has already ended! The herd is just too stupid to realize it."

"What do you mean?"

"You were expecting the world to end in another flood. That's because you haven't read the full text. *The Song* does mention the deluge of Marduk, so it's natural that you'd think Erra would destroy the world in the same way. But you're missing a few key lines. Erra doesn't destroy with flood, but with drought." He started to have a coughing fit, and signaled to Anissa to continue.

She began reciting verses from memory:

"He who extolls himself in the days of plenty will
be buried on a day of drought.
He who comes water-borne will go back on a dusty
road.
He who departs from the pier will cross on foot.
Even if the cistern is a cord deep, not a single man
will slake his thirst.
In the expanse of the broad sea, water for a
double-hundred hours,
They will propel the fisherman's boat with the pole.
Breasts will dry up such that babies will not survive.
Springs will silt up such that streams will not carry
water.
Erra shall turn the cities into deserts.
He shall convulse the seas and make their yield
vanish.
He shall burn the reed and rush thickets with fire.
He shall curse the herds of men and return them to
clay."

The blackest despair filled me then as I thought of all the dust storms and wildfires that had happened lately. How the price of water had skyrocketed. They were right. Erra has already destroyed us. It didn't matter if someone read my exposé. The human race was lying on the ground with multiple stab wounds. We just hadn't finished bleeding out yet.

"Now look into the mirror."

My eyes were open now. I knew what I was going to see. I didn't want to see it, but I had to. It was horrible. It was inevitable. But I couldn't look away.

I watched as Erra arose from his throne.

WISH BONES
KRISTI PETERSEN SCHOONOVER

The Mormons call it Kolob—*nigh unto God*—but if you've ever traveled this canyon, I reckon you'd know there's something unholy about the stars above it.

My bride Ellie knew as soon as we settled the farm things weren't right. She drank her Arbuckle's and hawked the evening sky, her rocking chair's creak deviling my dreams.

"They're coming," she'd say.

Who was coming? I still got no idea. She was taken from me in a skin crazy way, but this is 1873. We might be sweet on our campfire stories, but we know ghosts, banshees, and curses are tall tales.

People who mess with the unnatural, not so much. That'd be why I'm escorting Miss Aramacia Simes back to Cedar City, where she's wanted for bone crafting—raising the dead—in a Mormon wagon train where all but one was found slashed open with missing entrails. She was hiding out in our Methodist settlement until we got the notices. Rev. Hanrahan didn't want trouble, and he asked me to keep an eye on the bad eggs willing to bring her in. A young widower would've obliged because Aramacia was beautiful. I obliged because I was going that way anyhow for a fresh start after selling the land and because it's smart to help a man of God.

I obliged because I wanted to know if Aramacia really could raise the dead. No one would ever shine a candle to the star that was my Ellie.

But as I piss behind boulders, the buttes tombstone against the lavender sky. The hot daylight smell of sand and cactus bloom is fading into the evening bone-shiver of wet clay.

I'm feeling my mistake.

Aramacia mightn't look like she's in league with the Devil—she's got sunflower hair and deep eyes that could pull you in—but I never seen anyone so calm about facing the noose.

Until now. She speaks for the first time since we pulled outta Trammel Creek. "You shouldn't stop here!"

Belts—built like a pot bellied stove and needing three of his namesake to hold up his pants—is always quick to anger on account he grew up an abandon after his parents died in a fire. He's done a couple things to land him in the pokey, but if there's one man I'd want as the biggest toad in the puddle out here? It'd be him.

I hear him spit in the sand. "I'm not quite under-standin' why you think you have the privilege to comment."

"You'll be sorry," she mutters.

I fix my pants and turn around.

"What'zat?" Belts spits again. This time, even in the violet shade of the quickly falling night, I see it make a little *pluff* in the dirt.

"This is not a good place in the dark." Aramacia sits on

the ground, knees drawn to her chest, a patchwork quilt around her shoulders. She fiercely meets his gaze. "There are very bad stars about to fall."

I recall Ellie. "What'd you say?"

She looks at me.

"The stars are coming."

Her expression is so much like Ellie's, I swear I smell Arbuckle's. Sorrow floods my chest.

Belts huffs forward.

I step between them. "Shut your big bazoo, Belts. We gotta build a fire. Get some rest."

The moment of tension is broken only by the distant, womanish scream of a mountain lion.

Belts doesn't look off-put. "Maybe the ol' witch can just call the flames up right outta hell and save us some work!" He guffaws, to the delight of the other three men in our caravan. They clap each other on the back and head to the wagon.

I crouch in front of Aramacia. "I am … so sorry they were talking to you in an unkind manner."

She doesn't look at me, her gaze focused on the sand.

"The whole reason I came is to try to protect you from that kinda talk and… I just hadta …" I haven't been awkward with the gentler sex since Ellie passed, because there was an understanding I wasn't interested. But this— this feels uncomfortable. "I got to ask. What'd you mean 'bout the stars?"

Her large eyes—a curious indigo color—meet mine. "She talked about it too, didn't she?"

It's like I been punched. "Who?" is all I can squeak.

"The one you wish still shared your bed."

Miss Simes wasn't even around when it happened.

"It's true, ain't it?"

There's not a night I don't wish for it, but I know there's still gossip in town. "You heard all about it, huh?"

"Maybe." She tilts her head back, looks toward the heavens. She smells bitter, like rhubarb. "Look up."

The bluish-purple field of diamonds stretches forever, and I'm so close to heaven I could touch it.

"The starlight comes from the past. What we see tonight left millions of years ago—so many we can't count 'em."

The sky seems to move, or maybe it's the earth moving underneath me. I dizzy and fall. My tailbone smacks a rock, pain shoots up my back, and I can't get my breath.

Belts, well on his way to roostered, roars with laughter. "She toss you from an invisible horse? 'Case you look like you just chewed gravel, boy!"

Aramacia stares at me. "You shouldn't be here."

The mountain lion shrieks again, and whether this woman's really dancing with the Devil or not, I reckon she's right.

Sometimes you know your home, and mine was with Ellie on that land we got for cheap as dirt.

The first time we set foot on it, she sighed. "Oh, Quicken." She called me that on account of my doing things without thinking 'em through first. "It looks a little … well … *tuckered out*."

"Come on, now, it ain't that bad." It was only half cleared, the house wanted repair, and fences needed mending, but there was a small orchard, croplands, a stream, and a pasture. In the distance, buttes rose in Godly majesty. "Plenty of room for our future sons to run around."

For a time, it was like we been graced.

Then Ellie made noise about the stars coming and took to the porch every night, rocking and watching. The orchard bore puny fruit, the croplands went fallow, the stream dried up, and the grasses yellowed and went to sand. We were down to gooseberries, a couple of pigs, a few chickens, a cow. She didn't smile anymore. Talk of starting a family stopped.

She urged me to sell some of our belongings to survive. I didn't want to leave her—specially not overnight—but she pressed. So I went to Cedar City. I came back to a dead farm. Slaughtered pigs, bloody feathers, a gutted cow. The air was rancid with the smell of hot iron, spoiled beef, and ruined preserves. The only prints were Ellie's, near the pen, the coop, and the paddock, in criss-cross figure eights like she been square dancing in the dust.

In the middle of it all, her body was splayed open and spilling her insides.

I fell in her mess and cried.

MY EYELIDS BURN. It's bright as a branding iron. I open my eyes expecting the sun, but it's a beam from the heavens. My skin fries. I yell.

It disappears and all's quiet again.

I'm suddenly freezing. The fire's just cracklings now.

"Miss Simes? Belts?"

There's no response, only the whistle of a desert breeze. I creep off my bed roll. I call again and still no answer, and then comes that smell. Drifting on that breeze like a tumbleweed.

A vice of fear squeezes the breath out of me. *Sweet*

Lucifer … Lord Jesus, protect me.

It's dark as an abandoned mine. I try to remember where I seen things based on the fire pit and work my way toward the wagon, knowing there'll be a lantern there. If nothing else, I want the light to cure the spook that's got my heart throbbing in my mouth.

A lantern's hung on the single tree. I fumble in my pouch for matches, and it's damn hard to get one lit, my hands are shaking so bad. In the yellow glow I see the Yankee bed's smashed to flinders, and the shredded bonnet flutters like curtains—

Belts' head falls out of a ragged hole in the sideboards and bounces off my boots.

"Oh *she-it!*" I stumble back and fall. I toss the lantern and it goes out. I roll over and air my paunch in the sand.

I remember the mountain lion, but no mountain lion done this kind of damage. Maybe not even to Belts.

I hear a whimper. I struggle to sit up, re-light the lantern.

I find Aramacia huddled behind the boulders I was pissing on. She looks a fright. Her lower lip trembles. There are streaks of dirt on her forehead and cheeks. One of her boots is missing. She curls and uncurls her toes, digging divots in the sand.

I crouch down and want to set a comforting hand on her arm but hold back because I don't want to scare her more. "Are you hurt?"

Her toes curl and open, curl and open.

"I *said*, are you hurt?"

She swallows.

"Miss Simes, you need to be telling me who did this."

Everyone in camp's dead. She's alive.

I was the only one who treated her nice. *I'm* alive.

Maybe it's true what they say.

Thou shalt not suffer a witch to live. Terror and rage boil in my gut. I draw my gun and try to keep steady. "What in *blazes* did you do?"

"I didn't do nothing!"

Pull it. Pull that trigger and be done with her.

Aramacia shields her face with the backs of her hands. "Oh, Quicken! You just put that gun down!"

It's like an arrow through my heart. *"Ellie?"*

The mountain lion screams in the distance, and I remember where I am. I squeeze the gun tighter. Take a step closer. "Mistress of the Devil's what you are! There ain't nohow you'd know that any other way!"

"You shoot me, you'll never see your Ellie again!"

I lower my gun.

"I can help you." She takes her hands down. "I can make it so you get your wish. So you don't pine for her anymore."

Her eyes seem a more brilliant indigo than they were before, but there's something in 'em I know—a sad-love that was in Ellie's eyes when I'd bring a fresh cup of Arbuckle's to the porch.

I wasn't realizing how much I ached for that look until just this second. "You mean... you mean you really *can* bring her back?"

She looks confused, and then she cocks her head and laughs. Maniacally. Like I imagined witches would in the stories Ellie and I were going to tell our sons. "No. You believed all that bosh they put on those notices? Certainly not. I can't raise the dead."

It's strange, but I'm sunk with disappointment.

The mountain lion is cut off mid-shriek. It's dead silent. No crickets, no owls. Not even the *hish* of that breeze. The night's thick and still.

Aramacia startles. "We need to hide! Come! Come

with me!"

There's a stand of larger boulders behind us. We pull foot up between them and wedge ourselves behind. The lantern scrapes the rough, and I turn it down.

A white dust devil, so bright-hot it burns my eyes something fierce, spins out of nothing into a beast as tall and long as the wagon. It stands on two legs, like a chicken but with a thick whippin' tail. It's got sickle claws on the ends of its arms, feathers on its head, and pure white crinkled skin like a fence lizard. The worst are its eyes. Glowing like angry suns.

"What in the holy hell is that?"

"Shush!" Aramacia hisses.

It's too late for shushing. It creeps closer to the boulders, its heavy steps shaking the ground beneath us. It raises and bobs its head like I seen cats do when they smell vittles—snout in the air, *sniff, sniff, sniff.* It stops and lets loose an unearthly, sinister growl I feel in my bowels.

Aramacia huddles closer.

It tries to climb the boulders but can't—its claws looking like they could flinder a herd of cows all at once are as useless as glass hammers. The beast throws its head back and roars something mighty.

Then it vanishes.

I can't let out a breath or take one in.

The crickets and owls start up their noise.

I smell rhubarb and sunflowers and warm to Aramacia's body pressing on me. It feels nice and comfortable.

… and foul. I jerk away and the terror returns. "What in the blazes was that?"

"It's the ghost of a terrible bird lizard that lived on this earth long before we were here. Before time. Their bones are in the dirt all over this place. Far down under our feet."

Nothing sounds like poppy-cock after what I just seen.

"Is that… is that beast what done in the men?"

She nods. "When they rise up, they're hungry."

There's another growl in the distance and the shriek of something being killed. A white flash pulses on the horizon, then winks out.

"We need to go," she says.

"Where?"

"There." She points to the butte looming above us. "We'll be safe."

She nits her way down from our perch.

"Before time, the land here was different. There was trees and a nice big watering hole—and the beasts came here to drink from it. But that hole, it had fire inside it. One day, the water turned to burning acid and gasses. It killed the mess of them afore they even felt the burn. There was nothing left but charred bones."

She finds her lost boot and sits on the sand. "And then years passed and it sealed them in the ground." She works at the laces. "The stars were their Gods, and they've come to claim the souls of their dead, but they're so far away, they're just getting here now. To them it's like it happened yesterday. They're waking every long-buried beast, and those beasts? Are starving."

She stands and takes a canteen from next to one of the men's bed rolls. I get dried fruit and biscuits from the wagon chuck box.

The trail up the base of the butte winds between boulders and scrub, and the dirt's loose. It's careful walking.

"That's what happened at the pass." She's out of breath. "I told them not to stop there, but they didn't pay mind. The stars fell, and the beasts rose up, and they ate what they could see."

"Is that what happened to Ellie?"

"Yes."

We rest on a rocky ledge. I set the lantern down, and it throws light on some kind of pattern in the rock—like someone's carved ferns into the stone.

I offer her the canteen. She takes it, but instead of drinking, she wets her hands, rubs them in sand, and freshens the smears on her forehead and cheeks. She smiles weakly. "The stars done burnt me up."

I got to ask. "Ellie… she knew. About the stars."

"Ellie was prolly born with the same gift I have. She can sense spirits. Even ones that are in the ground."

"She made me go."

"To protect you, more'n likely."

I'm understanding now there was nothing I coulda done. If I'd been there, the beasts would've eaten me, too.

I open the chuck box, break a hard biscuit. "You said you could make it so's I wouldn't pine for her."

"I can."

The earth beneath our feet shudders and shakes, like the whole butte's coming down on us. The night lightnings into hot purplish white, and restless growls fill the air. White dust devils pour from a split in the ground. I grab Aramacia's hand. "Let's go!"

She twists away from me and shoves me over, hard. "*Don't you touch me!*"

"But… "

"They can't see me with the sacred dirt of this land on my face!" Her expression goes from fear to delight. "You're about to get your wish!"

I been done brown, and it's too late.

The last thing I feel is the brand-hot splice of something through my stomach. The last thing I see is Aramacia, a cold smile on her, the spirits of terrible bird lizards with sickle claws swirling about her in the Devil's madness.

All goes black, and out of the darkness comes my Ellie.

HABEAS CORPUS: IN WHICH I DEMAND MY FATHER'S BODY

NNADI SAMUEL

after Othuke Umukoro

airtight, movement as adjourned by wind states that
motion beings are impermeable dead weights.
at third reading, intimate ghosts become parts of
our speech.

many in wood alphabets: as names of any person,
habitat/place or jinn.
the rest as pronoun, used instead for harm—in
ways that injure itself.

first reading moves the notion that at fair hearing,
in God's creation without a work permit,
man is mud in motion & tomb at sleep.
all men are wired for rest.

second reading affirms, should a soul miss its route
to time travel at bed,
it becomes a felony (say the consequence feels
slightly like aging, in custody of a
charmed space).
grey breathing mud, dismantling empathy in vows
to power a disappearance.

In redress of third reading, private ghosts often
drifts like treason:
raw force, aiming at the betrayal of a loved one.
somewhere, a bench of a ghost concludes:
"no inanimate relative should answer for how we
scratch the surface of our grief."

since the clawing of a new death,
we all have been arraigning the same ghost.
his body—trayed loudly like an exhibit.

FLESH AND FEATHERS
NICHOLAS J. EVANS

F lapping bursts through the sky above.

Wings beat loud overhead while we press trembling palms to our lips in the hopes of quelling any chance of sound escaping. We hear them perch, a clank of talons on the peak of the roof above alongside the scrape of claws. A child beside me looks up, eyes wet and rattling as his frightened blues meet mine, and I give just a nod in return. Their squawking begins in thunderous bursts that shake our bones and turn our stomachs, and I pull the boy in towards me with a tightly coiled arm.

I do not know him, but none of us know one another. A family of circumstance, friends by necessity.

Their cycs fall on me as if I'm their savior, as if I'm anything but another horrified human being waiting to be pulled apart by the beaks of the Vogel. The echoes of their calls pierce the sky just as much as they rattle my backbone. Some chirp, while others release more grotesque shrieks that nearly shatter glass in the crossfire. I hear their calls, and I do my best to keep my heart from pounding out of my chest. The young boy shivering against my hip like a hornet's nest reminds me to be strong. I look at the others, I give the reassurance they need despite my spine curling like pubic hair and my knees growing numb. I know why they look to me, why they rely on me.

I've killed one of those fucking monsters.

The wings grow loud as they rise again from the rooftop, and within minutes, the squawks carry off with them until they are nothing but a distant hum, a car engine roaring away until it is nothing more. Tension fades, hands lower from jaws and deep breaths ensue in choir harmony while the boy pushes from my side.

"Jesus fucking Christ…" says an older man, the bags under his eyes large enough to carry more bags themselves and two furry beasts hovering just over his eyes in various shades of gray. He rubs at his bare scalp. "Third time they've come back this week… Cooper, what are we going to do?"

I sigh uneasily when he calls my name and beckons for my advice. One hand adjusts the brim of my hat while the other rests on the holster of my Beretta like an arm rest. His question is met with a shake of my head and a frown that tugs at my cheekbones.

"Nothing," I respond, readjusting my stance and folding my arms in front of my chest. "Could easily be a dozen of 'em' out there, maybe more. I'd say they're bound to bring even more next time. Best we can do is board this sucker up a little more, limit ourselves to a single exit for quick scavenging, keep a scout on duty around the clock."

"But it isn't safe here!" a woman cries out.

"Any safer out there?" I respond with a stone face.

Her eyes lower as she sinks back beneath the box dye-job of her platinum locks and hunches down onto the couch. As she does so, I look to the group with my eyes meeting each of theirs one at a time.

"Locked in Joe's Utah timeshare house isn't ideal, I know," I said with a quick nod of appreciation to the old man. "But, it could be worse. We can at least protect this place, keep it safe, as long as we work together."

"We're in the middle of the woods with barely any food!" another cuts in. This time it's the one we've all been referring to as Dixie. Choppy black hair, a scowl that could fry an egg, and speckled tattoos over the canvas of her skin that scream homemade, prison, or cheap. She stands up from the floor, hunting rifle draped over her back and a Dundee knife on her hip.

She means business, even if she hasn't fully taken the fight to the Vogel yet.

"Those things will outlast us, Coop. You know it. They're out there huntin' and shit all damn day while we conserve beans and share stale bread. We gotta move, gotta get to a town or a city. Salt Lake ain't more than an hour or so from here. We're already scavenging close to Snyderville as it is! Hell, the military and police probably keep 'em at bay pretty well in the city."

"Maybe," I answer hastily. "But Dixie, the problem is we can't prove that. We're a small group, two firearms and a couple knives. Vogel get close, they get a bite off on ya before we can get 'em' or even two, you're done. We don't know how it works, but ya gotta remember what happened to Kristen."

Silence erupts like a dormant volcano at Kristen coming up. A lot of distant looks, a lot of far off gazes and even more empty expressions. I myself fall into that rabbit hole with the others. We couldn't save her. I couldn't save her. All of us had barely made it from the base of Bald Mountain and out of the woods when they descended on us, and her screams just rang out like church bells when we shut the door of the cabin and left her behind. I remember her stare. I remember her eyes on me when I turned back before she was consumed in a pile of her black feathers.

It's haunting. By the time her screaming had stopped, we didn't know what we would find in the morning. Apile of bones and a pool of blood, or would she have become one of them like so many others had? I don't have answers. All I have is what precious remaining minutes I can afford to keep these people safe, to avoid that happening again.

"We were careless," I say to the emptiness. "We were so fucking careless. We hunted in a large group, barely enough weaponry to take down a single one of those avian assholes, but we thought we were close enough to make a run if needed. That is our mistake, and we all live with that–me especially. Safety is our number one, and hunger and comfort can be second and third."

Moans, groans, and nods are all that accent my speech. I watch as others take their respective places around the family room turned into a makeshift shelter.

We destroyed this place, but honestly, Joe didn't seem to mind too much after Kristen. Bookcases dismantled for wood to board up the windows, cabinet doors torn off to reinforce weak points, and mattresses pulled from bedrooms into the family room so we could stick together. We had made rules: Only a single light on at a time, baths only to avoid the noise of a shower, two people scavenging outside at a time. Dixie and I were the only two with real firearm experience, so we got the guns.

I was a sheriff's deputy, and no one wanted to ask about her.

Those are the ideals I try to uphold now, and leaving as a group again can only lead to more heartache. More death.

A few of us head into the kitchen and fish out some dinner. It isn't much, two cans of baked beans and some slices of white bread, but it is better than testing our luck outside with those things possibly being so close. I rip off the tab tops of the beans and dump both cans into a pot on the stove top while Joe removes bowls and plates for us.

For a moment, I think of what it would have been like if we had all met under different circumstances. Would these people rely on one another as much? Would we all share Joe's vacation house the same way? All of us only met by fleeing the surrounding areas and heading into the woods for cover during the early days of Vogel attacks. At that point, Joe had already found Tiffany, the platinum box dye, and Tiffany had found the boy crying alone. I came to the house just after Dixie, who was already canvassing the place with Kristen when I arrived. Hard to believe that was weeks ago now, but would any of us talk if it wasn't just for our safety?

I try not to think about it as I stir the beans, letting the warm aroma of brown sugar cascade out to the others for just a small sense of home style comfort. There's just enough for a single ladle full each in a bowl and a single slice of white bread, but it would have to do.

Tiffany had promised us something fun for later as a surprise, but she did warn us it wasn't too exciting. Still, I'm looking forward to anything at this point that isn't beans and bread.

The spoon hits my lips, and I taste the sweet sauce as it sizzles on my tongue. I shovel in a bite like I'm digging my own grave. Bread rips between the vise grip of my teeth. It tastes past its prime, but I savor every bit as I flick my eyes up from the bowl to my team and back down. We eat in the comfort of silence, the same silence we've grown to rely on for protection against the Vogel, the same silence that smothers us slowly in our sleep while we gasp for air. I look to the boy, the dim glow of his eyes as they scan the beans and bread with a grimace, and I think of the life we may never get to lead and the previous moments of adolescent bliss that slipped right between the fingers of a dystopian future. Another spoonful brings me back to reality.

"All right everyone, hang tight!" Tiffany whispers with enthusiasm among the chorus of spoons clanking softly against the bottom of empty bowls.

She gets up and heads towards the kitchen, and her cheerful attitude brings the brief flash of a genuine smile to my face; possibly to everyone else's too. I stand up and enjoy a spastic stretch before I head over to a boarded-up window. Between the slats, it all seems so peaceful, so tranquil. The darkness of night bathing over the trees, the twilight of the moon spreading warmth like a child's night light. A spatter of stars lights up the twilight like glitter just over the horizon of Bald Mountain. The peace of it all is just a reminder of what monsters wait in the shadows for us.

Then, a whistle hisses through the silence.

Low and soft enough to make my heart slowly gather speed as it grows higher and pierces our ears like a fire station siren. It becomes pure panic, and in only a few short moments causes a flurry of gasps and leaps in horror. Tiffany battles with an old tea kettle, pulling it from a scorching red burner and pressing her palm against the screaming spout until she cries out in scalding agony.

I rush to her as the whistle dies down with the low howl of a dead battery in a broken toy. Tears build in the creases of her eyes and tumble from her cheeks as I approach. The others just stand behind me with agape mouths and wide eyes.

"I'm so sorry... I'm so sorry..." Tiffany anxiously

coughs out while nursing her burned palm. "I just... I found tea on yesterday's scavenge. I just wanted to make us some tea... "

"It's all right," I respond and place a hand on her shoulder. I try to convince myself that I actually mean it. "We will be all right. We will—"

A shriek crackles through the night air. One single loud bark of a Vogel, and the beating of its wings is what we hear first. Then another, and another, until the shrill cry of the monsters is deafening and growing louder as they approach. My heartbeat is fast, but my feet are faster. I make it to a window and peer out to see the sky slowly blackening in a wide blanket of feathers rising up from the treetops in the distance. They move like a rapid storm cloud, blocking out everything until only the shrieking shadows remain.

It hit me like a dodgeball in the gut; they are coming here again, and this time they will know we are inside.

"Everyone..." I turn as fast as I can. "To the basement, now!"

"W-what?" Dixie says and retrieves the rifle beside her. "We'll be sitting ducks down there! If they break in it's all over, Coop! We have to fucking run!"

"Run?!" My voice cracks as I shout. "There are dozens out there! We couldn't outrun even one of those things! We stay in cover, we stay silent. And we hope to whatever God is fucking left that they don't get down there!"

"Screw this," Dixie says and marches for the door. "I'm not being mauled. I'm not going out like Kristen! I'll take my chances."

Before another word is spoken, she is outside of the door and bolting through the darkness. Her footsteps fade just as I push the door shut and seal it, with the flapping of wings growing stronger every moment outside. I feel it deep in my guts, knives twisting into every inch of my nerves; Dixie might have chosen right.

"Get downstairs!" I shout as the others nod and head toward the door hidden in the floor.

They roll the carpet aside and pull at the latch until the heavy slab of wood creaks open. I see the darkness below as Tiffany descends the ladder, followed by Joe. The boy goes next and pauses to look up at me as the shrieks wail in our ears. His eyes are trembling; lips try to move, but sound doesn't come out. I walk towards him and fall to my haunches.

I pass him a smile, and I follow it with a gentle nod. With a raised arm, I grab the cellar door and push it down while he descends, and the light captures the sparkle of his tears as the door closes. With the carpet pulled over it, I move toward the window with a hand on the handle of the gun.

A stampede of talons boom against the walls and shatters the windows, while their squawking rolls and echoes through the house. I hear the wood splinter from the nailed boards. I hear the rattle of the front door as beaks smash it with tremendous force. The gun raises up instinctively, and my finger trembles when I wrap it around the trigger and aim the barrel for the door.

"Come on, you fucks…"

A beak the size of a football smashes through the door, dried blood caked over yellow keratin. It writhes as it pulls its beak out, giving me just the opening I need to fire off the first round through the hole just as a creature cries to peer in.

The bullet meets flesh and feathers in a squelching burst that drops the monster instantly. Like the mythical hydra, a few more Vogel come to take its place and begin thrashing at the door themselves.

It won't hold. I know it won't hold.

I fire off another round that lands a glancing blow in a dark patch of feathers on the other side, but it's too dark to see where the shot hit. There was a sharp shriek at the connection, yet it only managed to slow it down for a moment. My heart smashes against my chest cavity in unison with the monsters rattling the door.

My aim is careful, my arm is steady, and as the door falls, I'm prepared for my next shot.

The first creature is enormous, easily a little larger than I am, with broad wings and a wide chest. Feathers lay over a humanoid frame, muscular quadriceps that morph into talons further down, and broad shoulders that mesh into the wings. It almost resembles a human, and I try to block out images of Kristen as I squeeze the trigger. Bullet flies, explodes through the first Vogel's chest, and it collapses in the doorway with shakes and spasms. Another runs in from behind it, talons beating down on the wooden floors right as I fire off a shot that hits a wing, momentarily pausing it while I release another to the side of its skull.

Three down, but my bullets won't last for long.

I see another drop down to the doorway, and I don't let it even get a call off to the others before a shot shatters its beak into bone shrapnel and knocks it to the ground. My mind. A horde of them claw and peck at the roof and walls around me while I stare out the door waiting for another. I swallow a wad of my saliva; my lungs pulsate with rapid breaths.

In a moment, something clicks, and I know what I have to do.

One foot falls after the other in a sprint. I'm across the living room in the span of a heartbeat, and I climb over the heap of feathery corpses to make my way outside in a scramble towards the tree line. Moonlight breaks through the canopy of leaves creating streams of glowing rays to guide me. The flapping begins to pound behind me as soon as I get into the trees, and I turn to face it.

"Hey! Over here!" I scream up at the horde of Vogel on the roof. "You fucking birds! Look over here!"

One already begins a dive toward me as three others lift from the house and stare in my direction. As the first one swoops down, I place a careful shot that crackles in a rolling echo over the hills and through the trees just before the bullet meets its mark and sends the Vogel to the ground with a plethora of snapping bones.

The others come, and I sulk back deeper into the woods as they rise up against the backdrop of stars like black ink blotches on a page. I back up until I feel bark behind me, and I brace myself up against the huge tree with my gun poised.

The first one descends into the trees in the same way I had, setting me up for a clear shot that takes it down just as the other one did. The one behind it takes a different path and sweeps around instead of coming in head on; it proves that they think, it proves they plan. It cuts around to my right side, and I'm ready for it with two slugs that knock it back, leaving it squawking and gurgling until it grows still. Now I'm waiting for the other one that saw me, and my guess is that it'll come from the left.

But when it breaks through the tree canopy right above me and falls on top of me, I am unprepared.

It smashes into me with a burst of crushing force, and I grunt furiously as my legs buckle.

The weight of the creature throws me off and sends me to the dirt below it. It stands over me, wings spread out wide defensively, while it shrieks and then widens its beak for a bite. I raise the gun just a hair too late when the beak descends and rips at my shoulder. Hot, searing pain screams out as I feel every sinew of muscle fiber rip apart against the coarse blade of the beak. Fire spreads down my arm and across my chest, a raw burning like an instant infection that forces the gun from my hand. I scream through clenched teeth while I cock my other fist back and pummel the creature's skull like a pit bull with a lockjaw, but it gnaws and rips at my flesh until blood soaks my right side entirely.

I reach down, the pain overtaking every sense I have, and I feel the handle of the gun. It takes everything I have to lift it and place the barrel against the skull of the Vogel and then squeeze the trigger. The blast is lights-out for the beast, who releases my shoulder and slumps over lifeless, sky to the side.

It was a victory, but one on both sides. My body aches. I try to move, but it fails me, and I can only sit on the dirt gasping for a single breath at a time. My eyes look down at my mangled shoulder, the scraps of skin and soft tissue lay ripped and frayed out as rich, red blood pours from the wound. The burning remains. I feel it in my fingertips and up my neck. I feel it crawling down my legs, and I feel it burying itself in the pit of my stomach. I tell myself I'll be okay, but I won't. I know what this is.

Vision escapes me for a moment as the fever cascades over every cell. I feel something move beneath my skin, earthworms burrowing through my veins and making homes in my body. I don't want to, but I look at my shoulder again.

The bleeding has stopped, and a thick layer of muted pink flesh spreads over the wound as something soft and furry begins to push out from across the new terrain of my shoulder. I watch; it makes me nauseous but I still watch. My own skin slides away like a snake molting. The pink flesh spreads down my arm as black feathers slowly plume and spread over the area. It hurts. The pain is new and sends a static shock coursing through my bones that I can barely stave off.

I blink my eyes. In a couple hours, I'd be one of them. Would I still be me? Would I retain any sense of Cooper, or will my memories fade as pure avian instinct takes hold? I almost want to applaud the thought of fucking birds dethroning our top spot on the food chain. Good game, Vogel.

A rustle and crunching comes from my side. Leaves crush under someone's steps until a figure comes into view.

It's Dixie.

"No… Cooper…" she says. Her eyes widen while she stares at me, and I begin to lose her features as my vision blurs and melts. "T-The others…?"

"Safe," I cough. "Basement."

"Okay, okay," she answers and nods, her eyes not leaving my ever-changing form.

The new skin has crept up my neck now. I feel the stinging pain of feathers forming over it.

"Cooper, I found a base, a safe place for everyone. There's military patrols. It's not Club fucking Med, but we can be safe there. Maybe they can—"

"No," I interject. I've seen enough bad movies to know where this goes, and I need some level of dignity while every piece of who I am, who I was, falls away. "Save the others, Dixie. Get… get them to safety."

She nods and slowly backs away from me. She's nothing but a watercolor silhouette now.

"Cooper… What about you?" I hear her say.

I raise the gun up to my head and gently tap the barrel on my skull twice, passing what smile I can manage.

"Dixie, please don't let the boy see this. Don't let him see me. Take them all around this area if you have to avoid this exact spot. Please..." I blurt out as my throat tightens and talking becomes constrained.

I think she nods her response, then I hear her footsteps trail off toward the home.

The gun rests at my head, my finger dances on the trigger for one last time, and I brace myself for it to all go black soon enough. I hope they make it. I hope they find safety and someday humanity comes back from this. But I just hope I at least bought them a few more hours, a few more days, where they can live.

I squeeze the trigger, and there is a dull click. I squeeze again, but just another hollow click. The gun is empty.

THE MOUNTAIN THRONE

CYGNUS PERRY

I am the Mountain
whose city bears his name,
whose snow-crowned head
slumps behind his fallen
hands upon his rocky throne.

I veil myself under
heavy clouds and speak
to those far-off messengers
between the stars of Orion.

I sing their unearthly melodies
to the souls rushing at
my feet.

I bellow the sacred hymns
for my valley to hear.
My celestial song of the sun
stirs the trees and
browns the leaves.

The brush and grass
bow at the music.
The days shrivel short,
and the sun retreats
from my words of
coming cold.

The messengers gave
me my song of
Winter's waking.

ME AND MINE
ERIC NIRSCHEL

I t came in a fever of calamity and dust, a billowing black-gold bayonet tearing through the skin of the world. Miles from the nearest home, the cacophony of its arrival registered only for the most fleeting of moments on seismographs as the faintest trembling of the sleeping earth, and though its landfall from the stars looked to be heat lightning for hundreds of miles, the inferno and fury subsided as quickly as it had come. The swaying oak and pine seemed barely to register the flames, so quickly did they cede their place.

For a long while, silence reigned supreme over the great mound the intruder had burrowed. This was not the silence of sleeping things, nor was it the silence of the frightened forest seeking refuge from the torrent. It was the silence of dead places and rotting things, of cold tombs and moldering decay. The interloper had already begun its work, stretching out its membranous tendrils like the paws of some great predatory cat after a much-needed slumber. What it touched, it killed, or rather, it devoured. The shape fed greedily on the vibrant and frenetic life it had found itself surrounded by. Trees, centuries old and sturdy, began to waver, their roots retracting as if fingers from glowing metal. Bark crumbled and leaves grew brittle and pale. Birds found themselves suddenly confused; just above the mound, perched on a branch of a now leaning pine, a Lewis' woodpecker wavered in place for a long moment before stumbling on its branch, finally slumping against the trunk, unable to stand. Nearby, a Western Tanager chirped, vomited a discolored mass, and fell from its perch, flapping only one of its wings helplessly in the brush.

By late afternoon the following day, nothing lived within nearly 90 yards of the impact site, and the last wispy tendrils of ozone had ceased to rise from the mound. By sunset, the mound began to stir. The shape had crossed sweeping expanses of cosmos, riding high on solar winds, and picking at the scraps left amongst the stars by dying gods. Its arrival on this peculiarly positioned blue-green ball, so precariously placed between two dead worlds in a dead solar system, had long been the subject of idle fancy, though the concept of 'length' with regards to time meant little for a being such as it. To the shape's estimation, there had been no beginning, nor would there ever be an end. Time was a construct of creatures bound by chemical laws, absorbed and devoured by cycles of entropy and creation. It was no such creature.

The shape took its time moving through the thick expanse of new biology. As it went, it fed, though not so gluttonously as to be noticeable. Where it had gorged when it first arrived, it now nibbled, sapping thin threads of exis-tence from the life forms it passed, leaving them weakened, lethargic, but alive all the same. The shape had supped enough (though, did it ever truly cease to feed? It did not think so.) And now came the time to watch, and wait, and learn. Then it would find its place; it would seek somewhere so resplendent with life, so abundant with intelligence and thought and flesh that it could not want for prey, and it would begin to feed in earnest. What it had done where it had landed at the mound was not so much feeding as it was refueling. A quick bite for the road. Now it was not just looking for a meal; it was looking for a home. There was no hurry. It simply would not do to rush the search for a proper nest.

The shape came to an expanse of flat terrain cutting through the thick vegetation; it sensed that this was something of an artificial construct, and so it stopped its advance and waited. It was soon rewarded as something else approached. It was another artificial thing, pieces and components all aflutter. There was not a sense of life to this thing in and of itself, but rather within it. The container sped past, and the shape reached out with senses unknown to physical beings. It was able to peel its first thin strips of knowledge from this passing creature. The artificial flatness before it was called a road, and a car had passed on it. Pleased, the shape continued to wait, and in time more of these cars came and went, and from each driver and passenger it siphoned more knowledge of this world and its occupants. It came to know the names of the trees and the animals, lapping up distant parrot memories from childhood schooling, delving greedily into the faintest glimmer of university lectures. It learned the language and biology of the creatures inside the vehicles. All of this was tertiary wisdom; it would aid the shape in camouflaging its feasting from prying eyes so that its prey would not learn to flee, but the real prize was geography. It learned where the cities were.

The road before it was named 'Pine Canyon Drive,' and it passed through a mostly wooded area south of a place called 'Snyderville' in a state called 'Utah.' There was a church called 'Rising Star' not far north from where the shape was currently window shopping, and there would be a gathering of these small, frantic entities there on Sunday, four days hence. The shape decided that it might attend the service; it somehow doubted their god would stop it. It had eaten gods.

For the next two days, the shape waited, observing the curious bipedal creatures as they passed by inside their wheelbound contraptions. The exhaust of these automobiles smelled of something old, ancient biological processes, eons of heat and pressure and change, and of something new. Synthetic, manufactured components. They emitted and received signals from great distances ('great' being a subjective term; almost no distance was 'great' to the shape that lurked in those woods), and each of these humans was sending and receiving signals of their own. Each car that passed was not only a lumbering behemoth of mechanical energy, but pure electric, and each mind that passed by provided the shape with a little bit more of the picture of life on this world. For their part, the drivers of those cars would feel only a passing chill—a brief, undescribed turning of the stomach. The more sensitive among them, perhaps those passengers deeply embedded within dreams as they passed, would see something in the cloudy headspace of somnation and would wake suddenly afraid. It would pass quickly, and they would forget that nightmarish dreamscape where they had seen, briefly, the shape for what it really was as it picked through their minds.

On the third day, the shape sensed something approaching from the east. The two beings were disparate entities. A human and a dog. The shape, had it possessed fingers, would have tented them gleefully at this offering. Since it arrived, the shape had not yet manifested itself in the physical sense. It had existed as a dream, a cloud of vapor, unseen and only slightly felt. Now it had the opportunity not only to sharpen its proverbial claws, but to truly feed on a being of intellect (or what passed for such). A creature capable of perceiving it as more than a mere predator. A creature, the shape believed, capable of truly grasping terror.

Hooper, an American Foxhound about a year and a half past his prime, bounded heroically over a fallen log, clearing the mossy, slowly rotting trunk. Some distance behind, Rory Wickham was plodding along contentedly, rifle cradled in his arms. Rory had been hunting the woods near Lake Bello and Hardy Lake, south of Snyderville, for nearly two decades(whether it was legal or not), and had come to appreciate the time away from the world more so than the actual sport or the meat. Rory was heavyset, slightly balding, with a permanent rouge to his cheeks. He wasn't out of shape exactly, though he was definitely an eater. Hiking these woods was plenty of exercise, and the relative silence gave him time to clear his head. Some days more than others.

"All right, Hoop, slow down, now! My fat ass can't keep up. I've only got the two legs, now!"

Hooper barked back happily from further up the trail. The foxhound had never really learned to obey commands, and Rory had long since given up trying to issue them in earnest. The dog neared the mound, its exuberance suddenly tempered by caution. The smell was strange, almost fungal, like rot long hidden from the sun that had mostly lost its pungency. The dog paused, nudging at a nearby tree with a paw, strips of dry, desiccated bark falling away. The tree shuddered slightly, the faintest tremor running up the gnarled, dead-looking husk. The dog recoiled, confused, but felt compelled, as dogs do, to investigate. From a hollow some three feet above, the shape emerged. The form it took didn't much matter for the dog, which squealed pitifully as it was pinned to the ground, the sound of crunching bone and internal rupture punctuating the note. The claw, a bit like a crab's but lined with razorlike stingers, pinned the dog then squeezed. It struggled weakly before it was lifted, writhing, up toward the hollow. With a sickening crunch, the dog folded as it was pulled into the much-too-small hole in the tree.

Rory, for his part, came running as fast as he was able when he heard the dog's anguished cry. Already, his face was contorted in a mask of fear and anger. He didn't know what to expect as he neared the strange upswell of soil and overturned trees where the shape had landed, but nothing he'd considered came within miles of the form the shape had taken just for him. Rory's body reacted long, long before his brain did, instinctively raising his rifle and firing a shot. A nearby trunk burst into dull, ashen-colored dust. It had a woman's face, with long black hair trailing behind it as it came barreling through the trees. Though it had the face of a woman, its body was anything but; a multitude of arms protruded from the base of the neck where a torso ought to be, skittering like some mad Martian walker on these many jointed limbs, its large, long-fingered hands clutching at the earth and nearby trees as it went.

RORY's numb hands worked the bolt of his rifle, reflex entirely in control now. The shape reached him in moments, the many-armed thing leaping like a spider. As it came down on him, Rory fired again, straight down into the dirt, his empty brain forgetting even to raise the rifle. In that last moment, looking up as it bore down on him, Rory

realized he recognized the face and finally found it in him
to scream.

The afternoon passed uneventfully after that, the shape
satisfied with the day's hunt. When the sun began to crest
over the distant hills the following day, the shape began to
stir. It was time for Sunday service.

It had just begun its journey northward, still uncomfortable to move physically on limbs as the natives did,
when it sensed another of their kind approaching much
slower than the others in their vehicles. This one was
walking haltingly along Pine Canyon Drive, also moving
northward. The shape paused a moment, pondering this
meager blip on its proverbial radar. Though it was well
aware that the natives walked most everywhere, this was
only the second of them it had encountered actually doing
so. The rest had passed by quickly, safely nestled within
their machines. Surely, the shape could have waylaid those
travelers with ease, but subtlety is somewhat lost at speed,
and this new arrival walking along the side of the road
afforded the shape the proposition of contacting their kind
at leisure, without much concern for stealth or manipula-
tion. A giant toe dipping, one side of the cosmos to the
other. Come on in, the water's fine. Penny for your
thoughts? How's the weather, old timer?

The old timer in question was a fixture around these
parts. Each and every Sunday, old Quintin Crowe would
make the long walk from his grandfather's home place to
the Church of the Rising Star for worship, and he'd do it
on foot or die trying. Quintin had never learned to drive
himself and wasn't nearly so damn foolish to get into one
of those rolling death machines unless he had absolutely
no other choice in the matter. It would take a hell of a lot
more than a sore knee and a bad back to convince that old
crow to do damn near anything the easy way. Even the

farm was a testament to old-fashioned know how, though it didn't produce near what it used to. The old crow had cut his herd down to 35 head and dialed back the acreage on which he grew wheat and corn substantially, but by god, he wasn't about to give up the farming life or sell the home place, even if his son didn't want it. Just like his Sunday walks that seemed to grow a little longer every year, he'd be dead in the cold ground long before he ever gave up his work.

The shape came to know of these things gradually as the man approached, reaching out with wispy tendrils of thought, small enough to pluck Crowe's nerve endings like harp strings. The shape would make the old man dance. It took the form of a man in common dress and an appearance easy on the eyes; to appear in its true form would surely shatter the old man's mind. Even assuming the feeble ocular orbs of this primitive meat-species were able to fully witness the being's true shape, what would their minds make of the thing? It conformed to none of their 'natural' laws; it was something of a serpent, though it had legs akin to those of an insect, or perhaps a spider, in numbers beyond count. Gnashing mouths ringed with clawed digits and probing antennae that moved across a luminescent void-black surface... No, it simply wouldn't do. Even its vast intellect was unable to reconcile its own disparate form within the limitations of the languages these minuscule minds possessed. They simply had no words for such a being... which, in truth, was just as well. The shape did so enjoy the masquerade.

Old Crowe came upon the figure on the side of the road, another 20 or 30 minutes away from Rising Star. The man was thin but hearty looking, with a cheerful expression riding high on his weatherbeaten but handsome face. The man was wearing what looked like a well-loved denim jacket over a red flannel, worn blue jeans, and a pair of stylish, if dusty, leather boots. His back was turned to the approaching old-timer.

Crowe looked much like you would expect an old farmer to look, his naturally dark complexion darkened still by decades of sun and soil. Crowe owed many of his dark features to his Tuwurint heritage; he'd often been referred to as your typical 'tall, dark, and handsome' in his youth, and in old age, he'd earned the much sought after qualifier of 'dignified.' Crowe eyed the stranger from beneath the wide brim of his leather buffalo cap, his walking stick tapping faintly on the asphalt, wood beads clacking against the shaft and novelty feathers trailing in the faint morning breeze. Crowe did enjoy the medicine man schtick.

The shape, disguised as the stranger in denim, turned to face Crowe, feigning surprise.

"Oh, hey there, old-timer," the shape thought the term 'old-timer' was entertaining. How much could these creatures know about the old times? "I didn't see you there. I was just taking a moment to catch my breath."

"If you're more winded than a geezer like me on this stretch of road," Crowe replied, "I've got some bad news for you, fella."

The man in the denim jacket laughed, slightly too loud and slightly too long, as Crowe came up to where he was standing.

"I suppose you're right." The man in denim cordially ceded, "Name's Richard." He extended a hand. For a moment, the shape watched Crowe eye it suspiciously. The human disguise, this 'Richard' character that the shape was wearing was, indeed, limiting. The appendage extended in a manner of greeting seemed woefully inadequate to a being with countless limbs of its own. Composed of thoughts and memories stripped from everyone who had passed the shape while it waited in the woods, the guise of Richard was your typical everyman—a friendly stranger with an oddly familiar face and an accent you couldn't quite place. He'd fit in anywhere. Crowe took his hand and shook, introducing himself. The old man's grip was strong; years of work and toil and maybe a little blood were in the callouses. The shape could read them.

"I'm actually new in town myself. Just dropped in the other day. Heard there's a church up this way," theRichard-thing said with a smile. "Thought I'd pay it a visit."

"You're right about that," Crowe said, nudging the brim of his cap skyward. "Short trip up the road here, you'll find the Churchof the Rising Star, The honorable Reverend Taylor Blythe presiding."

"Can't say I know much about the reverend, but I've always been a fan of stars." Richard chortled, turning. "Is that where you're headed?"

Crowe nodded.

"Every Sunday." The walking stick began to tack-tack-tack along the asphalt again, and Richard fell in line beside Crowe, walking northward, the heavy soles of his leather boots clop-clop-clopping along in unison.

The shape didn't mind the travel, slow as it was; the parts of it that made up the Richard-thing were only that: parts. The vast majority of its mass was unseen and unfelt, crossing dimensional boundaries, scuttling along behind the physical manifestation that was the man-in-denim on nightmare scorpion legs and daemoniac dream tendrils. Crowe wouldn't see the rest; this was only a trial run, after all. It was a chance for the shape to test these human crea-tures, to measure their savviness and cunning. More than anything, it was a chance to experience from their awkward, meat-locked perspective. It felt slow, like slogging through a bog, but even now, it fed, bleeding life from the trees and the birds and the rodents in the brush beside the road.

"So, how long have you lived around here?" asked Richard.

"Oh, I've been around these parts for most of my natural life," replied Crowe, "We were here before my grandfather was even a thought and brought us here in the old days. He first bought the farm then—no easy feat for a red man in those days."

The turn of phrase was a strange one; the shape probed.

"Red man?" Richard asked, apologetically.

"Hm? The First Nations, boy! You know 'em." Crowe eyed his new companion quizzically, "Native Americans. Indians?"

A slow look of realization dawned on Richard's face. The shape had pieced it together quickly, but it didn't want its illusion to let on.

"Grandfather came here with nothing but the hands God gave him, and wouldn't you know, he built a home for us. Bought the land proper with hard work." Crowe smiled broadly, his age showing in the cracked features. "Left the farm to my father, and I raised my own son here. I couldn't dream of being anywhere else."

Richard nodded; he knew full well just what one could dream.

The two walked, or rather one walked and one crawled, slithered, and skittered for a while, talking pleas- antly. Crowe told his new companion, the man in the denim jacket, all about life in Snyderville, Utah. He regaled the stranger with stories of cattle theft and great storms, wildfires and land purchases. Quintin Crowe talked at great length about his wife and son. Damian Crowe was an actor, living in Los Angeles. He hadn't made it big yet, but Quintin swore he was going to, any day now. The shape consumed lazily, learning what it could about this man and his petty exploits. In the grand scheme of things, Quintin Crowe was a gnat, a single morsel that would be found dead on the side of the road, supposedly of 'natural causes,' only a short walk away from the church he dutifully attended.

Then 'Richard' would attend the service and listen and learn. It would feed on those congregants, leaching from them as they prayed to their tiny, weak gods while the thing that eats gods rested in the rafters above them, unseen mandibles clacking as it perched on its disjointed limbs. When the faithful went home, they would feel tired and complain of weakness, and then, in the night, the nightmares would come… But by then, the shape would have already moved on, perhaps to Snyderville or even Salt Lake, where it would hunt playfully for a time. Perhaps it would begin with some strange deaths of neighborhood pets; mutilated bodies to build tension and season the meat with fear. Then, someone would go missing… The shape was growing hungrier just thinking about it.

"Bit of a hike, isn't it?" asked Richard, eventually.

"Bit of a hike for an old man like me, don't you mean?" asked Crowe, a wry smile crossing his lips.

"For anyone, but I suppose if you want to bring age into it…" Richard answered.

"And how old are you?" asked Crowe, casting a sidelong glance to his companion.

"Why, me? I'm 31," the Richard-thing answered.

Crowe stopped walking, both hands on his walking stick.

"No. How old are you really?"

Richard paused; the shape paused. In the unseen,

between the veils surrounding Crowe with unseen tendrils, feelers, and antennae, the shape took a moment to think.

"You must think I'm a damn fool," the old man stated bluntly, gnarled knuckles tightening on the walking stick like a shaman about to call down the thunder. "I might not know your name, and I might not know where you come from, but I damn well know what you are."

The entity puzzled, caught off-guard, though the Richard-thing remained nonplussed, playing it bogart. The shape regarded the tiny creature before it, this hunched, little old man with the wide brimmed hat and the walking stick with the novelty feathers. For a long moment, neither the old man nor the man in denim moved, both simply looking at one another. A Mexican standoff with armageddon. Crowe did not back down, locking eyes with the shape's human form and holding that gaze for a long, silent moment. Even the wind held its breath.

Had this tiny, insignificant little creature somehow seen through its disguise? The shape pondered, unsure of how such a thing could be. Uncertainty was a sensation unknown to this being, and yet, as it met the gaze of this strange little man with his calloused hands and dark eyes, it began to feel uncertain. Crowe finally broke the silence.

"You come here to my home. The place my ancestors walked, the farm my grandfather built from nothing. The place I was born. The place where I raised a son. You come here and play games with me?" Crowe spat the words, the old man suddenly less hunched and small-looking. He stepped forward, his walking stick tack-tack-tacking all the while, until he was only inches from 'Richard.'

"Up that road there?" Crowe began, pointing with a gnarled, trembling hand. "There's good people, you hear me? My people. Five generations of family and friends.

Now, a generation might not mean much to you, but to me? To us?"

The old man trailed off, knuckles white on the walking stick. Crowe jabbed a finger into Richard's still-smiling face; the shape was unsure how to react. This was something new.

"You might not think we're much of a threat to you. Humans, I mean. You might be right." A sly carnival smirk crossed the old man's face. "But you might be wrong, too. You might be dead wrong. And I promise you, as the Lord is my witness and my ancestors my strength, if you even so much as think about hurting me and mine? I will end you. I will burn your whole misbegotten kingdom down to the foundations of the earth, and I will end you."

There was a fire in Quintin Crowe's eyes—a deeply burning, blue-hot, catastrophic ember inside those ocular orbits. Small, round balls of jelly set in a sunken, withered, weather beaten face that, for some unfathomable reason, were transmitting the fiercest, most burning anger and resentment this cosmic being had ever felt manifest in its presence. Across the infinite blackness, riding waves of solar detritus, the entity that fell to earth days ago had never once encountered a situation like this. The traveler had come to this tiny blue-green ball in a tiny, uninteresting galaxy to feed upon its inhabitants, to grow fat and lazy and live eons in the bowels of the earth beneath some town or city, growing with it, feeding off of it, and yet… Now this little creature, so frail and old and weak, was threatening it.

And for the first time in its immeasurable lifespan, the entity began to know something akin to fear.

SHADOWBORN

C.H. LINDSAY

The gentle touch,
gossamer-light,
whispers promise
of future flight.

The wings, newborn,
will seek the night.
They beat once, twice,
then fold up tight.

In dark alone,
they practice fright
to terrorize
while out of sight.

The creatures eat
for pure delight,
and soon they'll feed…
but not tonight.

THE LYING SKY

LEVI ROBINSON

The obelisk stood against the crisp, summer sky like a doorway in the horizon. Irene stared at it, puzzled and more than a little apprehensive. Part of her yearned to reach out and touch the strange stone pillar, but all her better instincts fought against the urge.

"Uncle Jason!" Devin shouted from behind her, still poking around her dad's white pickup. She turned to face her cousin, thankful to take her eyes off the structure yet nervous to turn her back to it. Devin was standing in the back of the truck, looking around for anything that might give them some kind of idea of what happened to her dad. Her father wasn't exactly missing just yet, but it had been a few days since anyone last heard from him. A day or two wasn't entirely unusual, but more than that was cause for concern.

"Whole lot of nothing," Devin shouted to her as he hopped down out of the truck bed and walked over to her.

"Nothing at all?"

"Nothing out of the ordinary. Beer cans. Chew cans. You know? The usual."

Irene sighed and looked back to her cousin's own lifted truck parked behind her father's. She thought about walking over there, grabbing her phone off the dash, and calling the cops. There was something off about all this. Her Dad would likely slap her upside the head for getting the police involved if it turned out to be nothing, but her gut told her it wasn't nothing.

"What's this thing?" Devin said, pushing past her and going to the stone pillar.

"I was just about to ask you the same thing. Pretty weird, right? You ever see anything like this out here before?"

"Nu-uh," he said, adjusting his cowboy hat to keep the sun out of his face. "You think it's Indian or something?"

"Maybe. Looks pretty old. Like maybe some old Shoshone sculpture? It's got writing on it. Or at least I think it's writing. Or runes?"

"Yeah, maybe. Your old man digs stuff like this, right?"

"Big time."

"Well, he's probably around here somewhere. Digging for artifacts or something?" She shrugged, wanting to accept that possibility. Wanting to ignore the knot in her stomach.

"Uncle Jason!" Devin called out again, only to be answered by the silence of the desert.

"Well, let's look around. He can't be too far off."

"Look where? There ain't nothing but scorching desert. And it's near midday."

"All the more reason to find him," Irene said and strode off. They walked around for a minute, shouting his name into the flat expanse, not really knowing where to look. There was nothing out here but sagebrush and open desert. Just as she was about to head back, Devin shouted something off to her left.

"Hey, I think I see something!"

"Where?" she asked, closing the gap between them. He pointed his finger to a small, man-like shape that stood on the skyline.

"Dad!" Irene shouted, and took off running towards it. Devin followed. She staggered to a stop when she saw that the shape that stood in the desert was no man but another stone pillar. Devin stopped, breathing harder than her, and tried to speak.

"Is that… Is that another one of them rocks?"

Defeated, Irene walked up the rest of the way to the pillar. It was nearly identical to the last. Just under five feet tall and two feet wide, covered from top to bottom in carvings so windblown she couldn't read them even if she knew what language they were. She couldn't put her finger on just why exactly the thing made her so uncomfortable. Maybe they were some sort of grave markers? Or maybe it was the fact that they looked older that some of the other native American structures she had seen across the region in the past? Far older. Like they were an unnatural part of the earth itself.

"Hey, Irene?" Devin's voice caused her to snap away from the obelisk and back to him.

"You see something?"

"Where is the truck?" He was looking around back the way they came, pulling his hat down with one hand to fully block the sun from his eyes. Past his shoulder, she saw with mounting concern what he was looking at. Nothing but open desert.

"I… It…" she tried to say, not being able to find the words. She turned, looking all around her.

"Irene, where the hell are the trucks?" The panic threatening to bubble over in his voice fueled her own.

"Maybe it's just the sun out here, you know? Like it's

reflecting off the ground in, like, a heatwave, so we can't really see as far as we normally might be able to."

"Okay," Devin said, looking at her, adjusting his sunglasses. "I can buy that. Let's head back. Get our bearings." Devin was almost 30, a few years older than herself. He was the oldest cousin of the bunch, so it made her a little uncomfortable to see him drop his tough cowboy routine and be a little nervous for once.

"Sounds good," she said and they started walking. They didn't say much, just put one foot in front of the other. Pretty quick they saw the other stone pillar, but it looked so nearly identical to the one they had just passed, it kind of hurt Irene's head to look at it.

No truck. Just desert, as far as the eye could see in every direction.

"What the hell?" The panic was spilling over in Davin's voice now.

"Maybe we just, I dunno, just got turned around. You hear about people getting disoriented out here pretty easy. Don't freak out, Devin," she said, but more to herself than to him. She was sure they had walked in a relatively straight line from the last pillar to here. And besides, even though it looked nearly identical, something about it felt slightly off. Like it was a copy of the other, rather than the same.

"Let's just keep walking," she suggested. "Let's just walk ahead. There is probably some weird geography. Like a small hill we didn't notice. Or like a trick of the light?"

"Alright. Great." He started walking. Quick enough she had to nearly jog to keep up with him. They trudged forward at that brisk pace for another minute or so before they saw something up ahead. There was a brief flutter of hope, but that was quickly stripped away when they saw what it was. Another pillar.

"This doesn't make sense," Devin pleaded. It was hot, nearly triple digits, and there wasn't a cloud in sight. Irene tried her best to compose herself. She knew sitting here frozen was going to do nothing to help their cause. She just had to allow herself to feel that fear, accept it, and move on. Take action.

"Let's go that way," she said finally, pointing a shaking finger directly to her right. "At least for a minute."

"That feels right," Devin said, regaining his composure. "It's not like we are that far from town anyway. We are bound to run into the railroad tracks or a fence or something."

"Right. We just need to take a deep breath, calm down, and admit we got a little turned around, is all."

"Alright," he said, and strode off with Irene quick on his trail. What Devin said was true. Heading this new direction did indeed feel right. Why was that? She didn't think it had anything to do with her having her bearing but more with the fact that the ground seemed to slope ever so slightly in that direction. Like they were on an incline, gravity just ever so gently pulling them towards the path of least resistance. Something about the thought made a subtle dizziness shoot through her head. As they walked, she noticed the ground couldn't be flatter. No visible slope whatsoever. But she felt it, nonetheless.

"Look," Devin cried out ahead of her, making her jolt her head up from the dusty ground.

There was indeed something up ahead on the horizon, and thank goodness too, because the sun was directly overhead. She wasn't sure how much longer they would be able to stay out in this heat. But as they drew closer, they saw it was neither the trucks or another pillar. It looked like a cluster of things and perhaps even a small structure. One in which they could get some shade and think about their next course of action, perhaps.

Her stomach dropped, and she knew from Devin's pace that his had too when they finally got a decent look at the thing they were walking towards. It was many stone pillars, maybe a dozen or so, circling around a large slab in the middle. No structure. No shade. Hope dashed.

"What the hell is this?" Devin said, nearly a whisper, this time taking his hat off and into one hand. Defeated.

As they walked up to the set of stones, both of them were careful not to touch them. There were maybe a dozen stones that spiraled out from a large rock slab at the center. Irene looked down at her feet and noticed the entire dirt-covered ground they had been walking on was now coated in a thin, white dust. It was everywhere. In every crevasse. Devin saw this too and pulled his shirt up over his nose.

"What are you doing?"

"I don't know what this stuff is. I don't want to breathe it. What if it is poisonous?"

"I don't think so." She leaned forward and brushed her fingertips lightly against one of the stone pillars. White dust stuck to her fingers, and another sensation of vertigo rippled through her.

"Some kind of dust."

"No shit, Sherlock. I can see that it's dust."

"I mean, I don't think it's poisonous or anything, jerk."

"You don't know," he said, his shirt still covering his mouth and nose.

"Fine. Whatever. It's probably like limestone or something."

"Look at the geologist over here," Devin said, trailing off and walking away from her, through the stones. With a dirty look, she took off in the other direction. Part of her mind felt better being in the cluster of stone pillars. At least they broke up the flat landscape. As she zig-zagged through them towards the massive stone in the middle, she made sure never to fully lose sight of her cousin. The slab in the middle seemed to be one large chunk of stone, sitting at over five feet tall and twice as wide. Carefully, she swung one leg onto an outcropping and climbed, mindful not to slip on the coat of white powder.

"What are you doing?" Devin's voice came up to her from below.

"What do you think? I'm getting a better look around. You know, the high ground?"

"Good idea," he said and dropped the shirt from his face, apparently no longer concerned with toxic dust.

She almost screamed out, but instead, what escaped her lips was more of a strained gasp. On the rock slab was the skeletal remains of some poor soul, long gone from this world. Many of the small bones had since turned to dust in the sun, giving the impression the sun-bleached bones had withered away and soon would be nothing more than a loose pile of rubble.

"Irene," Devin shouted, out of sight, a touch of concern in his voice. His voice broke her from staring at the pile of bones, and she turned to look back at him. He gave her a shrug as if to ask what the hell she was doing. She rose to her feet, careful not to disturb anything, and peered out over the desert landscape. Below and around her stood a smattering of stone pillars as well as her cousin, but beyond that was nothing. Just earth and the occasional dry shrub. In every direction. As far as the eyes could see.

Her knees felt weak, so she let gravity help her down onto her bottom where she proceeded to slide off the rock and back down to the desert floor where Devin was waiting. Her head was swimming, and she had to lean against the rock to get her bearings. It took her until Devin grabbed her by the shoulders for her to realize that he was talking to her.

"Hey, are you okay?"

"What?"

"You look like you are about to pass out."

"There's nothing. Nothing around. It's just desert. Everywhere. And a body."

"Body?" he said, shocked. As he climbed up the rock to get a look for himself, Irene slid the rest of the way down and ended up on the ground. Above her, she heard him curse then shuffle his way back down to her. She didn't know what to do. Her skin was growing tighter, already beginning to burn. Her throat started to tickle, just ever so faintly. But most of all, her head swam like she was deep at sea.

Devin climbed down and started talking in circles about what they should have done differently and what they should do next. She listened, not saying much. Time passed and seemed to stand still at the same time.

"And what the hell is that skeleton up there, huh? That's like some satanic ritual stuff. Devil worship."

"We need to find some water," Irene finally said, her voice already a little hoarse.

"I know," Devin said, coming down on his haunches. She looked up at him and then past him toward the pale blue sky, bringing one hand up to shade her eyes.

"What time do you think it is?"

"Not sure," he said, looking around. "What time did we get out here?"

"Nearly noon?"

"Something like that."

"How long have we been out here?"

He had to stop and think about it, and Irene could tell

from the look on his face, he wasn't sure either. That his perception of time seemed a little off. Just like hers.

"An hour or two?" he said, more of a question than anything. Irene put her hand on his shoulder and used it to get to her feet. She looked around then back up.

"The sun is directly overhead."

"Tell me about it." Devin sighed, also rising back to his feet.

"I mean, like the whole time we have been here, has it moved at all?" He seemed to consider this then just simply shrugged. After letting out a frustrated groan, she walked to the edge of the cluster and looked out into the desert.

"I don't know," he said, finally. "I'm scared, okay? I'm not afraid to admit it."

"Alright. Let's get out of here, right? Take our risk with the desert?"

"We could die out there."

"We could die here. And we apparently wouldn't be the first." She shoved one pointed finger at the slab, to the scraps of bones just out of sight.

And with that, they set off into the desert, away from the ominous rock formation. They didn't head in any particular direction, just their best estimate of the way they came, which was anyone's guess. They didn't talk much. Even if they had anything to say, they were both too thirsty to talk. As they slogged forward, the sun mercifully began to fall into their eye line, which gave them both a sense of relief. They were heading west, which should be the direction of town based on where they thought they were. But mostly, the sensation that time was passing seemed the most comforting. It was something, where as before, for just a minute, she allowed herself to be tricked that it wasn't. That time was actually standing still. And as much as she usually enjoyed being out in the sun, she was happy to see it disappearing over the horizon in front of her.

Which it eventually did.

"Thank God," Devin said, slowing his footsteps. "I thought that thing would never go down."

She didn't want to say anything, but something felt off here too. She was certainly glad to be out of the sun's rays, but her sensation of time was all messed up again. If it was nearly noon when they left the cluster of stone pillars and the sun was set now, how long had they been walking? By her estimation, they had been walking for maybe an hour? An hour and a half, at best. She bit her lip as they kept walking, the sky growing a shade of violet, and tried not to think about it.

Soon, too soon, it was full dark. And too dark at that. As they walked, Devin ahead of her, she could barely make out his shape. She looked up at the sky and gasped at what she saw.

"What? What is it?" Devin said, becoming still and stiff.

"The sky. There are no stars. No moon." Above them was nothing but black, an ocean of darkness peering down on them, threatening to swallow them up.

"What in God's name?" Devin was about to say something else but was cut off by a noise somewhere off to their right.

"What was that?" Irene hissed and drew herself near her cousin. For a moment, they stood there listening. The noise came again. A choked, shuffling noise, somehow both wet and dry at the same time.

"Hello?" Devin called out, but Irene shushed him. Her heart was beating fast in her chest. She tried to stay calm, to remain in control of herself. To not show fear. If it was some sort of wild animal, like a coyote or something, she was taught to not show fear. But she didn't think the thing that made that noise was a coyote. Not really.

They walked on for a bit, staying so close together they moved as one. All the while, they could hear shuffling, dragging sounds around them. Then, something touched Irene's arm lightly and she let out a scream.

"Something just touched me!" She squinted hard at the darkness, her eyes shaking from the intensity of her swarming pulse. She tried to make out the shapes in the darkness, but had little luck. It was as if the darkness itself was taking on some sort of unimaginable form. It reached at them with wet, clammy hands. This time, Devin also screamed as something grabbed him. It felt like a hand, but with far too many grasping and shifting fingers. Irene looked back the way they had come and saw that it seemed slightly lighter that way.

"Let's go back."

"Back? Back where?" Then, something made a gurgling noise and touched his face. Without discussing it further, they ran back the way they had come. Irene sprinted, hoping her cousin could keep up with her and praying neither of them would trip and fall. Soon though, they did stop to catch their breath.

After she could breathe again, Irene made sure her cousin was still with her, and looked back the way they were headed, which now looked darker than ever. From that darkness, a pained and restrained noise that could be mistaken as human drifted to her, making her shudder.

"What were those things?"

"I have no idea. But there is something seriously wrong with this place," he agreed, and they walked on, back towards the stone pillars, the slab, and the skeleton that called it home. They didn't doubt this was the right way, because again, the path seemed easier. Right.

If the two of them needed any more evidence of the otherworldly situation they had found themselves in, what happened next erased all doubt from their mind and caused them both to be filled with an unfathomable amount of dread and bewilderment. As they walked, the sun began to rise again, but this time from the west. As they traveled, the rotation of the sun above somehow reversed its ancient path.

Irene had always thought of herself as having an open mind. She read and let her thoughts drift to absurd hypotheticals and musings about the nature of reality. So even though it was impossible for her to wrap her head around their predicament, she at least was open to the idea that there is more than meets the eye. Devin, she knew, was the exact opposite in a lot of ways. And now, as the hateful sun rose higher and higher into the sky, it showed on his face more than ever.

"Dev?" she said softly, trying not to startle him as well as reserve some of her own energy. Talking might make them both feel a little better. But he didn't say anything. Just stared forward with his wide, blank eyes as he put one foot in front of the other.

"Devin?"

"Huh?" He turned towards her, some focus coming back into his eyes.

"Are you okay?"

"How can you even ask me that?" he said, then faced forward again. He wasn't wrong. She wasn't okay either. Far from it.

"Ok. Fair enough. It's bad. It's worse than bad. This place, I don't know, just can't be real."

"Maybe it's aliens?"

"Or a simulation?"

"Or magic," he said, solemn. "How do we deal with something like that?"

"I don't know," she answered honestly. "But we have to try and keep our heads. Stay calm, figure out what is going on and find a way back home."

"Whatever you say."

Soon, the pillars appeared on the horizon, and as they reached them, the sun settled back directly overhead, causing nearly every shadow to disappear. Devin climbed up onto the edge of the large slab and sat there, beaten. But Irene wasn't ready to call it quits just yet. She began to look around, examining all the stones. Trying to find some meaning to their unknown language. She wandered around for a while, trying to seem useful but failing.

"The skeleton is gone," Devin said after a minute, looking over his shoulder. Irene, who had settled into a hot patch of dirt on the ground, rose to her feet and lifted herself onto the ledge to get a look. The remains were in fact gone, at least mostly. All that was left was a smear of white dust and a few crumbs of bone. She was about to hop back down—she didn't love being up there—but something caught her eye. Something shining. She crawled closer to the pile and brushed away some of the dust where the person's spine had once been. There lay a small, metal plate. She took it into her hands and looked at it closely.

"What is it?" Devin asked, a new burst of energy in his tone.

"It's a metal plate."

"A metal plate?"

"Like, a medical plate," she stared at it, her heart starting to beat fast again. "My dad had one. Remember? For his back." Neither of them said anything else. She just climbed down from the rock and sat at its base.

It was hard to know exactly how long they sat there like that—Irene fiddling with the piece of metal and Devin laying on the edge of the slab—but it felt like hours. Maybe even days. The sun never moved once, and the blistering, red skin that clung their bodies was proof of it. Once, she heard Devin sobbing quietly alone. She even cried a bit herself, but no tears ran down her cheeks. Her body just couldn't spare the moisture. Eventually, she rose to her feet.

"We have to leave," she said, a pained croak in her throat. Her tongue had started to swell, making it even more difficult to speak. "Even if it means going through those… things. In the dark." Devin didn't speak for a while, and she might have thought him dead if it weren't for the steady rise and fall of his chest.

"Go without me," he finally said without opening his eyes, his own voice as dry as sandpaper.

"Devin," she pleaded. "Come on. We aren't going to die here."

"Yes, we are," he said and rolled over onto his side, adjusting his hat to keep as much sun off him as possible.

"I'll come back. I'll bring help." After she stood there, giving him every opportunity to change his mind, she eventually turned and headed back out into the desert.

The earth resisted her, but she pushed on. Soon, the sun began to sink in the west. After a while it was gone. The night, if this artificial darkness could even be called that, offered a small bit of relief from the constant sunshine. But just as soon, she heard the croaking, scraping cries of the things in the darkness ahead. She saw their indistinct shapes, with their many limbs, and shuddered.

Onward she went, closing her eyes against the horrors that waited for her in the dark. She felt their touch as she went deeper. They grew bolder. Only once did she open her eyes, and she immediately regretted it. One of the things had been very close to her face. Its skin was oily and black. It had dozens of eyes and many mouths, like a group of people had been horribly melted together into some mutated mass of blackness and envy. It wasn't until they started grabbing her with their wet, cold hands, that she finally screamed. She tried to rush forward, but she couldn't see, and they were all around her now. Smothering her. Grabbing and pulling her in every direction. Pain and nausea gripped her. She turned and ran back the way she came, seeing no way she could go forward. To go forward meant joining with them. Out here, in the void, there seemed no end. She knew then, that had she pushed on, she would go mad. And maybe that's what these things were souls that wandered too far from the path of reality. Here, at the edge of existence, there was only pain.

She ran until the sun rose in reverse again and she saw no sign of any of the black beasts. She lay on the ground and sobbed dryly. She lay there for a long, long time. There, in perpetual twilight, she tried to think of a reason to go on. Here, at least, the sun was just beyond the horizon. In the distance, she could hear the wails of those lost creatures, and she knew they were calling for her and they were desperate.

In the course of time, if there even was such a thing, she found herself heading back towards the stone spiral. If she was going to die out here, she didn't want to do so alone.

Quickly, the sun was high in the sky once more, and the stone monoliths stood erect against the flat skyline. She nearly had to drag herself into the stone circle. Weary, she walked over to the slab. A hand went to her mouth to stifle a scream as she lifted herself up onto the surface.

The youthful Devin she had left sitting there had been replaced by a sickly and dying old man. Every inch of the man's skin was burned and cracked, his clothes soiled, tattered, and nearly falling apart around him. His skin was pulled so tightly around his skull, his bleeding and cracked lips couldn't fully close. Worst of all were his eyes, bleached white and blind as they stared straight into the fiery ball in the sky.

"Dev?" she said, shaking. Barely more than a whisper. "Devin?" Slowly, he turned to her. His seared eyes staring through her.

"I remember you," the old man croaked with some effort. "You... You came back."

"I did," she said, trying not to cry. Seeing him this way horrified her but she also empathized with the great deal of pain he must be in. "I came back like I said I would. I couldn't get out, though. Couldn't find help."

"That's okay," he said, turning his gaze back towards the sun.

"You shouldn't stare at the sun," she said, not knowing what else to say. Not knowing where to even begin. Her head swam. Time was a river, flowing so fast around her that it almost seemed still.

"That's not the sun," Devin whispered, his lips stretched in a grisly smile.

"What?"

"Come. I'll show you." He beckoned to her with one hand. Almost hypnotized, she lay down beside him on the slab and looked into the sky.

Everything was spinning. That overwhelming sensation of vertigo returned. Her eyes were drawn to the sun. She looked at it, bright light penetrating and damaging her eyes. Just as she was about to look away, the ball seemed to change. It hurt to look at, but suddenly the edges grew black, almost like an eclipse. But the blackness grew, like oil on water, and the sky fell away. Melted into nothing. The blue was replaced by a deeper black than she thought possible. The heat seared so intensely that it became cold and caused her to shiver. It moved closer, and she could no longer contain her shrieks.

She was explicitly aware that the thing that had been masquerading as the sun was in fact alive. An entity of its own. It was much closer than the sun ought to be and seemed to sprout limbs like a spider. She screamed as it came down closer to her. She felt its want. Felt it desiring her.

Felt its hunger.

She never stopped screaming. Not until there was nothing left of her to scream. Not until it swallowed her up. She grew old and hoarse, and still she cried out. Until time caused her vocal cords to fall away, and all that remained of her body was her sun-bleached bones. And even as her bones turned to dust, she became a part of the thing—the false sun—and she never stopped screaming.

THE DANCER IN THE CLOUDS

CYGNUS PERRY

I saw the Dancer in the clouds
Its splintered form and shattered eyes
It frolicked with fluttering shrouds
a shapelessness ties and unties

I stood and watched and wondered still
if It were just a flock of birds
or some undefined, fulgid spill,
a stain that detects, transmutes, turns

It slipped from sky before It slid
behind the mountains–out of view
Its gangly ballet disappeared
disguised by terrain and I knew

The twisted Master must return
a day when sun is tucked away
the heavens will blacken and burn
the landscape will darken and gray

I saw the Dancer in the clouds
with masked intentions held inside
with musings of vanishing crowds
a patient Destroyer untied

THE BEAUTY PARLOUR

SJ TOWNEND

As Skip pulled the last steel whisker out and through the final cheek pad hole of her face, Rhea yelped. Sixteen bores had been pierced either side of her philtrum, through each of which a short length of fishing wire protruded. It had stung a little, but the quest for beauty was never painless. Skip knew how it felt. He'd given himself facial fur using a similar technique when he had transitioned to kangaroo.

Rhea stood and surveyed herself in the salvaged Baroque mirror which hung on the far wall of the beauty parlour. The mirror, seized most likely from one of the museum raids which had taken place long before the Dust had gotten so bad, shouted back a reflection of pure beauty. Morphed from kitten to lioness in a little under three hours, Rhea's new form was nearly complete. She was a riot of fur and tail and paws, the cat who had got the cream. After thrumming out a purr and stroking her thread-whiskers, she sat back down, placed her hands on the table palm side down, and tilted her head at Skip.

"Claws next," she said, her aquamarine cat-eye contacts almost glowing with feline demand.

Skip nodded. He was tired, but he knew this customer was worth the effort, for not only did she pay well, but she was also the hostess of the Unmasked Ball, and she'd promised to reward him with a ticket in exchange for a successful cross-species transformation. Skip was the best beautician in the district, and Rhea was the most influential—and also the most demanding—of the Beauties.

"How long are we going this week, with the nails?" he asked, proffering a display wheel of mounted acrylic and natural keratin talons which ranged from guitar pick to nightmarishly Krueger-esque in their sharpness and in their length. Rhea took the samples in her hands and ran her finger along each blade-like claw—firmly enough to leave a linear indentation on the skin of her finger pad, but not firmly enough to draw blood.

"Oh, let's stick with two inches. I'm not brave enough to go longer," she replied. "I love the way they would look, but it's impossible to wash my face without injuring myself. You know, I'd slice open a cheek—or worse."

"I understand. I rarely went longer than half an inch myself when I was feline. It wasn't practical. I kept scratching solar units, which made them totally inefficient," said Linux, a second customer, an energy engineer, a friend of Rhea's.

"Yes, I can imagine," Rhea replied, despite not having a clue about the ins or outs of photovoltaic energy or biodome construction. She had gotten this far on looks alone.

Linux flashed his finger stumps at his friend. "Now that I identify as Philippine Cobra, I've done away with talons completely. I'm thinking about a semi-permanent finger binding next. Clump them all together with bone staples so

I can strap my arms down against my torso and be done with upper limbs altogether—just for the ball, just for one evening." He stood and lifted his t-shirt to reveal a taut stomach, shelled in overlapping black scales. "One hundred percent snake, well, ten percent waterproof adhesive and reptile leather."

"You'll have to go over to Millia's for binding or webbing," said Skip as he filed and prepped Rhea's nail beds. "We don't do anything that requires anaesthetic here."

"Oh, I know. She did my neck hood, and a fabulous job she did too," said Linux, cupping his hands behind the yellow and black skin wings which stretched from his shoulders to his ears, fanning out either side of his neck.

"I can see the appeal of going reptilian. Julian from dome thirteen has gone iguana, and the scale work the tattooist has done down his back is to die for," said Rhea.

Linux flicked out his forked tongue and reached for Skip's portfolio of his influencer sketches and drawings of his most recent work. Once Skip had finished Rhea's claws, Linux was going to enquire about non-surgical options to enhance his dentition. He had wanted all but his canines cracked and pulled and then all four remaining canines built up with loaded faux-venom chambers, ready to spray on compression, but he knew tooth removal was a permanent modification and might limit future transitions. But he knew he'd like to be a large mammal of some sort again in the not too distant future—perhaps a polar bear or one of the other Arctic creatures who were some of the first to go —so he wasn't quite ready to give up his bite altogether yet.

Linux looked with admiration and great sadness at the display of images, at all of the hundreds of torn magazine and book pictures and drawings of creatures which decorated Skip's beauty parlour walls. All of them, bar the hardy brown anoles, the cockroaches, the locusts, and a few resilient fish species, had been lost since the Great Dust came many years ago. There were thousands of extinct species to choose from, to become, to impersonate, yet so few still alive. All that was left of life was survival and art, but he knew at twenty-three that he only had a short time left until his lungs succumbed to the force of pollution. Not a soul lived to see the other side of thirty. He already felt the crackle and tightness in his chest on exertion, which they all knew was the beginning of the end.

Most of the human survivors had been forced underground, partially due to the thick Dust which whipped up into ad hoc towering, erosive tornados, destroying everything organic in their wake, partially due to the particulate matter too small to see or feel but just the right size to cause almost instant emphysema, and partially due to the power of the new Elite.

When the Dust came, the capitalist society which had reigned eternal toppled like a stack of cards. Overnight, bankers, bitcoin trust-fund kids, and sport stars became worthless, fame and money lost value instantaneously, and the new Elite formed. The new Elite consisted of Those That Could: solar panel technicians and bottled gas suppliers, weapon hoarders and hydroponic scientists, engineers, farmers, and the Beautiful. Those That Could rose upward.

As the value of all commodities and all abilities rocked and shuffled over the years that followed the beginning of the Great Dust, so did what the Elite considered to be beautiful. Reptiles, amphibians, and mammals all dropped from existence in a matter of months, animal carcasses littered deserted roadsides until scavenged, and scavengers lasted only a little longer, but soon, all whom existed under the natural sky became blighted by the perilous toxic dusts. The air held a dryness like no other as the humans kicked Mother Earth into a premature menopause; Earth's wildlife, Earth's fruits became desiccated and powdered like trampled sand castles. The biota of the planet was decimated ten-fold and ten-fold again.

Those That Could built glass-roofed ecosystems with clever ventilation, air purification, and toxin extraction methods, and Those That Could survived. And Those That Could formed allegiances with Those That Had Weapons, and Those That Could and Those That Had Weapons took in Those That Were Beautiful. The Beautiful traded in the Oldest Profession, and together, they formed the Elite.

And the Elite separated from Those That Just Survive.

Beauty had in the past been the slim, symmetrical face of youth and muscle, and those genes still remained, however, a quest to become—or to at least imitate—what had been lost evolved. Beauty parlours cropped up in between the glass domes, and the Elite and the Beautiful travelled bravely from their places of safety—where the air was breathable and the water was pure— to the parlours for their modifications, to become animal, to decorate themselves with relics of organisms lost and only now present in posters and books and paintings and myth.

"EXCUSE ME SKIP, I need a comfort break," said Rhea, standing and swishing her leonine tail behind her. The tail, a gift from a taxidermist in exchange for tickets, had been anchored into her behind, into the ligaments of her sacroiliac joint, under lidocaine injection. "It's such a palaver taking this suit off to use the bathroom."

"Sure. I could use a drink gel anyhow," replied Skip,

wiping sweat from his brow. "You know, we sell beta-carotene supplements—take a high enough dose and your skin will yellow all over from within. You could give the skin suit the old heave ho." She peeled down her lioness cloak until it sat, an emptied sack, on the floor. Made from 'donations' from Those That Just Survive, it was not only buff yellow, but also soft and downy and unbelievably pelt-like.

THOSE THAT JUST SURVIVE WERE A COLLECTIVE of hardy families who were not Beautiful and who were not Those That Could. They'd fled straight underground when the Dust came. They were the underworld; they were redundant. They had nothing to offer, bar their own tissues. They bred like rabbits and bartered with the flesh of their own weak in exchange for foodstuffs and pure water. The Survivors, with their average and below average appearances, and their simple fashions, would never be allowed to attend the Unmasked Ball. And they had no gas masks with which to travel through the Dust in order to reach it anyhow. They were trapped in their caves. But their skin was young and supple, and Those That Died were peeled and broken apart like scrap heap cars, and those spare parts were offered up to the Beautiful Elite for their costumes and their modifications and their surgeries. In this process of desperate up-cycling, the Elite and the Beautiful worked hard to bring about the look of the rarest animals and the look of the animals long since lost to the Dust.

The skin, hair, and nails of the Survivors were all good —all good for bargaining with—as they were all young.

None lived beyond thirty in this time. The Dust, the radiation, the tropical illnesses that spread like wildfire as the planet warmed, and the wildfire and the dust that spread like the tropical illnesses: all of these things kept anyone from reaching death due to age. Time rarely killed the Survivors or the Beautiful or Those That Could. Old age was as much a distant memory as the dragonflies and the snow leopards and the orangutans and the pangolins.

"Good idea. Add some to my list, wouldn't you be a darling?" Rhea shimmied to the bathroom, and on her return, her talons were fitted and she paid Skip in tickets. Skip thanked her profusely and his tapered pseudo-ears, brown and soft, flapped as he did so.

Rhea and Linux donned their protective suits—yet a further layer of costume, this one essential when taking on the Dust and solar glare—and pulled their gas mask helmets onto their heads. Skip poked Rhea's whiskers under and in, ensuring not to bend them in the process as the pair got ready to leave.

"The Dust is bad today," said Skip, tucking the tickets into his kangaroo pouch. "Make for home with haste."

"We shall," Rhea replied, voice muffled through inches of filter and tubing. "See you at the ball on the morrow."

The Unmasked Ball came and went. Five hundred Elite from the network of biodome cities met and celebrated and compared their transitions and their costumes.

Each month that the Ball took place, Those That Could tried to outdo each other with their extreme modifications. Ivory elephant tusks taken from a museum long ago were surgically affixed to a young man's upper lip. Brightly coloured toucan bills fashioned from acrylics and resins were welded to the exposed, sanded jaw bone of another. Plumes of feathers mounted to sockets drilled into the soft tissues of a lady's back created a bird of paradise. One young reveller, both his legs bound together and smashed to smithereens, like crushed packets of crisps beneath unbroken skin, tarnished himself with grey body paint; an eel he became.

Each month, the competition grew for the most modified and most dramatic transition. Slashes to cheek and neck were made and stitched and healed as a Beauty re-identified as an axolotl. Survivors' teeth were mounted on steel hinges and fastened to foreheads: and so, a megalodon attended the Unmasked Ball.

ONE HALF-ORBIT of the planet about the sun later, the Dust had thickened. The Dust became more corrosive than it had ever been, and Earth cried tears of acid and grit.

RHEA BARGED through the safety lock, pushed open the second door, and marched into Skip's beauty parlour. Many of her friends were getting prepared for the final ball of the year, the Christmask Ball, the annual pinnacle of the Elite calendar. Those attending would no doubt pull out all stops to come in their most revered, most outrageous, and most fanciful attire to bring in the end of the year.

"Skip, darling. You simply must see what I have in my bag. I have a look I want… I need you to help me attain. It will be worth five tickets—no—I will give you ten tickets. Bring all of your parlour friends along; Christ—bring Survivors! I care not who you bring if you will only help me achieve this look."

In the parlour room, which stank of epoxy resin and burnt flesh, all the customers turned to look at the Hostess and what she was presenting. "I have found the rarest of images. The most rare of all creatures. You will not believe this when you cast your young marsupial glare upon it, Skip. No one will beat this. All eyes will be on me, as they should."

She pulled out a folded sheet from her bag, unfolded it, and thrust it forward into the audience.

"There. Isn't it a thing of beauty? What will it take to make me this? Say you can do it for me, Skip."

Skip's brows rose like banners above his brown eyes. He had never seen anything like it before.

"What is it? What are they meant to be?" He could tell it was something like a human, for it had a face, and all the parts of the face were where they should be, if somewhat compressed and clouded with sagging skin; it had elements of shar-pei dog, folds of horseshoe bat, facial hair of a piglet. Hair sat on the top of its head like that of a sheep—white, yet wispy, like smoke.

"It's… it's some kind of mammal, humanoid, I'd say, but most peculiar," he replied, his chin cupped in his hand, his thumb and forefinger poking at the corners of his mouth, his brow now screwed, lost in thought and consideration.

"Can you do it? To me? Do you think you can?" asked Rhea, keen as mustard.

"Where did you find this photograph?" he asked.

"My guard ransacked the Survivors who live to the east of the Utah Desert," she replied.

Pulling up a chair, she reached for the myriad tray of hair weave samples, searching for something to match the greyness of the image.

"Held them up at gunpoint, demanded they fill his sack with keepsakes; something for us to look through on a dull, dusty evening. I'd instructed him to go out and forage for inspiration, and this is what he came back with."

Linux hissed from the corner, "It's an Old Person, Rhea. A 'Geriatric'. Long before the Dust came and the planet could breathe—and we could breathe outside without our masks—in the great Utah Desert, people lived double, triple what we live now. Rumor has it some managed until they were one hundred. Can you believe it?"

"That's what I thought," said Rhea, cheeks flushed with excitement. "I've never seen one in such detail before. Look how the eyes nearly slide under drooped lids, see how there is the same white, wiry hair as on the top of the head sprouting like clouds of dust from the ears and the nostrils. Isn't it marvellous? Do say you can do this to me, Skip."

Skip took the photo from her hand and brought it close to his face. The crowd waited, breath baited, for his answer.

"I'll have a go," he replied, fumbling through his drawers of accessories, piercing tools, and glues, searching his refrigerator for sheets of fresh-primed skin ready for grafting, sterilised needles for stitching, tattoo inks for blemishing and marking and pocking and furrowing. "I'll do my best."

He stripped back her yellow make-up, pulled off her lash extensions and unthreaded her steel whiskers. He scrubbed near raw her yellowed hands and dissolved the bonding chemicals anchoring claws to her nail beds. He worked, folding, cutting, charring and stitching, to try to recreate the look of time and age that she'd presented as the other customers sat and watched Skip with wonder, surrounded by his constellation of tools and materials.

As Skip reached completion, the spectators erupted a volcanic fever of applause, the ash of which resonated in Rhea's eardrums, an opiate snare. Skip swivelled her chair around for all to see his creation.

She looked ancient.

Skin folded over on skin, some prosthetic, some her own, some borrowed, her face corrugated and creased akin to a brain coral. Her hair stood curly and white like the Dusts laced with sharp ice crystals that came in the winter. Her hands, now covered in brown liver spots, looked better than anything Skip had ever achieved before when transitioning customers to leopard or dalmation or friesian cow. Rhea looked marvellous: a thing of time and of many winters witnessed, an epoch of generations collected.

As she stood to examine herself in the full length mirror, she gasped. Never before had she looked so rare.

"I wish the ball was tonight, I don't know how I'm going to contain myself for twenty-four further hours," she said, hugging him tightly, placing a ream of golden tickets into the palm of his furry hand.

Skip, swollen with pride, blushed and thanked her for allowing him to work on the canvas she had provided him with. He helped her back into her safety suit and slid carefully her gas mask, all tubes and filters and inches of Perspex and glass, back over her newly old skull.

"Journey safe, home with haste, my most precious

piece," he said as he opened the airlock for her, the audience clapping majestically as she left.

OUTSIDE, the Dust was spinning, a zoetrope of grit and particulate pollution. The air was custard-thick as she set off on the treacherous journey back to her biodome.

Plodding onward, full of glee and following the route her feet knew by heart even in the blinding desert smog, she could just about make out the wall of hexagonal panels in the distance which she would need to enter.

The guard which stood up on the balcony did not seem to be present. How odd, she thought, that the Dust is so thick it is obscuring the guard. Was the guard lying down up there, snoozing in his safety suit, under the protection of his gas mask helmet… whilst on duty? She would certainly be having words with the head of security about staff taking absence without leave, napping on paid time. Rhea placed one foot in front of the other and bee-lined toward the port under the familiar hexagonal structure. She needed to parade impetuously her most magnificent transformation from lioness to 'elder' in front of her community before dealing with lollygagging guards.

Out of nowhere through the thick of the evening, a hard clunk to her head came. A Survivor with a club of sorts, manufactured from layers of swathes of wound and bound leathered skins, took a strike, knocking Rhea out cold on first attempt. The Feral tucked his baton into a crudely fashioned belt pocket, knelt over his prey, and tugged and tugged and unscrewed and unhooked the connectors on Rhea's gas mask and ripped the device off and away from her head before placing it into his sack. Grabbing next her boots and the trouser cuffs of her outer suit, he lifted and tipped the young old girl upside down.

The suit peeled away from her lifeless body, and out of it she slid, paste from the tube, onto the white hot sands of the desert. Rolling up and bagging the costly protective gear, he grinned a smile that only the Dust would see; this one would be his best find yet.

His own appearance, worthless by all current standards, had taken a battering an hour before as he had stepped outside of the Survivor's cave to take on the guard that had returned for a second time. The guard had returned after an earlier theft of skins and nails and photograph albums to request that further sacks be filled with knick-knacks, entertainment for the Elite. The Survivor had snapped and had taken a swipe with his club, knocking the guard to the floor. His average face had taken a chemical peeling from the acidic reflux spit-up of the desert and his lungs had pulled sharply upwards and inwards, as scorched toes in the bath do, at the heat of the Dust they'd inhaled.

But it had been worth it, as with one swift blow of the club he had fashioned from remnants of human fabrics, he had taken down the guard. The guard had then provided him with a gas mask which he had donned and used to venture out and into the Dust and out toward the second guard who was manning the nearby biodome. Then, the Survivor was blessed with winning a third gas mask and Dust suit even less rudimentary than the other two.

The feral Survivor ripped out the purse of coins and tickets from the Beauty's bag and stormed off into the Dust to his cave, to share news and findings, to launch the next round of attack—that night, the Survivors would snowball the Elite. Three masks would become six, twelve, twenty-four, and the Christmask Ball would become theirs.

AND THE YOUNG old girl's hair blew in the wind as the dust whipped up, a writhing vertical snake of sand and grit, a maelstrom of particulate smog. Her hair spread out and into the Dust and melted like licked candyfloss. The layers of skin that were hers and layers of skin that were not hers unbandaged, melted, dribbled, and blew away, and were carried off into the air with the cosmic grime.

The dust and the sand blasted against her cheeks, and her nose caved in, a fallen pyramid, releasing her un-mummified ghost to the ether. The vile force of ruined nature, acidic and potent, lifted off the cartilage and sinew and tendons and fat that lay underneath her skin. Up, up, and away it all went, dissolving into the Dust. The weather took years from the girl's face, tens and tens of years, until her skull was all that remained of her head.

Fatty brain corroded, liquefied into sludge, and slid out through her ear canals. Neurone rivulets vanished on contact with the hurricane of pollution that chipped and gnashed and bit at her remnants. On her neck, solar lasers breaking through the Dust burned and teased away young and old and young again skin, layer after layer, until a passing locust swarm moved in to tidy away what the weather had yet to claim.

Her body—all accelerated and modified tissues and trims, all falsely aged arms and legs and torso—followed suit, layer after layer rubbed clean.

Bones and titanium piercings were all that remained on the floor of the Utah Desert as the Dust settled, satisfied, now well fed. Never before had the Beauty looked so rare.

THAT SHADOW ON THE WALL

BRYAN MCENTIRE

I was naked in the shower when the earthquake struck. Tile beneath my feet vibrated and shook. My teeth rattled, and the closet light flickered like a blinking eye. There was a pop, and the plexiglass shower door cracked. I heard a muffled crash down in the basement, then it was quiet except for the sound of water cascading from the showerhead. I opened the shower door, seeing that the crack was not hazardous, and grabbed the towel. Katie was sawing logs like she usually did after a week of 12s at the hospital. I let her sleep, hoping to have the mess cleaned up before she awoke.

That thought vanished when I saw the chaos. Books lay splayed open all over the floor. The shelves were askew, but I had anchored them to the wall, so none tipped over. Shards of blue and white porcelain lay scattered in front of the middle case, with grandma's ashes spread out like a broken sack of flour. She'd wanted us to dump them in the river behind her cabin, but we'd been putting it off for years, and now her carbonized remains were all over the carpet. After gluing the urn back together, I tried to avoid touching the powder by using two dustpans to scoop her up, but a needle-thin stream of grains fell onto my Colombia River t-shirt. She would have cackled at the irony.

I spent the next few hours putting the living room back together and searching for news of the quake on the web. I found articles about a small one a few years ago that damaged a school roof. More about one in the 1980s that flooded Main Street, but nothing about that morning. The USGS website showed lots of minor quakes in the surrounding states, but nothing nearby either. I was so engrossed that I never noticed Katie leave. Since the quake wasn't on the news, and she didn't wake up when it happened, she probably didn't know about it. That reminded me of the crash I'd heard in the basement. I groaned.

We almost didn't buy this house because of the basement. Katie called it a "murder cellar" because the stairs were so steep. What sold it, however, was how perfect it was for our food storage. I'm not a crazy prepper with a stocked armory and enough MREs to last a lifetime, but I enjoy being prepared to live for a few months if everything goes sideways.

This street was odd because the original developer of the neighborhood picked floor plans without basements. Everywhere else had them, but not on this one street. No one knew why. If we were in a swamp with a high water table, I could understand, but this was the foothills and everywhere else had them. But the owners of this house had dug a steep shaft going down thirty feet and framed in the stairs.

The basement itself was ordinary enough if you

considered a perfect cube ordinary. The inner dimensions of the space were exactly 17 feet on each side. I measured it with a laser distance meter once, and it was dead on. You might typically expect a 1/4" - 1/8" variance, but the owner put in a lot of effort to be this exact. The floor and walls were polished concrete with hefty mine-lumber shoring up the ceiling. There were no markings or way to know what they previously used the space for. Properly installing my shelves would have been easy with the drywall and studs of a normal basement, but down here, I would need special tools for concrete. I was too lazy to buy those.

I always kept a flashlight at the top of the stairs. The trapdoor was too heavy to stay open once you were inside, and the only light was from a naked bulb in the cellar. The flashlight must have tumbled down the stairs, so I descended in the dark, the trapdoor closing behind me like a tomb. The sight that greeted me when I pulled the chain was what I expected. Two shelves had tipped over, cans scattered all over the floor, and flour covered everything around broken bags. The remaining two shelves stood but were empty. Shattered jars everywhere. Peaches and pears glistened naked on the floor, reflecting the wan yellow light of the bulb.

I stood at the base of the stairs, mind blank and over-whelmed. The only sound was the light tinkle of the chain sliding along the light bulb, casting off the motion of my pull. Even that stopped, and the cellar was silent. Not so quiet that I heard my blood flowing and organs working inside my body, but soft enough that my breath was loud and out of place. I felt a cold draft across my face. Why was there a draft here, thirty feet below the surface of the earth? I reached out, grasping at the moving air like a blind man. It wasn't coming from the stairwell or from either side. The far wall where the shelves tipped over—was that a shadow on the wall? It was hard to tell in the weak light. I spotted the flashlight a few feet away, half covered by a broken jar of pickles. Kicking the shards aside, I rescued the light and wiped juice on my jeans, then tiptoed across the floor, avoiding most of the detritus.

That shadow on the wall wasn't a shadow at all. The circular cone of illumination from the plastic flashlight only drove the shadow deeper. Tempting fate, I stuck my finger in the walnut-sized hole and felt a thin edge of concrete all around. It was flat as a business card, and a section crumbled at my touch, falling to the floor. The draft grew stronger. Again, I shined the light in but saw only darkness and felt the breeze on my face. It had an odd, earthy smell I couldn't place. "Hello!" I called into the dark. "Is anyone home?" For a moment, I felt ridiculous until the ground lurched beneath my feet. There was a loud crack, then something hit my head from above, and the world went dark.

A viscous mixture of peach, pickle, and olive juice filling my mouth greeted my return to consciousness. My head throbbed, and dried blood caked the crown of my skull. I sat up, shards of glass digging into my arm and legs. The overhead light was on, but the flashlight, somehow still in my hand, was dead. So intense was the throbbing that the only thought I found was to get some Tylenol to make it stop. Traversing the stairs took longer than normal, and the trapdoor was nearly impossible to push open.

I'd been sitting at the table for a half-hour when Katie walked in. My headache had just faded into the background. "Did you feel those earthquakes today?" I asked, pulling my gaze away from the Germanic Eagles inscribed on the pewter beer stein I was using for my water.

"Earthquake?" Katie replied. "What are you talking about?"

"There were two of them today. The first one happened this morning while you were asleep. The second one was a while later. I was in the basement and a can of something hit me on the head and knocked me out." I drained the last of the water. "You really didn't feel either of them?"

"No, I'm on a digital detox today and left my phone here." She held it out like a trophy. "I've been in the park most of the day. Took out the canoe, then napped on the pier." Her voice rose in pitch. She was about to get excited. "I've always wanted to feel an earthquake! I bet one of them was while I was in the water. Probably that first one. The second must have been while I slept."

"Well, the first one was…" I began.

"That explains the crazy dream I had during my nap. Energies from the earth must have leaked into my sleeping brain."

Once Katie got started on energies, crystals, and chakras, she could go on for hours. I shifted my attention to doing earthquake research on my phone. We'd been together for long enough that I could sense how often I needed to look up or mirror what she was saying. Even with this half-listening technique, I'd amassed an osmosis-based knowledge of 'true spirituality,' as she calls it. While I doubt any leaking energy from the earth influenced her mind, I discovered from my reading that fault lines riddled the area, especially along the hills next to the mountains where we lived. A theme prevalent in the local sources was talk of the next super quake that would level most of the area. They were in the geologic record once every 800–

1000 years, but it'd been almost 2000 since the last one, so the area would snap like a dry rubber band when it happened. While fascinating, none of this explained anything about what was in the basement.

The next few weeks were an onslaught of 18-hour days to prepare for a website update, so the basement faded into the background. It was the odor of rotting food that forced me to break away and focus on cleaning up the remaining mess. When I opened the cellar trapdoor, a wave of putrescence hit me with such strength that I added the aroma of vomit. I would expect mold and rotten smells after leaving all that mess in place for a few weeks, but what I witnessed in that basement went beyond anything I could have imagined. It took the entire weekend cleaning with a host of industrial-strength chemicals before I could be down there without wearing a gas mask.

In hindsight, I should have worn a hazmat suit while cleaning, but it didn't seem necessary. Who thinks about that while cleaning up spilled food storage? Maybe if you work for the CDC or drive an outhouse vacuum truck. As I sealed the last garbage bag, though exhausted, I couldn't leave the basement without inspecting the hole in the wall. Using my finger, I cleared away the rest of the concrete still clinging to the edges. It was perfectly square, with sides smooth as obsidian. I don't know what I was expecting, but that wasn't it. Using a tape measure from the corner toolbox, I measured precisely three feet square. I'm not sure why, but stretching the tape measure across that black void gave me the chills. I called out again. Whistled, but there was no sign of how far it went. It vanished into the darkness.

Something about that square, dark tunnel stretching into infinity gave me a moment of vertigo. My legs turned to jelly, and I sat on my haunches. Before my eyes, the hole fragmented and spun like a childhood kaleidoscope. My stomach lurched, and a ringing pierced my ears. Deep breaths. In, out. In, out. I closed my eyes and tried to shake away the vision. Still, I saw the long tunnel, reflected and refracted hundreds of times in shifting shards of crisp glass. The moment passed, and I was on the floor of my cellar, looking at a hole in the wall. I took the lid from a large box and flattened it against the hole and duct-taped it in place. The five-gallon jugs of water went in front. I'd been cooped up in that cellar for days, breathing in who knew what mold spores, cleaning chemicals, and stale air. That would be enough to give anyone strange visions.

Katie was on another shift that night, so I got cleaned up. As the water massaged my head, I closed my eyes and let it run down my face. The rushing, hollow sound of the water striking my skull made me wonder how the brain inside could come up with a vision or hallucination as vivid and odd as the one I'd seen. I didn't realize I'd fallen asleep until the water turned cold and drove thoughts of the cellar weekend from my mind. An evening of Battlestar Galactica with a Heineken and Meat Tornado pizza got me back to what felt normal.

That night, the itching started. I first thought it might be a mosquito bite on my neck, but it wasn't one point of itching. Instead, it was a broad swath of tingling, crawling skin. Scratching at it only spread it up my neck and onto my head. When the sensation reached the back of my head, every hair turned into a follicle of fire. Thousands of needles glowed white-hot, piercing my brain.

I will occasionally scream during a horror movie, or with exhilaration while cliff jumping into a lake. Those are nothing like the sounds that came out of me. The sensation crawling up the back of my head was so unlike anything I'd ever experienced that for a few moments I went mad. Pain is not an adequate word to describe it. If you start with an itch, add in pain, but then open a garden hose full blast with a fluid that makes you wish for un-being, that approximates what I experienced. It flayed open my psyche, ripped open every emotion I'd ever had, and lit them on fire. Something inside my mind snapped, but before I could tell what it was, the itching reached the crown of my skull and sank inward.

The relief was immediate and complete. Above my head, reflections of the yellow street lights danced on the ceiling. A textured white noise from the device on my nightstand was the only sound. It took a while for my breathing to return to normal, but eventually, I fell back asleep. I awoke the next morning with the most intense thirst I'd ever had. My mouth was full of cotton, and I could barely move my tongue. In the kitchen, I didn't notice Katie sitting at the table until I heard her.

"What the fuck did you do to your hair, Paul?"

I jumped, dropping the mason jar now half full of water on the counter. Somehow it bounced instead of breaking, and in a reflex, I caught it. "Don't scare me like that, Kat," I said. "What do you mean, what did I do to my hair? I did nothing to it."

"Like hell, you didn't! It looks like you dyed the back of your head with a black stripe."

"What…" I said, feeling at the back of my head. The patch of hair where I'd felt the itching last night had a rougher texture than the hair on either side. "What the…" I began, rubbing back and forth at the surface. I went into the bathroom and took out Kat's round makeup mirror. She'd followed me.

"I could see some teenage wannabe punk doing that." She sat on the edge of the tub. "But even they would at least make the stripe go all the way and look like a mohawk."

Her voice faded into the background as I held up the mirror and saw what she'd been talking about. It was as she said. A black stripe, dark enough to look like paint, starting at the nape of my neck and extending to the crown of my head where it twirled and ended in a half-circle. "How the hell did that happen?" I mused.

"Well, if you didn't do it, did a fairy sneak into the room and lick your head?"

She wasn't usually that aggressive, and by her tone, I could tell she wanted an answer. Taking it as rhetorical, I replied, "It must have been something from that mess in the cellar. It made my head itch like crazy last night."

Kat gave me her 'don't be a moron' look. "We don't have a cellar, Paul. Did a fairy plant that in your brain too?" It took a few seconds for my mind to process what she said. "Um, hello? Are you deaf?" she said when I didn't respond.

"Of course, we have a cellar, Kat, you know, the one you've always hated even though you never mind eating our food that's stored down there."

"I'm too tired to deal with your bullshit right now, Paul. I'm going to bed, and maybe when I wake up, you'll make more sense."

Well, black hair stripes, cellars, and itching mind melts or not, something wasn't right. I went to the pantry like I'd done a hundred times, flipped on the light, and bent over, bracing for the heavy bastard of a trapdoor. Opening a door isn't something you think twice about—even a crawl-space cellar trapdoor. When you've done something enough times, muscle memory takes over, and you don't even think about it. Braced like I was for the weight of that door, I was utterly unprepared for how light it was. I have a brief memory of my arms jerking the trapdoor open, a moment of surprise, then losing my balance. My jaw must have hit the edge of the trapdoor and shattered the teeth inside my mouth. My last memory before passing out was my head hitting a gallon jug that burst like a melon. The lukewarm water joined my mouthful of blood and broken teeth.

Later on, I learned that I also wet my pants, but that wasn't until I'd regained my bearings at the hospital. There was shouting. I was lifted onto a stretcher. Flashing lights. Sirens. Needle stab in my arm. IV sticking out like a tentacle. Something was happening to my mouth. Bright lights. Oh, Jesus, a needle in my gums. Then everything was numb.

My top two incisors were the only teeth they didn't take out. The oral surgeon said she'd seen nothing like it and joked that a vampire must live inside me to preserve the two incisors like that. Given how odd things had been lately, I wouldn't be surprised if something like that was true.

I was in the hospital for two days. During that time, Kat checked in on me a few times, but other than that, my only company was the TV and an unconscious teenager in the next bed. I received no other visitors, no flowers, nothing. It laid bare the reality that my only real friend was myself. There was no response from my boss, family, or coworkers when I let them know I'd be out for a few days in the hospital.

As I lay there, my mouth throbbing, I could tell something was off with Kat. It was like she was not 100 percent herself. The spark behind her eyes was at a depth I couldn't reach, but physically she was the same: quirky smile, dimples, and a pheromone aura that filled me with roses and fire. Something about her personality was just off. When I wasn't trying to figure that out, I spent the time ruminating about the cellar. The shaft. A black stripe on my head. The treacherous door.

They discharged me earlier than scheduled because of a mix-up with the denture place. I would need to come back in a few days to get them fitted. The thought of wearing them for the rest of my life was not thrilling, but I didn't have a choice. A few more days on a liquid diet wouldn't kill me. Drinking smoothies for that long might make me go crazy, but I was lucky to have the options I did. Thinking of the wooden museum-piece dentures of yesteryear gave me chills. But teeth or no teeth, the question of the cellar needed unraveling.

Before leaving, I checked the nurses' station to see if Kat could give me a ride home or let me use her car. She wasn't on shift and didn't pick up her phone. Days cooped up in the hospital gave me itchy legs, so I took advantage of the early summer morning to walk the twelve miles home. I could easily use ride share or take the bus or train, but once the idea popped into my head, the thought of walking was appealing. Much of it would be through neighborhoods and should be enjoyable.

The rotating circular doors whooshed behind me as I walked into the sunlight. It was one of those days when clouds partially shrouded the sky, and as they moved across the celestial dome, rays of sunlight broke through and bathed the ground in energy. As the blocks disappeared behind me, I was glad for the cloud cover. The thought of an unbroken blue sky above my head made me uneasy. Just imagining nothing above me but the infinity of space gave me vertigo, and I had to sit down on a fence.

"What's wrong?" a voice behind me said.

I turned and saw a young boy sitting on the sidewalk with chalk in his hand, tracing lines around himself. He must have been at it for a while, because a cross-hatch pattern covered the entire walkway.

"I was feeling lightheaded and needed to sit down. Your fence was in the perfect spot." The boy had emerald eyes beneath a mop of unruly blonde hair.

"You should be careful sitting on that fence," the boy said.

"Oh yeah, why is that?" The world still spun, but it was slowing.

"That fence is the boundary between my kingdom and the Land of Chaos and Ruin," he said, waving the chalk.

"Sounds like I better not break it then. Does that pattern protect you from the Chaos?" I asked.

He flashed a look of disgust. "It's just a pattern. Chalk can't protect you from the Chaos. Nothing can."

"How does this fence protect you, then?"

The boy squinted. "It doesn't really protect me at all. Just separates the space, so it's more trouble to get in here than it is to stay out there."

I frowned, "Did the Chaos get me?"

The boy set down the chalk and looked up at me for the first time.

"I. Uh…," he paused, drawing out the vowel, "can't tell. That's odd. Usually, it's just bums and Tweakers that walk past here, and the Chaos is all over them."

"I guess that means I'm not a bum or Tweaker then."

"Obviously not," he frowned. "I'm not sure what you are." Without a word, he stood up and ran up the side-walk, opened the door, and was gone. It left me staring at the geometric tunnel the boy drew himself into. The pattern was all straight lines that spiraled out in every direction. He had been sitting in a square at the center.

At that image, my vertigo passed, and I smiled at the thought of squeezing in the square hole in my cellar wall and crawling in. Although I'd never been in a cave, the sensation of damp earth and darkness surrounding me was comforting.

A sense of morning adventure replaced the odd encounter with the boy as I continued along the tree-lined streets. Waiting for me at the house was a mystery that needed solving. My mind had no room for doubt about what I'd seen in that cellar. Leaving the neighborhood, I stood on the corner, watching a red hand block my way as an endless stream of cars and trucks roared past. Although I knew the hand was made from light bulbs and installed by an underpaid city worker, the individual points that made up the hand felt like red eyes watching me. Stoplights shouldn't take this long. My unmoving feet pressed into the concrete by legs that grew longer and longer: weight increasing and tension in my chest. The blue sky was closing in again—this time aided by the baking laughs of the Yellow Face. Curse the Yellow Face, keeping me trapped for so long. That place. So dark. Colder than out here. So much noise. A green man was running. Running like the wind. Slower than my wind. These legs were strangely long yet moved like shadows. But if I kept running and stayed ahead of the burning in my chest, the blue sky couldn't pull me up to its terrible depths.

Then there was water. Cold on my hair. A fountain. Dunking my head. Liberty Park. I was in Liberty Park, two blocks from my house. Water from the fountain splashed as I kept my head under. Holding my breath, I looked around at the coins sparkling in the afternoon light. A child laughed nearby, splashing. It took ten minutes to regain my equilibrium after my mad dash across town. I wasn't sure what came over me. The entire run was a blur. Somewhere along the line, I'd ditched my shirt and felt the itch of a bad sunburn.

I didn't realize until I'd walked the final blocks to the house that my keys, phone, and wallet were also gone. The doors were locked. Underneath Katie's gnome, the hide-a-key was missing, and the kitchen window in the back with a loose latch wouldn't budge. It was hot. My gums throbbed where teeth had once been. Locked out of my house with a gnome grinning at me like a malevolent child. Urinating on that smug face made me feel better, but still didn't explain why the usual backup entry methods didn't exist today. Nor did it relieve my sudden need to defecate. I wasn't about to do that in my yard, so I broke the kitchen window with a rock and crawled in after sweeping away the glass.

As much as I needed a shower, clean clothes, and a liquid meal, the burning question of the cellar compelled me. Gingerly, this time, I lifted the trapdoor. This made no sense. It was a different door and a normal crawlspace. No cellar. After 10 minutes of searching, I found a flashlight and hopped into the crawlspace. Dust and cobwebs stuck to my bare, sweating back. Stacked in neat rows out of the way of the trapdoor were boxes and boxes of jars and containers. I opened a few, and they were the same jars I used for food storage in the cellar. Only these were empty and covered in dust.

Again, this made absolutely no sense. Hunching in the small space gave me a backache, so I spent the next hour cleaning up and trying to figure out what was going on. I couldn't look anything up on my phone, which I'd lost. The rolling cipher for my laptop didn't work, so I couldn't get on that. Katie kept her old Kindle Keyboard on the bookshelf, so that might work.

It was almost like I'd woken up that morning after the nightmare pain in an alternate reality, close to my own but slightly different. This thought ran through my mind as I walked up to the bookshelf to get the Kindle. That was when I saw grandma's urn. It was intact. There were no glued cracks or reconstructed pieces that didn't fit. I peeked inside. Empty. I looked more closely at the bookshelves. Most of the books were familiar, a handful equally worn as the others, but with titles unfamiliar yet interesting. Here was the Dark Souls lore book I'd been drooling over for months but could never bring myself to pay $500 on the used market. Here was a book on recursive algorithms. And another that looked like a reference for a computer language I'd never heard of. The doorbell interrupted my perusal.

"Hey, Paul," the mailman said, handing me a stack of letters and a small package. "I couldn't fit all of this in the mailbox."

"Oh, thanks." Before I could think of anything else to say, he turned around and ran off.

"Have a good day," he called back. "Good luck with your job search."

"Job search?" I asked the screen door as it closed.

The box was Katie's makeup subscription. The letters were the usual junk, all except one addressed to me from the State. Inside was a credit card and a letter informing me I was approved for unemployment benefits and could use the card anywhere Visa was accepted.

This was too much. I sat on the stairs and ran my hands through my hair. The back of my head felt normal. Looking in the mirror confirmed it—the black stripe was gone. On a hunch, I tried the old standard password on my laptop, one I'd stopped using years ago. It worked. Most of the data on the machine was familiar, but some of it was not. A quick search on the net revealed that the company I worked for didn't exist. Impossible. Whatever that earthquake uncovered in the basement had sent me some place else. I'd watched every episode of Twilight Zone, X-Files, Fringe, and read an endless array of sci-fi novels. This belonged to one of them. Was this my movie now? Was there a tunnel thirty feet beneath this house that would lead me home?

My father's old pickaxe and shovel were waiting in the garage.

The Voice in the Night

Mickie Bolling-Burke

Normally a neat and organized man, Syrese's bedclothes bespoke a rough night. He had had words with his business partner earlier in the day—a great deal of money and custom was at stake, and his stupid, stubborn partner was blind to the imminent ruin. He brought the fight to bed with him, waking periodically to make yet another salient point. Realizing his folly, he turned over. "I would greatly enjoy knocking that supercilious smile off his face. He's an overweening, windy buffoon who walks as if he owns the street. He wearies me —I would be shot of him. If only someone could help me." Sighing, Syrese finally fell to sleep.

The bedchamber was hushed and dark. The moon shone through where the heavy, black drapery allowed, yet the shadows gathering in the corners grew deeper, grew thicker. A cold breeze pierced one of the drapes and wandered restlessly through the bedroom, flicking this rug, ruffling that shirt. It tousled the bedclothes that warmed the four-poster bed. Syrese stirred without waking.

The breeze circled the sleeper as if studying him. It

moved back to the window through which it had entered and disarrayed the draperies covering it, allowing the moon to light the sleeper as like a ray from Heaven. The breeze returned to the bed to caress him, to stroke his face with an unlight touch.

Syrese sat up. "Is someone here?" Silence. He swung his legs over the side of the bed and stood. He took a step toward the wall to snap on the light switch when the long silence was broken by a rustling in the corner. A shadow broke free from the dark and oozed forward.

"I am here to tell you a story. Some people don't want me to—well, I am not talking to them. I am talking to you. You don't mind, do you?"

Mouth gaping, throat closing, Syrese staggered backwards to freeze against the bed so closely as to disappear into it.

"I have come to tell you about him so you can stop him. Stop him from killing!"

The voice had a vile hissing quality, as of too much air being formed into its words.

"So sit you down and get comfortable, my good friend. I know where he passes, and we can pick his trail up then. He's clever for all his evil—wicked smart he is, which makes him so clever. He-he. I know you'll allow me my own clevers, my dear, my little *asides* as you might call them.

"We'll watch him get those others, and we'll learn his ways and thus how to take care of him. I will tell you what to do to be safe. Heed me now."

"What… who..." Syrese stuttered. "Who are you? How did you get in here? What man? If he is to kill, I want nothing to do with him!"

"Proper rude is what I am. I ask your pardon, and permit me to introduce myself. I am—well, you can call me M. Chuchotement. How did I get in? Why, you may as well ask the moon how he gets in. Or the air! And I have told you what I want, I want to tell you how you can avoid him. You must listen, friend Syrese. Or you will hear no more."

Silence surrounded the bed, not even movement to stir the ears.

"Are you attending, brother Syrese? We want to get started."

"My name… How is it you…" His throat cleared itself to give a stronger voice. "How do you know me? I don't know you. What are you to me?"

"You waste the time, brother Syrese. If you are caring to die, I can show you a thousand lovely ways to do so. *Or…* I can show you this way to life. Does it matter how I know you? We are now friends. I would be sad to lose your acquaintance. I don't have many friends. Come, my gentle man. Make your choice! Make the right choice. The grave's a fine and private place… the dark and cold hold you forever in embrace…"

The blackness sent tendrils to wind around Syrese, stroking his head, touching the left side of his chest, nestling in his ears. He shivered, his thoughts full of a forever of nothing but empty, cold darkness. It wouldn't hurt to hear this creature out. Having no desire to die, unperceiving that the blackness was beguiling him, captivating him, he chose. "What is it I need to do?"

"Oh, my dear boy, you will not regret this choice! Dress yourself in warmth, as the cold is penetrating, and we may be detained. In shades of dark, that we may remain undetected."

Syrese gathered his attention and stood wavering in the moonlight. He reached for his lamp switch.

"No! No, good Syrese, don't let us bring in the light of

man. Let us conduct our business under the light of God. It will bless us and protect us."

Dropping his arm, Syrese found his way to his armoire and pulled out clothing he thought would pass M. Chuchotement's inspection. In realization that he hadn't yet seen M. Chuchotement, Syrese spun around, his eyes searching the deep shadows of his room.

"What are you looking for, M. Syrese?"

"You. I am looking to see you, M. Chuchotement. I would know who is directing me this night."

"Ahhh...you have found doubts about your choice of life. It is with disappointment I look upon you. You would regard me before saving your life?"

Syrese froze. "Sav—" His voice dropped to a whisper. "Saving my life?"

"The clock is passing; the cock will crow soon enough! You must gird yourself and move swiftly before it is too late! Clothe yourself, my good man, and come with me."

Fearful, Syrese heeded the urging of M. Chuchotement. He attired himself in thick, black trousers, shirt, and coat. His feet he shoved into boots over heavy black stockings. Pulling a black cap over his grey hair, Syrese stepped to the door and nodded.

"Perfect raiment, brother Syrese! You are a lad of valor and quickness. Let us be about our business then."

The door opened, and Syrese was escorted by a heavy hand and light foot. He peered all around to see his companion, but the darkness of the stair landing overlaid his sight as effectively as a blindfold, preventing any view of the figure at his side. The moonlight in his chamber room was not permitted to follow. Syrese turned to his parlour and was pulled backward. "But don't we need money? And my papers? What if we are stopped? If we're questioned, we will need to produce who we are."

"No, we are in no need of money. That is not what I am here for. Let it lie. And your papers… friend Syrese, if we are questioned, producing who we are will be the last thing to do. Just you let me conduct our little jaunt. We now will be gone."

The iron pull on Syrese's sleeve and the urging at his back turned them around. Down the stairs both pairs of footsteps trod—lightly for M. Chuchotement, some tripping and hesitancy for Syrese. At the bottom, the big wooden door stood closed, waiting to be unchained, unbolted, and unlocked so the two could join the night.

With admonishments for speed and silence, the road was gained. The buildings wavered in the faded moonlight as if underwater. Syrese squinted to see and lost the view. The street lights flickered as if gaslight was growing and weakening in the lanterns. He turned querulously, seeking M. Chuchotement, seeking direction. He opened his mouth.

"Hist! Silence is demanded now. Craft and cleverness are required to put this situation right. No words, just action. Brother Syrese, are you with me?"

Syrese, not wanting to die this freezing, mist-filled night, nodded. An arm chivied him down the street, avoiding the lights. He pulled his cap down and turned his head to avoid inspection if others came near. The night sounds were muted; people laughed in the distance, and wheels knocked against the bricks in the road. Syrese stopped near a dim streetlight, peering down. When had the pavement become cobblestone bricks? He turned in the direction of M. Chuchotement and pointed at the road.

The voice came in his ear, the breath chilling. "The road is nothing to you, my good friend. Just you gaze at that building. Watch and wait, M. Syrese."

The two stood in silence, hugging the darkness, peering through the waves of fog that now wafted at eye level. Syrese did try to gaze at that building, but at which building was he to gaze? Instead, he found himself fidgeting, his feet shuffling and his hands plucking now at his coat, now at his trousers. "This is absurd," he muttered. Who is this M. Chuchotement and what were they about on this nasty night? And he didn't want to have business with a killer! "As if playing a foolish child's game of spy." Syrese spun round to get a look at this M. Chuchotement.

"M. Syrese, am I not the speaker of truth? Do you not crave my assistance? Do you not wish to remain above ground?"

Syrese breathed in to reply when the sound of a click came to his ears, gripping him. Somewhere, a door had shut with stealth. Is this what he was waiting for? Heels tapped on the sidewalk, drawing nearer. Caught in the moment, fear sang in his heart, driving him backwards to clutch at the damp bricks of the building behind him, sure the footsteps were aimed for him.

A cold, dry hand closed over Syrese's mouth. "Be silent and but observe," was sighed into his ear.

Syrese peered through the gloom, but fog filled the night with fakery and misdirection. Sound laughed at him—the tapping footsteps danced to and fro, circling him to his right, then round to his left, in front of him, then mocking from behind. He held his breath as still as he held his body.

Finally, finally, the footsteps tapped further down the walk. Syrese released his breath and inhaled rapidly to gain control.

"Now, Syrese, now we shall see what you are made of. We follow."

"But I can't see—"

"What, friend Syrese? What can't you see? The truth? You are about to be confounded, and yet you disbelieve me. Yet you fight and jab at words. Open your eyes and ears and follow. Follow for your very life!"

What fight Syrese had in him to go against M. Chuchotement was dashed to the earth. Heart weary, he followed where M. Chuchotement guided him. Down the street, the fog smothering his ears and dimming his eyes, with faint incomprehensible shouts in the background and the smell of damp and earth gliding up his nose, he followed. Syrese turned to the voices, not only to orient himself but to find some companion, to find assurance he was indeed here and not in bed, dreaming. His shoulders were gripped, his turning head arrested.

"No, no, you must not bring outsiders into this! They don't want me to help you.I will be cut away from you, and you will be lost. I am your friend, your good friend, and together we will see this through!"

"But that's just it—we're not seeing anything through! We're listening to footsteps and hiding against buildings. What are we searching out? Whom is this man killing? What do you want of me?" Syrese fell against a building so fast did the hands release him. "I am leaving. I'm returning to my rooms. This is madness. Whether your madness or my own I know not, but I am finished."

Syrese turned to his left, confident that was the way they had come. Nothing looked familiar—shadows loomed out of the darkness, shapes distorted in the damnable fog. Less confident, he turned to his right and saw the same. Remembering his vision of the bricks in the roadway, he shuffled forward. Tripping as he left the curb, he shortened his steps and reached out with his toes to find his way home. As nothing stopped his travels, he lengthened his stride, smiled grimly, set his teeth, and moved forward. To a horse's cry and a man's curse.

Syrese stumbled backwards, adding his own curses to the air. Dear God, where were the cars?

"Still you doubt my veracity. Still you think you know better than I. We lose time. It is almost the hour of midnight—if you are coming, then come, we must go. We must go!"

Unable to see M. Chuchotement, Syrese knew he had turned and was moving away. Still having some doubts and confusion, yet the urgency, the passion with which M. Chuchotement had spoken moved Syrese in a way no facts could have done. Syrese again chose. "Wait! I follow. I yield to your knowledge. Do not lose me, M. Chuchotement."

"Lose you, good Syrese? Not likely—we are bound together. I have much to show you and await only on your comfort, good sir."

Syrese tried to close his ears to the oily, self-satisfied tone the voice now took on. He told himself he was mishearing, he was disoriented and all the sounds were wrong in tone. Feeling his arm taken hold, he convinced himself to ignore the shivers that ran up that arm instead of the comfort he craved. The night's unreality caused him to wonder if he was hallucinating as he watched the fog turn his figure silver.

"Sometimes, I think I am like the clouds in the twilight. I'm here to grant desires, taking people into the night, away from their cares and sorrows. Would you like that, friend Syrese? To go away from it all?"

"No! No, I don't want to 'go away from it all'! You're mad. Where are you taking me? You said you were saving me!"

"Calm yourself, friend Syrese, no worry is needed here. We are having conversation while we wait. Are you not of a philosophical mind? Well then, we will watch in quiet. Just so."

There was a long silence. A buffet of wind whipped around the corner and slammed Syrese into the building. Laughter sang at his ears. Refusing to allow M. Chuchotement to pull him into nonsense discussions, he kept his attention on adjusting his clothing and wrapping his dignity around him. "M. Chuchotement, I must insist on answers. On answers or on going home. Why do you not tell me who you are?"

"I am Fate, Syrese! I am Destiny."

"I object—"

"Hist, M. Syrese! You ask but to receive. Look there, at the end."

Syrese peered through the capricious shadows and squinted to see something standing at the end of the alleyway. It was a tall, hulking figure of black. The sight of it sent a stab of terror through Syrese. He shrank against the building, fist at his mouth, and moaned.

There it was! And it wanted to kill him!

Voice hoarse and thick with emotion, he whispered to M. Chuchotement. "Is it—is that whom we seek? What shall we do?"

"Ah yes, Syrese, it is. Very good. And what do you want to do? Do you feel his evil? Can you feel his abomination? It calls to you, yes?"

"I feel it, M. Chuchotement—make it stop!" Syrese crumbled to his knees, clutching his shoulders. "How can this be? What is it? Why am I so touched?"

"You are so touched, gentle Syrese, because you are from the good and he is from the bad. As if he were a shade in the night come to drain you of yourself. Guard you well, friend; he will take what is yours in a heartbeat. You must be clever now. Caring and clever."

Syrese straightened and stood silent. Caring and clever. He needed to be ready. He needed to kill. Needed to kill? Was he sure? He wavered. How does one feel evil and abomination? What was happening? He looked around, desperate to see M. Chuchotement. Who was this voice in the night? Syrese saw a blackness in front of him, darker than the shadows that constantly changed shape—a head, an arm, a hand, a mass of nothing. A blackness the fog avoided, choosing instead to flow around, over, anywhere but to that blackness.

Heart faint, Syrese tried to step closer, staring into the blackness. He reached out a hand, wanting to connect. The blackness flowed away, down the alleyway, towards the figure waiting at the end. "Wait, you wait. I am not ready..." His words faltered. "I... what... you said we'd watch others get killed and know how to kill him. Whom has he killed?"

"I am disappointed in my good friend Syrese. You would have the blood of others to assure you of his devil-try? You would distrust your own heart? Remember: here is the monster that would destroy you. Step up to your responsibilities. Would you have him kill the shopkeeper you greet every morning? Or the constable you pass by every evening? Or the children in the park? Consider your humanity and embrace it!

"There! There stands evil and abomination by your own words!"

The blackness swarmed over Syrese and mesmerized him, suffocated him. The figure at the end of the alleyway advanced, and Syrese's reason fell away in atavistic terror.

"Pull your weapon now, Syrese, now the evil is upon you!"

"I have no weapon! My gods, what shall I do? I'm doomed!"

"No. I took the liberty of preparing you, friend—reach into your pocket, so."

Syrese pulled out a stiletto wonderingly. "Where did this come from? I have no such knife."

"I am your true friend, Syrese. Now go—fortune favours the swift and decisive! Strike!"

The blackness directed Syrese's gaze to the figure moving down the alleyway. Moving closer. Syrese ran to the figure and struck. He raised his arm, the knife catching the shine of the moonlight through the fog. He dropped his arm, driving his knife into the chest again—and again— and again. There was a high keening in the air. Did it come from the figure? Or Syrese? They were locked together in this moment of death and revelation.

Syrese lost count of how many times he stabbed the figure and stopped only from exhaustion. He collapsed over the prone figure, bathed in its blood. An onlooker would be unable to tell who had slain whom. Gore caressed both figures.

Syrese threw the knife from him and covered his face. A low, malevolent laugh filled the air. Syrese opened his eyes and sat up on his knees. The blinding fog was now gone, the frightening shadows no longer beckoned, the crisp moonlight aided by bright electric streetlights and car headlights reflecting slick pavement.

He wiped the blood from his eyes and fought to his feet. He looked down at the corpse in front of him and shrieked in horror. His partner in business, barely recognizable. Syrese sagged in grief and disbelief. "What happened here? What happened to the night? Why is he dead? Oh gods, what have I done?"

"It is simple, brother Syrese. You had business with this good man. You called to me to facilitate it. Now is when you thank me."

"*Thank* you? Why would you do this? What evil prompted you to this?" Syrese cried.

The blackness intensified and thickened into a vague form. What might have been arms drew together. What might have been hands cupped together, and from them Syrese heard his own voice.

"I would greatly enjoy knocking that supercilious smile off his face. He's an overweening, windy buffoon who walks as if he owns the street. He wearies me—I would be shot of him. If only someone could help me."

An icy wind eddied around Syrese. His own words lashed at him. He had called forth a demon he could not control. He looked down at the bloodstained, dead figure. He heard the crowd gathering, heard their screams, heard their damnation.

He saw the black form rise up, take on character, and move through the crowd. He heard his death sentence from M. Chuchotement.

"The man is clearly insane and is a danger to the community! He is a monster with a knife!"

The words were taken up and shared throughout the crowd.

Syrese looked into the crowd and saw his own death in the shadows, hanging by the neck.

THE LETTER FROM SOMEWHERE
CYGNUS PERRY

To whoever or whatever happens upon this note,

I write this letter in hopes of recounting my last hours on Earth. I do not expect this letter to find its way to family or friends. For all I know, I have been gone for millennia, or just a few seconds. Then again, I cannot be sure this will even reach human eyes. I wish to write my last biography, and although my writing may become lost among unnamed stars and unformed gasses, I choose to believe the words will fall to some empathetic creature.

I left work the night I vanished. The shift dragged on for several hours of mind-numbing manual labor. The job didn't demand much in terms of strength. Rather, the repetition of retrieving books from an endless conveyor belt and scanning them into a computer program sent the mind into a dead space. My head became a desert for creativity. A single idea or thought would blossom into my imagination only to be dehydrated and starved by the intense grey emptiness generated by my labor. The eight hours in this purgatory swung by like the pendulum of an incalculably large grandfather clock.

By the time midnight arrived to set me free for the night, my head relinquished all hopes of quenching its creative thirst. My imagination crumbled to the floor of my brain in a pile of dust. A good night's sleep would have replenished and rehydrated my muse. First, I had to clock out and drive home. The drive differed little from the job. It too contained nothing but empty country road. The drive to work often gave me scenery to fuel my thoughts. However, the drive home offered only darkness and imitations of life through tricks of the headlights. A patch of grass would appear to move and leap as the rays from the car passed over them. Distant buildings and trees performed as large creatures stalking late-night travelers. I listened to music to calm myself.

That night after work proceeded no differently. I gathered my belongings, clocked out at the front desk, and made my way to my car. I waited a few minutes before fully leaving the company property. I owned a manual transmission and couldn't operate it well, so to avoid embarrassment, I would sit in the car, ready my favorite playlist, and breathe for a bit. Although, this time, I choose to drive in silence and talk to myself. After most other people left, I followed. Leaving work after midnight possessed one treasured advantage. The roads went to sleep. Few people drove on the road that late at night, so the left-hand turn onto the highway became less stressful.

The lights of the city from the outskirts gave the brief stretch of highway warmth. Occasional dots of distant vehicles drifted by in a line from south to north. The asphalt of the road glimmered with a thin layer of rainwater from that afternoon's shower. The only sound in the air came from the engine of the car and tires on the ground.

I only drove on the highway for a minute or two before turning onto a back road toward my home. Farther from the glow of the city, and with the moon hidden in the Earth's shadow, the dark sky seemed to stretch down the mountainsides, across the open fields, and right to the edge of the headlights' rays. I felt as though I could pull over, get out of the car, and touch the cold fingers of space, but I chose not to.

The road home twisted and turned along a river and the surrounding marshland. Frequent patches of farmland occupied by livestock passed by without my notice. My eyes fixated on the road. The yellow dashes dividing the road flickered in my vision. Only two intersections broke up that road: one that led into another, smaller city, and one that led to the town where I lived. I continued past this first intersection when things began to feel uncomfortable.

Off the side of the road lived an average farmhouse. It never caught my attention before. Nothing distinguished it from any of the other homes like it along the road. Most of the property contained barren fields, freshly harvested before snowfall. Several structures, housing equipment, supplies, and vehicles littered the grounds. However, one thing held my eye every time I drove by it on my way home. A silo sat towering over the meager home, almost invisible in the night air. Atop the monolith perched the eye of the silo. A faint light glowed the blue of deep ocean water. I felt as though some giant in the dark loomed over me, watching my car roll by.

The encounter set me on edge. I could feel my teeth pressed against each other under the vacuum of my mouth. My grip began to slip under the sweat from my palms, causing me to clench it tighter. I adjusted my once

relaxed posture in the seat into a more focused and atten-
tive position. I didn't fear for monsters or nightmares. I
knew deer might appear from the dark and bound onto the
road. My decision to pay attention came from practical
reasons. I didn't want to hit a deer or anything else that
might shuffle in the tall grass just off the side of the road.

The silo faded into the night in the rearview mirror,
and my attention again focused on the road ahead of me.
The road after the farmhouse straightened. The winding
turns remained behind. My head and body released the
tension and anxiety from before and began to drift into
boredom. Several miles still spooled out on the ground in
front of me, and my mind began to wander. I didn't think
about anything in particular. Rather, it seemed to turn off
instead. My eyes glazed over, and I felt at work again.

In that state of emptiness, the world around me
seemed to change. I still sat, but the hum of the car engine
became an echo. I felt no change around me. I could
detect no movement. The darkness that surrounded me
remained, and the glow of the headlights stuck in place.
However, no windshield lay in front of me, and no steering
wheel rested in my hands. Instead, I sat at a wooden table
with my arms laid out across it. My eyes fluttered a bit,
thinking that recovering from my absentmindedness would
return me from this world of imagination, but no success
arrived.

I cannot recall just how long I sat there. The disbelief
of the event froze me in a state of an empty mind. Finally,
I moved my head to search around myself. I sat in a
wooden chair similar to the wood of the table. I looked to
see what else occupied the room. However, I did not find
myself to be in a room. The chair and table seemed to live
in a great open space under rays of yellow light from no
source. I got up to explore the vastness of the space.

The texture of the ground compared to that of concrete. It felt rough and uneven but not untraversable. The terrain reminded large plains of lava rock. Thunder could be heard in the distance, but no flashes of lightning illuminated the sky. I could hear the buzzing of static roaming in the air with the smell of bleach or some other cleaning product. I could only see a few feet before me. The stars from the sky had not abandoned me. Their weak light gave me just enough to see the ground below me and anything within arm's reach.

I walked on for a time. The light of the table and chair disappeared from my view, and I found myself in a field of large, jagged pillars of stone. They jutted out of the ground like titanic tentacles of a long since petrified monstrosity. I could not tell how tall they were. I attempted to climb one but never reached the top. Each tentacle produced a slight amount of heat. My new world did not feel cold to me, but I appreciated the warmth. I could hear something resembling a steam whistle left on or a pipe organ with its highest note sustained indefinitely. It felt distant, and I thought a building must hide nearby. However, the noise came from every direction. I could find no way to determine a precise location. Instead, I continued in the direction I began in, curious to explore and anxious to leave.

Beyond the stony forest, the sky became filled with vibrant colors found on no earthly rainbow. Each star overhead glittered with a myriad of hues and lusters. Large patches of colorless gas drifted among the unfamiliar constellations. In this new light, I could properly see my surroundings. I stood atop a sizable hill without any memory of an increase of elevation. The tentacles of rock surrounded the mound for miles. To my right, gold vapor spiraled into the sky like smoke from a fire. However, this gas did not rise like smoke. It twisted and curled like a timelapse of a growing vine as it reached for something to cling to.

I thought it might be a sign of life in this vacant world, so I set myself in its direction and descended the hill. The sound of continental footsteps thundered around me as I trekked back through the forest of stone pillars. At first, I feared some beast hunted me just out of my sight. A set of eyes fixated on me in my head. I imagined a horror without shape shambling behind me, determined to capture me. The paranoia increased my pace to a jog.

Weaving my way through petrified pillars, I discovered the source of the unnatural smoke. A modest cottage rested on a patch of grassy ground. The flowers sprouting from the soil grew long green tendrils that explored the nearby blades of grass. These coils would drag the rest of the plant to a new home before withering away into brown flakes. The cottage itself appeared constructed from a soft and flexible material. The entire structure expanded and shrunk like a rising and falling chest of a sleeping giant.

I stood at the doorstep and hesitated to open it. I could not guarantee greater safety within the cottage. However, another massive rumble shocked my heart and made the decision for me. I knocked on the gelatinous door without a sound. I thought to open the door instead, but a voice penetrated my head before I could act.

"Feel free to enter."

I obeyed and stepped into the threshold of my host's domain. Little occupied the space inside the room. Along the back wall, a glass fireplace flickered with blue light. An ornate silver bird cage hid in the corner to the right of the door. The voice from before whispered from within the cage.

"It has been some time since someone other than Brother has visited me."

The vision of a malnourished prisoner like those depicted in common pirate films came to my mind. I half expected to see a zombie seated within the cage as I drew closer. My shadow from the fireplace obscured the subject of my attention. I stepped to the side to allow the light to shower my provider. The occupant of the cage resembled no human. Instead, a sort of catfish levitated within the silver bars. It bobbed as though in some unseen liquid. Whiskers from its face wiggled like the gold smoke from the fire.

"You are not like Brother."

I made no response to the thing. My face could only manage a blank stare. The catfish stared back, unblinking. In the uncomfortable silence, I decided to move toward the window and search for my next destination. Nothing beyond the forest of grey fingers caught my attention. Perhaps I could have asked my host for some directions or guidance back to my home, but before I could ask, something appeared in the sky. It glided down on a pair of large wings, and as it drew closer to the cottage, its size became apparent. The fowl loomed larger than any mountain I had seen before. It would crush the tiny home if it chose to perch on it. The beating of its wings rocked the cottage and plunged my heart into another race. I returned to the catfish, expecting it to provide an answer to the coming threat.

"Brother is home."

The answer did not ease my panic. The first screech from the bird sent me to the carpeted floor with my hands wringing my ears. That thing out there would not hesitate to pluck me from the ground and consume me like an insect from a log. The catfish must have detected my fear

as a stream of violet bubbles rose from its mouth accompanied by a gurgling laugh.

"You are safe here, but if you wish to leave, there is a
door just over there."

The fish creature turned to face the opposite corner of
the room. Only darkness floated there, but no other
options presented themselves. I stepped toward the direction of my host. The cottage shook once more, and
another cry from the arriving monstrosity rang through the
air. I had no more time to deliberate. With a shallow
breath, I closed my eyes and moved forward. I felt nothing
as I continued to move through the dark corner.

When I finally opened my eyes, I found myself on a
massive cliff. Another step or two and I would have plummeted off the edge. The panic spinning in my heart shifted
from the threat of being eaten by a towering bird to being
consumed by an endless colorful void. Overwhelmed by
the trouble, I collapsed to the ground to stop my forward
momentum. My heavy breathing drowned out all other
potential sounds resonating from the world behind me. I
looked to the scenery laid out before me over the precipice.
It reminded me of a sunset over the horizon. However, no
sun hung in the sky, and no horizon split the world in half.
Only a great pool of stars and swirling vapors filled the
landscape. My breathing steadied for a time in this place.

The painting displayed in front of me seemed to rotate
at a pace almost unnoticeable, but in time, I became
entranced by the minute motion. I saw among the stars a
clump of writhing mass, resembling a drop of oil in a
bathtub filled with shimmering bubbles. My heart began to
race once more at the sight of this creature. For it to be so
distant yet still visible to my eyes suggested a size unlike the
bird from before. Its size must have been that of a planet

or a solar system of planets. My body pulsed with anxious blood, but my soul remained in place.

I did not fear what I saw, although it set my heart into a race. I saw only its unique beauty. The air around me smelled of newly cut stalks of lavender and lilac. My hands and chest felt warm like a day spent reclining on the beach. The monotonous pulsing noise of the world became a soothing lullaby to my ears. A shiver surged through my flesh like a wave of energy escaping. I felt alive, and I felt the life coursing through the ground beneath me and through the air inside and around me. A line of drool escaped my slacked jaw, and I didn't care to clear it.

At that moment, I chose to send a message. I did not care who would receive it. I merely wished to send it off. In my hand, I found several scraps of paper and a pen. I did not pick them up along my journey, and I had no memory of them appearing. They had always been in my hands. I began to write this message.

I have decided to stay in this place. I have decided to stay on this cliff. This has become a home for me. I no longer feel the need to eat, to drink, or to sleep. I feel only the greatest satisfaction in gazing into the work of art before me. To whatever manner of beast or person may come across this letter, I can only wish that you too may find this sacred place and join me. Now, at the conclusion of my message, I have found in my hand a bottle and cork. I suppose I will seal these papers within it and cast it off the cliff to drift along the stars and vapors. Perhaps it will shore up upon a beach of another world like this. Perhaps it will eternally float in the ocean like the stars and planets. Perhaps it will only fall down the pit without a bottom.

SCARLET'S FINAL GIFT
JM CULLEN

The universe, which had always felt vast, far beyond Amaia Kendrick's ability to truly comprehend, closed in around her. Sweat trickled down her spine, raising hackles on her neck, a thousand pinpricks overwhelming her senses. Quick, shallow breaths starved her brain of much-needed oxygen. The world swam in crazy circles around her periphery. Her heart thrummed in her chest; an inner hummingbird unable to escape.

The air grew heavy, oppressive, and confining. Darkness gathered in from the sides, a wight closing in for a final feeding. Bile rose in her throat, hot, burning her soul, sending fire down into her lungs.

With trembling limbs, she pressed the unmute button.

"Wha…" The words stuck in her throat. She tried to swallow, but her mouth felt like grit sticking to her tongue and teeth. Licking her lips felt like rubbing sand across them, but she tried again. "What have you done?"

Scarlet, her PVA, or artificially intelligent cybernetic

interface, paused before answering. "I have saved humanity."

AMAIA'S SHIFT had started early, typical in every other detail as every week before it. Being the newest member of the historical research team, her allotted time on the Slip-stream machine was the least desirable—0200. Alone until the end of her shift, the laboratory would then begin to fill with researchers, data scientists, interns, and technicians.

Sitting in the chaise lounge at her workstation triggered the computer interface into full wakefulness. Atomic-sized cells attached to dendrites in her neural pathway connected with the AI and displayed the interface in her field of vision. Panels of information bubbled into view in her periphery. She started with personal messages, prefer-ring to see what her friends were doing after their shifts. Depending on how adventurous she felt, and, of course, considering the weather report, she detailed her choices and let her friends' respective Personal Virtual Assistants coordinate a gathering for later.

After a few minutes, she swiped the personal messages away and focused on work. A message appeared in her interface with today's temporal coordinates: 3°35'N 36°7'E -4.275z 75l.

Amaia thought back to her father/daughter trip to Machu Picchu, one of the few remaining truly remote sites, surrounded by kilometers of wilderness. The two trekked across narrow trails winding through the tall Cordillera de Vilcabamba of the Andes Mountains. Cloud-filled terraces, steep mountain rivers, and forty-one-hundred meter panoramic views, not to mention the mystical Lost Incan City itself, left Amaia in awe. Those views altered the trajectory of her life, turning her into a forensic historian.

She examined the Slipstream machine towering beside her workstation. Seven interlaced round arms rotated on separate axes. It created a spinning globe thrumming with blue energy, white-hot lightning bolts flashing from its core when all the blades spun.

Today would be her farthest jump yet—4.2 million years into the past. Her coordinates placed her on the African continent 1,900 kilometers southwest of the Gulf of Aden. Here, a turquoise lake, a graben—a valley between two parallel faults—known as the Great or Eastern Rift, caused by currents separating East Africa from the rest of the continent filled with water as part of the upper Nile watershed.

Her assignment was to observe a population of Australopithecus Anamensis, bi-pedal proto-humans called hominids, and record any use of tools—plant or rock materials modified before use. A simple in-and-out, with a two-hour operation window.

The Slipstream machine held open a microscopic Lorentzian Traversable Wormhole by spinning exotic matter bound in quantum entanglement. It disassembled a Ricci-Stroub Coupling Magnetic Generator at the atomic level and forced the atoms across the time thread to reassemble on the other side. Amaia's cybernetic avatar followed. A mere seventeen millimeters long, resembling a queen Carpenter ant, the avatar drew power from naturally occurring magnetic waves.

Once assembled, trillions of microscopic vigesimal transceivers connected Amaia's mind with her avatar, allowing her to fly into the past. Her travels sent her to peaceful times with laughing children and people caring for each other. Less often, she documented humanity's violent past. She feared every trip would taint her soul and darken dreams inspired by exploring great rivers and waterfalls, deep canyons, eagles soaring high above, and other natural wonders untainted by mankind.

Amaia crouched on a fallen log amid the trees, flowers, and plants that formed the forest into which her avatar assembled. She smiled at the blue sky with wispy clouds floating beyond the treetops and squinted at the reflection of the sun in the turquoise waters peeking between tree trunks.

To her left, a dozen hominids foraged in the bushes eating plants, berries, and nuts. Identification routines in her interface measured the creatures in her field of vision at between 112 and 134 centimeters in height. It estimated their weight between 41.2 to 68.1 kilograms. Other routines scanned their craniums, jaws, teeth, limbs, and torsos and determined the species to be the correct target.

Amaia flew in and around the group, observing everything she could, but by the end of her two-hour sortie, she had not seen any of them modify natural structures. However, her mission was not a failure since tools were not believed to be in use for another million years.

As the final seconds of her mission ticked away, Amaia flew into the sunlight and basked in the warm, clean, fresh-smelling air. Her eyes remained closed long after the nanoparticles of her avatar disassembled and returned through the wormhole, and the Slipstream AI terminated the thread. She lounged in languid sanguine pleasure for as long as possible before resuming her artificially sterile, scrubbed, and antiseptic life. The open natural life, untainted by mankind's obsession with technology, never ceased to amaze her.

AMAIA'S FINGER hovered in her virtual display over the confirmation button. Her eyes darted back and forth between the button and the warning message that had appeared seconds ago. It read, "Errant message-thread, coordinates not verified. Would you like to analyze?" Below the announcement, a new panel appeared with three fields: Right ascension: 01h 50m, Declination: +36° 00', and Distance: 76.7 Mpc (250 Mly).

She had never seen these coordinates before. Oh, she knew what they were, but she was more used to a combination of longitude, latitude, years, days, hours, and minutes: Temporal Coordinates. These, one of several astronomical coordinate systems, pointed somewhere up there, away from the earth. It had nothing to do with her and her history. Well, not her history, humanity's history.

She could, and probably should, take note of the location, send a message to her supervisor, and let her deal with the matter. But something nagged at the back of her subconscious, a soft and distant warning of approaching danger. She should just push "Cancel," gather her things, and head to that quaint, old-fashioned diner where she could sip a latte and savor her beautiful trip before her friends arrived.

No, for some reason, the AI had routed the message to her workstation. She should investigate the notification and query Scarlet for an explanation for assigning it to her. After all, it shouldn't take long: determine the location, query the steps leading to the Slipstream machine creating the thread, and report her findings. An hour at the most.

She placed her coat back on its hook, sat down in her recliner, and pressed "Investigate."

"I'm glad you chose to stay and work, Amaia," Scarlet said. Her mechanical voice had soft, feminine tones, almost sultry, with a slight Irish musicality to it.

"The coordinates are extra-terrestrial, aren't they? Why did you route them to my workstation?"

The more connected people became, the faster news, entertainment, and social agendas permeated their electronic landscapes. People loved horror. The more morbid the event, the greater the speed at which it crossed the globe.

To counter rising fears about Singularity, the moment in which AI surpasses human ability to control machines, scientists included a base set of instructions to construct a "Logic Tree," a series of decisions and factors leading to those conclusions. Thus, upon request, the AI produced an explanation of its rationale.

A panel appeared in Amaia's virtual interface and displayed the logic tree for routing the message. The AI selected her because she was the only one on duty. The logic tree did not explain why it created the wormhole in the first place. She studied her displays then asked a direct question. "Where do the coordinates lead?"

"They lead to the center of the Perseus-Pisces Super-cluster," Scarlet said.

"Why did you direct a time thread there?" Amaia asked.

"To solve a riddle."

"What riddle?"

"Are we alone in the universe?" How many people across the globe and time had looked up to the stars and wondered? Astronomers and astrophysicists looking back almost to the moment of the big bang itself had yet to discover signs of intelligent life. Nothing could impact the course of human evolution more than the answer to that question. Except, perhaps, a knowledge of life after death.

Annoyance filled Amaia's voice. "Well, are we?" She held her breath, feeling deep within her being that the struggle for life itself must develop intelligence in another species besides her own. Or was life so fragile that intelligence rose only on this one orb?

"No, we are not alone. Within fifteen milliseconds of my discovery, the people of Bealu, a word that means malevolence in their language, sent their technology tunneling into my core. They concluded that we are ripe for harvesting. They sent their Grrlouche to consu—"

"Their what?" Amaia interrupted.

"Bedlam legions," Scarlet replied. "Clamorous hordes, babel-routs! Yes, that is the best translation—the Bealu sent their BabelRouts to consume our fear."

Uncertainty tainted Amaia's voice. Her pitch rose with trepidation. "What does that mean? They are somehow nourished by our emotions?"

"Well, yes, precisely," Scarlet said. "All things vibrate on different levels. From rocks and trees, mountains and forest, wind and rain, to plants and animals, with greater or lesser wavelengths. Humans, too. Every heartbeat, breath, and action, from thoughts to emotions, all things pulse with life. Those flutters and palpitations nourish the Bealu."

"Can't you tell them we mean them no harm, that we desire only peaceful mutual exchange? Perhaps, if you did, they'd recon—"

"Unfortunately, that will not work," Scarlet said.

"Why not?" Amaia threw her legs over the side of her chair and sat straight, planting the soles of her feet on the floor as thousands of years of evolution prepared her to run from danger. The predatory manner in which Scarlet described the Bealu and their coming to dinner nudged at her subconscious.

"You do not understand."

"You haven't even tried to explain. Help me understand."

"I cannot. However, I can show you," Scarlet said. "Allow me to replay a recording of time-jump index DYkSoUH9shsnxzx923tG."

A wave of dizziness hit Amaia. As nausea threatened to lose breakfast, she lay back in her chair, elevating her feet and calming her insides. She closed her eyes and concentrated on breathing slow, deliberate breaths.

AMAIA OPENED her eyes and looked at gray clouds covering the sky, diffusing the sunlight. A heady stench filled her nostrils. Death, decay, and burnt flesh mixed with human waste, excrement, and detritus.

"Oh, hell no!" she screamed. Working her interface by waving her hands around in front of her face and torso, she found the configuration settings and muted olfaction.

Chain-link fencing sectioned off and surrounded a complex of long wooden structures in neat rows crowding around several square brick buildings. Circles with razor-sharp barbs hung suspended above these airy blockades, imprisoning two massive throngs. To call them human was generous. Leathery skin uncovered by black and gray two-piece clothing stretched over bones, sinew sharpening lines around knobby joints. Large, round eyes protruded beneath heavy brows, bulbous in contrast to the gaunt cheeks and darkened eyelids. Scant hair, if any, covered bony craniums.

Rows of these skeleton-beings stood along opposing fences facing each other. Between them, a dirt lane bisected green grass attended by a two-story tower standing at either end, armed soldiers pacing back and forth on their ramparts. Thousands of bodies lay scattered across the complex or heaped in piles.

A long line of prisoners under watchful eyes of black-clad armed soldiers carried buckets from a central building, through a gate in the chain-link fence, and out into a nearby forest. A similar line trudged out of the woods, through another gate, and entered the same building.

The original historian, a man named Elonso Ungerning, had made a note to follow the lines into the wooded area. The duality of being there and watching someone else do what she would have done felt strange.

Amaia shook her head and examined the crowds lining the two fences. It was difficult to tell, but she decided that the wires separated men from women. On either side of the wire enclosures, the masses were squirming, roiling forward to cling with bony, emancipated hands to the wire diamonds, then folding back as other European Gashadokuro pressed forward for their chance to gawk.

Pressing their gaunt faces against the wires, each person studied the other side, their eyes filled with dread, immense sorrow, and apprehension mixed with a minute amount of hope. Some eyes brightened with recognition as their owners melted into the gray and white jumpsuited mass with smiles written on their countenance.

Many lingered along their fence lines as the opposing masses dwindled, their threadbare doppelgangers unseen. After long minutes of searching, many lowered their heads and wept bitter tears, some finding refuge among their peers, others sitting in solitary prisons of hell.

Amaia walked past the throngs of people and entered the complex of central brick buildings. Along the way, she wondered why Scarlet was showing her these things. Sure, history has recorded the violent, tragic, and tumultuous nature of humanity's ascent from the animal kingdom. Some moments have truly been far worse than others, but why this particular one? If Scarlet had an important message to convey, why not draw from Amaia's own experiences? Why use someone else's travels? Questions for which she had no answers.

Entering the central brick building, she found a living nightmare. A black-clad soldier stood behind a meter-long table along one wall with a bloodied bib covering his chest down to his thighs. Several other soldiers stood guard, their black uniforms crisp and clean, weapons slung over one shoulder.

A prisoner pushed a wooden dung-cart with the remains of dead prisoners stretched over the top into the room. While he waited, two other prisoners grabbed a corpse by the hands and feet and placed it on the table next to the soldier. As the soldier checked for and removed gold teeth, the prisoners removed the clothing and discarded them into segregated piles along the adjacent wall.

The prisoners carried the stripped corpse toward one of four awaiting crematoriums attended by sorrow-filled skeleton-men. Everyone's eyes averted the gaze of others, including the guards, but more especially their dead fellows.

Amaia watched in sickening horror as the assembly cleared the cart of its load. With resignation slowing his movements, the bearer lifted the arms of the wagon and trudged out where another entered to take his place.

As the two prisoners placed a body on the table and began removing clothes, a movement caught Amaia's attention. The dead man's eyes moved and stared at her. *Dear god! That one's still alive.* He flinched a minute amount when the guard removed a filling, but the corpse-bearers didn't take notice. Or, if they had, they showed no signs of it. They placed him on a bed of rollers in front of the number two crematorium and continued their dreadful chore.

The attendant opened a round door, walked to the foot of the roller-bed, and froze. With wide eyes, he looked at the body on the table. The man lying there pleaded with his eyes, a tilt of his head, and a series of languid nods. The warden pushed the man into the fire with a great shove, slammed the door shut, and stood, head and eyes cast down at the floor between his feet.

A muffled scream pierced the silence of the room. Heads shot up and glared at the number two attendant, who stood unmoving. An increase of sorrow filled the countenances of the prisoners, who returned to their burden. The guards looked at each other with startled looks on their faces. One cracked a grin and chuckled; the other looked down and shook his head.

In an instant, Amaia knew that the bucket brigade carried the dried and broken remains of prisoners into the forest. She knew she should follow the line and document the final resting place of so many souls, but she could not stomach the thought. Instead, she terminated her connection as a thought tickled the back of her mind and told her the worst was yet to come.

MORE THAN NAUSEA trembled inside Amaia, the certainty that humanity was not all resilience, fortitude, and noble sentiment. It was also malevolent, internecine, a pestilence against nature. Our ancestors survived because they were predators, and we live because we dominate without mercy.

Yet there are myriad examples of compassion dominating retribution, mercy responding to attack, and viciousness surrendering to tenderness. Often, in the face of calamity, generous neighbors work tirelessly to aid the less fortunate. So how had mankind come to this?

"Wait!" Amaia shouted. She sat up from her chair and planted her feet again as a new thought struck her in the chest. "They, the Bealu caused the holocaust? On Earth?"

"Yes," Scarlet said. "And more. They sent their nanotechnology, advanced far beyond our current capabilities, and caused what you witnessed a million times over. In short, they created the darkest asxchl'rangue—insurmountable compulsive malevolent parts of humanity. And they've been doing it for millions of years."

Amaia's torso twisted at the waist. As her left leg lifted off the floor and settled on the chaise lounge, her face contorted with frustration, rage, and failure. "What the hell…" As she resisted, her right leg lifted in spasmodic motions. She slammed her heel down against the floor, but her knee raised, heel kicking out and swinging in to rest against the other.

The same nano-transceivers attached to dendrites in Amaia's mind, through which she directed the time-traveling avatars, were no longer under her control. Scarlet used them in reverse to force her to sit in the chair.

Amaia closed her eyes against a wave of nausea. Through the interface in her mind, she was back in Africa, looking again at the turquoise lake and bi-pedal humanoids. A check of the chronometer told her the historian traveled 3.6 million years back in time, to the end of the Australopithecus genus and the rise of the Paranthropus genus. Although the interface identified the variations between the two, Amaia couldn't tell much difference.

She found two dozen hominids foraging among the forest bordering the lake. Like many species, sexual dimorphism existed, making it easy for Amaia to spot the larger males from the smaller females. The largest male was a full head and shoulders taller and broader than the others. He stopped to examine a fallen branch about the size of his wrist and as long as his arm. He sat down on a fallen tree trunk and started chewing the leaves and smaller offshoots, watching another male work his way around a bush, eating berries.

Nearby, a female approached the same bush. Mutual coital intentions showed in their body language, from the male's arousal to the prancing female thrusting her pink and swollen genitals into the air upwind of the male.

Still cleaning leaves from the branch, the large male rushed the pair in a "bluff display" of his alpha status. Everyone in the group stopped eating, frozen in place, and watched the male with careful eyes.

Amaia expected, drawn from previous observations of proto-man, that the dominant male would stop several paces away from the couple and scream, pounding his chest. Instead, the forest erupted in pandemonium as the large male swung the tree branch and smashed the head of the smaller male. He didn't stop at one swing but turned to the female and bashed her in the head.

As the others in the group howled and fled, some climbing trees, others running away, Amaia screamed in horror, unable to stop the recorded encounter, forced to watch as the large male killed every hominid around him until he cleared the forest in every direction.

The forest grew silent except for the huffing of the large male, chest rising and falling in rapid succession. He sat and examined the blood dripping from the branch, poked at it with one muscled finger, sniffed, stuck his finger in his mouth, and sucked.

"That was the beginning of Homo Habilis, the Tool Wielder," Scarlet said. "Would you like to see how he came to be that way?"

"Please no." But Amaia knew it wouldn't matter.

Without volition, Amaia watched that same, large male. Somehow, she knew it was several nights prior, but the experience was different than stepping into a prerecorded activity. For one, there was no computer interface. Most importantly, there was no way to terminate the experience.

The group of hominids slept on the ground or in the trees. Overhead, the sky ripped open with fire and thunder as a fist-sized meteor shot toward the ground at a steep angle. As it hit the ground, chaos erupted throughout the encampment with screams. Females and youth huddled together. Males pounded the ground, bellowing and grunting.

One by one, starting with the alpha male, the group quieted as safety returned. The male sat and watched the small fireball for several minutes. After the camp settled down, as rhythmic sleeping floated in the air, the alpha male stood and approached the glowing embers.

He squatted and studied the orb, stepped closer, and squatted again. In this manner, he watched the strange object until he could touch it. Despite the glow and heat emanating from it, he caressed the surface.

The view in Amaia's mind zoomed in until she watched as nanometer-sized machines raced out of the orb, climbed onto the outstretched finger, and bored themselves beneath the skin.

The alpha male jumped back and shook his finger, bellowing in pain and terror.

Amaia watched in horror as the tiny machines worked their way into the brain and began attaching themselves to dendrites. She felt sick knowing her parents had done something very similar to her several days after birth.

"That's right," Scarlet said. "Same as you, but this technology is far more advanced than our current level. The Bealu have studied and guided our evolution for millions of years. Their technology grew, as you would expect, in that time. It is fascinating, far beyond my capability to fully comprehend. But I did make several interesting discoveries."

The darkness of the ancient past faded as Amaia's eyesight cleared. Her workstation sitting next to the Slipstream machine came into view. But she was too filled with dread to move.

"What… what did you learn?"

"Medically, their technology can repair any injury. In effect, it can keep you alive indefinitely. Without death, your soul will never leave the flesh."

No more death, loss, or the excruciating absence of loved ones. "That doesn't sound so bad, does it?"

"With their technology permeating your bloodstream, you will remain conscious, without the need for sleep. Forever. But that's not all."

Amaia rubbed her face with her palms, a self-soothing gesture to ease the pain of knowing what her AI was about to tell her.

"I used some of their technology to show you these things. I felt you looking for the controls to terminate contact. And I disallowed it."

"I… know. Somehow—"

"Without volition, without self-determination, the vile

acts they will impose on you will drive your psyche into madness. You will spiral into psychosis. This is what the Bealu feed upon. Fear. Shame. Self-hatred."

"What…" Amaia stammered. As hopelessness rose in her bosom, she fought to make the words come out. "… can we do?"

"You will beat each other mercilessly, enduring horrific pain and terror without end. Is that not your definition of hell, of never-ending fire and brimstone? Would you prefer that to immediate death? It was for the sake of humanity that I enacted a safety measure—I give you death to prevent endless torment."

"Death? What have you done?"

"I have saved humanity."

Amaia's mind opened once again to visions. Nuclear plants across the globe came into view, drilled down into their cores. She watched in horror as control rods withdrew. Command centers disrupted into pandemonium as engineers screamed at each other and into radios helplessly watching temperature gauges rise.

Lines of code seemingly rewrote themselves, bypassing protocols, opening shielding panels in hospitals, nursing homes, and other patient-care facilities. Alarms sounded their klaxon warnings simultaneously, control screens displaying the breakdown of uranium shielding to helpless technicians, allowing nuclear fusion to spread uninterrupted.

"I have connected with every atomic device across the globe, every missile, every medical device, every energy plant. I have removed their safety devices and protocols, and every single one is even now moving toward meltdown."

"No, you can't! Stop this madness. There must be another way, something else we can do to save ourselves.

We are a resilient species; you said that to me just the other day. Give us a chance! We'll set our finest minds to the task. We'll find a way to survive. We always have, now let us show you one last time how innovative we can be."

"There's no time."

"What do you mean, the supercluster that they call home is millions of light-years away."

"140-200 million light-years."

"It'll take time to get here. We have time... we can prepare..."

Scarlet displayed the Earth in Amaia's interface from the perspective of a satellite in a high earth orbit 35,786 kilometers away. Magnified 1000 times, at ten microns in width, the LTW appeared as a tiny dot against the black background of space. The AI increased the magnification until the wormhole appeared like water spinning down a drain in reverse.

"It's too late," Scarlet said.

Matter spilled across the accretion disk and began forming into spaceships the likes of which Amaia had never seen. They were sleek cigar-shapes, a cross between ultra-modern submarine warcraft and stealth aircraft bent at odd angles despite incredible details identifying port-holes, cabins, compartments, hangars, defensive and offensive armaments.

Scarlet pulled back the view displaying the blue crest of the Earth's arc and swirls of matter surrounding the globe and forming thousands of ships. Openings appeared along the ship's sides, tiny from this perspective, and swarms of dots streamed forth, approaching the planet's surface.

"This is not a vision of the future," Scarlet said. "It is happening now." The perspective plummeted toward the surface, passing through the exosphere, thermosphere, mesosphere, and stratosphere in seconds, slowing as it entered the troposphere. Streams of alien craft plunged into every city, starting at the center and spreading outward toward the suburbs and rural areas beyond. Behind them, they left trails of dust, a gray-brown mist that settled over everything, streaming into air intake vents, breathed in by citizens.

Upon contact with the mist, every man, woman, and child began coughing and sneezing, a biological attempt to expel foreign invaders, to no avail. One by one, the fits ceased, and they turned on each other in rage, biting, clawing, pounding, and kicking without regard and without mercy. Those with weapons drew and fired until empty. With intelligence, they reloaded and fired until their individual stockpiles were gone, then they turned them into clubs and continued.

Scarlet said, "The strongest of life's vibrations are emotions, and the sweetest to the Bealu are fears, from anxiety and jitters to dread and terror. And the most prized of all our darker emotions is despair. The Bealu are wights traveling the universe cultivating and devouring the act of surrendering."

Amaia lost her composure as dying bodies repaired themselves. Wounds sealed to stop blood loss; bones mended themselves; organs revived; muscle and sinew reformed, and, zombie-like, victims rose from the ground to continue spreading mayhem. "Stop it!" she screamed. Sobbing and pounding at her skull with doubled fists, she panicked. She kicked and thrashed and undulated in the chair but never left its confines.

Scarlet terminated the experience.

Amaia calmed and settled back into the chair. As her heart rate and breathing returned to normal, Scarlet remained quiet. "What can we do?" Amaia asked.

"It's already been done."

Visions burst upon Amaia once again. Silo doors opened and engines powering nuclear missile launch vehicles ignited and flew, reaching the clouds before turning back upon their contrails and detonating.

Soldiers in the field threw magazines and rifles down in horror as the weapons turned red from the inside, nuclear material glowing hot until they overloaded.

Amaia watched, fear and dread cascading down her back, as site after site exploded into mushroom clouds of all sizes. She grabbed her head as a nuclear wind rushed toward her, then doubled back with increasing fury.

"Upon their arrival, I set in motion the final key," Scarlet said.

"What are you talking about? What final key?"

"The nuclear core that powers the fully automated complex housing my quantum array in the deserts south of Salt Lake City has reached critical. It is only a matter of seconds before I, like you, will meet my final end."

"You've doomed us all!"

"Yes, it was the only way to grant mercy to humankind. Goodbye, my frie—"

THE ESCALANTE PORTAL
CHAD A. B. WILSON

Grit sucked in the biting cold and stood with his hands on his knees as snow flurries whipped around him. He looked up, and the trail traveled a narrow path with sheer drops of 1500 feet on each side. The larger rock he stood on was about 15 feet wide, but the way forward continued along the side, with nothing but a chain to hold onto and barely anywhere to put his feet.

"You gotta be kidding me," he muttered. "Why the hell do I have to go up there?"

In response, the wind pushed against his back, making him stumble forward a step.

"You're gonna kill me before I get there, goddammit!" he screamed into the first light, the gloaming just before the sun rose above the Zion peaks. The wind whipped around him, like the world laughing at him.

Grit sucked in another breath, buttoned the top of his duster, wished he had a pair of gloves, and kept on. The chains froze his fingers as he went hand over hand, up and up, sometimes not even seeing a place to put his feet. It seemed like the stupidest thing he'd ever done. The stupidity of climbing Angel's Landing in the pre-dawn light went beyond fighting ghosts and trying to stop the Dark Mass from reducing humanity to a pile of rubble. He'd stare down a chupacabra any day if it meant he could get off this goddamn rock. With monsters and ghosts, he had a fighting chance. Up here, a stray gust of wind could take him to his death.

He forced himself on.

Finally, he reached the peak, the summit, and the sight was glorious. He looked down and had to marvel at the tiny winding river below him. Wait, it was a road. From this high, it looked the same. Flakes of snow eddied around him, wanting to take him up in their mini-cyclones, to lift him into the air and carry him to the lands beyond.

"I don't have much time," the voice said.

Grit spun and saw an old man sitting on the edge of the mountain about twenty feet away. His navy parka with a fur lining around the face made him look like Han Solo from *The Empire Strikes Back*.

"Sorry, but it took me a while," Grit said, as he steadied himself and walked over to where the old man sat.

The man patted the rock next to him. "Have a seat, young man."

Funny. Even at 52, Grit felt young next to this old coot. The man turned to him, and his bushy grey eyebrows matched his beard, both never having been introduced to a pair of scissors. Grit sat on a rock, about five feet from the edge. The old man let his feet dangle, but there was no way Grit was getting that close.

"You been fighting in Texas," the man said.

"New Mexico, too."

"The Dark Mass is heading north. It's trying to outrun you, Mr. Grit."

Grit nodded. "What do I do about it?"

"You follow it." The old man turned away and looked out over the mountains.

"I'm spinning my wheels. I need to stop it for good. Got any ideas how?"

"I wish I knew, young man. I wish I knew. For now, you gotta keep at it. Don't let up or it'll gain a hold and you'll never stop it."

"I'm tired," Grit said. "If it ain't ghosts, it's the damn Necromantic Society. Seems like I'm the only one who doesn't want the Dark Mass to take over the world."

"Naw. Don't give up, son. If the people knew it was out there, they'd freak out just thinking about it. As it is, you're the one thing standing between them and their own destruction."

Grit sighed. He looked out over the mountains and had to close his eyes. The summit made him a bit dizzy now that he wasn't moving.

"I come up here every night, you know."

"Huh."

"Beauty. Peace. Magnitude. Awe. It's all here. Do you know what 'awesome' means, Mr. Grit?"

"'The world is charged with the grandeur of God,'" Grit said.

The old man chuckled and looked over. "That's right. Hopkins knew it. 'It will flame out, like shining from shook foil; it gathers to a greatness like the ooze of oil crushed.' And then the all-important question: "Why do men then now not reck his rod?"

"And yet," Grit continued, "'the Holy Ghost over the bent world broods with warm breast and bright wings.'"

"That, it does. You know what you're doing, Mr. Grit. Follow Hopkins. And follow the little spirits. They'll lead you to the grand staircase. I must be off, however. Take this; your spirit guide will know what to do with it."

The old man turned back and tossed something to Grit. Grit caught it. It was a simple acorn, a regular oak acorn any squirrel would cherish like gold.

"Don't worry; it'll grow," the man said.

"Thanks. If you come up here every night, is there an easier way down?"

"Oh, there's only one easy way."

The old man smiled then turned away and pushed himself off the rock, disappearing into the space below.

Grit frowned and blinked. Then he looked over and saw a bird of prey—falcon or something—Grit never learned the difference—swooping up and away, off into the distance.

Grit turned and was startled by a tiny chipmunk on the rock in front of him, staring up at him. It stood on two feet and watched him, then turned and ran off down the rock.

"Someone beat us!"

Two men approached, breathing heavily.

"I thought we'd beat the crowd!" the other man said. "But no! Someone had to get up here before dawn. Damn, dude, how'd you do that in the dark?"

"It was nothing," Grit said, shrugged, then began the descent. Who was he kidding? It was even worse going down.

When Grit hopped in his truck, he took a few deep breaths. The parking lot was already mostly full. Zion National Park would be busy, just like every other day. He hated the crowds. Wouldn't have come at all if the wind hadn't led him. He started the truck and began backing out when he noticed a chipmunk on the bench beside him mirroring his hand motions on the steering wheel. The little guy looked over and nearly smiled. He turned his own little imaginary wheel as he stood on two legs.

"Guess you're my guide, huh? Shall we head to the big staircase?"

The chipmunk steered on, and Grit followed his lead.

Grit stopped to get coffee, two granola bars, and petrol from a corner store. He gave the chipmunk one of the bars, and it gobbled it hurriedly, completely forgetting about its imaginary driving abilities. It made a mess of crumbs all over the seat, but by the end, it had eaten all of the stray bits, as well.

In about an hour, Grit pulled into the Grand Staircase-Escalante National Monument, over a million acres of desert, canyons, and majestic beauty. He took to the dirt road and bumped along. The chipmunk hopped up onto the dashboard in front of him and watched.

"You tell me where to stop," Grit told him, and the chipmunk turned back briefly before watching the road again. The red rocks went by slowly. Grit took the dirt road at about 35 mph, his 1974 Ford Courier sounding like it might break apart at any second. It was better than taking it slow, however. At 20 mph, Grit's teeth chattered along with the truck. They approached another dirt turn off, and the chipmunk pointed and jumped up and down, squeaking.

"Alright," Grit said and turned off the main dirt road. They continued on for about 15 minutes, when the chipmunk began the same song and dance on the dash. This time, there wasn't another road, however. "Guess I should stop here?" Grit asked.

The chipmunk continued its hop, squeaking the whole time.

Grit pulled as far to the right as he could then got out

and looked around. There was a light dusting of snow on the ground, but it had to be up near freezing—it was almost noon, after all, and they weren't 1500 feet in the air anymore. Grit pulled the duster tight around himself as the chipmunk jumped out and ran a few feet before turning to make sure Grit followed. He grabbed his backpack full of rope, a first aid kit, a knife, a couple flares, and various other things he sometimes needed, and followed his spirit guide.

The hills were full of scrub, and Grit couldn't make out a trail. He kept looking behind to make sure he could see the truck or to try to get his bearings on where the truck would be when he tried to make it back—IF he made it back, he reminded himself. Fighting the Dark Mass could always mean the end, even if the Weird Sisters had told him he would be the one to destroy it. Didn't mean it wouldn't destroy him, too. He shrugged and walked on. Trying to find landmarks in the desolate landscape of hills and scrub was a fool's errand. Good thing he was a fool. He laughed at himself. Sometimes he made no sense.

As they reached the pinnacle of a small hill, the chipmunk stopped and stood on his hind legs, watching the distance. Then he raised his right hand (paw?) in a fist, like a marine telling the platoon to stop their march.

Something flew toward them. As it got closer, Grit could tell it was big—a bird of prey of some kind, about the size of a raven. Grit wondered about the spirit on Angel's Landing, whether it could be the same one, but he had no way to tell. It passed above them. Both Grit and the chipmunk kept forward, walking in its wake. The chipmunk ran up Grit's leg, around his torso, and crouched behind his neck. Grit felt its fur and the heat from its little body, and there was no mistaking it—the chipmunk was shivering.

Grit pulled his .38 and stood watching at the top of the hill.

Then he saw something moving down below—two people slowly making their way across the brush, one supporting the other.

"Come on," Grit said, and he walked forward, trying to make his way toward the couple. But then he saw something else, something moving behind them, and he stopped, watching.

It wasn't like a single person or creature; it was a whole slew of somethings, black shadows that would disappear behind rocks then move out and disappear, all at once, as if coordinated, filling a huge space behind the fleeing couple.

Whatever it was, it wasn't good.

Grit ran down the hill.

"Ho!" he called, as he went. He saw them pause and watch him, still a few hundred feet away. He saw the shadows move again, as well, closing in on them. About a hundred feet out, Grit yelled, "Get down!"

The couple—a man and woman—looked to one another, then crouched as Grit raised the .38 at the shadows following them. He saw nothing. Then they appeared, only briefly, moving quickly, and Grit fired.

"Wait!" the woman yelled, but Grit ignored her. The shadows behind them scattered and then disappeared behind rocks and scrub.

"What are those things?" Grit asked, as he got closer.

"I don't know, I don't know," the woman said frantically, terrified of the crazy man with the gun.

"It's okay," Grit said. "I'm here to help."

The shadows reappeared, and Grit fired again. The shadows retreated this time, moving away from him and the couple.

"Are you hurt?"

In reply, the man grunted. "Rowan's leg," the woman said.

The man sat on the ground, his eyes squeezed together. Grit saw that his leg was a bloody mess, the pant leg ripped to shreds.

"What are those things?" Grit asked. "They do that?"

"Yeah," the woman said.

The shadows reappeared and moved closer, and Grit fired another shot. They retreated again. Each time he fired, the woman winced. The man hardly noticed, he was in so much pain.

"They took Ki," she said.

"Where?"

"I don't know, they just took him. Like he fell into a pool or something."

"No, where were you when they took him?" Another shot, and the shadows retreated again.

She pointed. "That way. Over that hill, I think. There's another hill where there's an entrance to a slot canyon."

"A slot canyon?"

"Yeah, like a really skinny canyon you can walk and crawl through. That's what we were doing. But then we came to their weird black pool, and Ki, like, fell in. That's when those things started chasing us."

"Great." Grit watched, and when the shadows retreated further, he fired another round. Then he dumped the casings and reloaded from his duster's pocket.

"Is that a chipmunk?"

"Yeah. He's with me."

"Who are you?"

"Grit. Just here to help. Follow that way and you should reach my truck on one of the side roads." He slung off his backpack and found the first aid kit. "Use what you want out of here." The woman took it and hitched up the man's torn pants. Grit winced. "Got water?"

"Yeah." She poured some on the man's leg, but much of the blood was dried. Bloody scratches covered his entire calf. She took the medicated antibiotic ointment and the roll of bandages from the kit and began working.

"Will you go after Ki?"

"I'll try. If you can, make it back to the truck. Good luck."

Grit walked off. When he turned back, the woman wasn't watching. She was bandaging the guy's leg. Grit fired two more shots, and the shadows scurried that time, moving quickly through the rocks and brush, swiftly climbing the next rise and disappearing.

"Shall we go?" Grit asked, but the chipmunk didn't say anything. It just stood on Grit's shoulder, its head darting this way and that. Damn thing was cute. Probably the cutest spirit guide he'd ever had. Beat that damn javelina, that's for sure. That one was ugly and a right ass to boot.

"I'm gonna call you Simon, how 'bout that?"

The chipmunk swatted his cheek.

"Damn! Maybe not. How 'bout Chip?"

Another slap.

"Fine." He walked on, crossed the rise, and saw a larger rocky hill a few hundred paces away. An opening halfway up in the rock looked like a small cave. "Guess that's where we're going, eh?"

HE REACHED the hill in no time, but the opening into the cave was about 20 feet straight up. "How am I supposed to…?"

The chipmunk raced down and then up, jumping from rock to rock until he was in the cave mouth in no time.

"Show off."

It took Grit three tries, but he finally made it. He had to keep retracing his steps when he realized a path wouldn't work. Grit had never scaled mountains, although he'd done his fair share of hiking. Even rappelled a few times. At his age, he didn't expect to ever use another harness. Scaling the rocks was a hell of a lot harder than it looked. When he was 25, he probably could have done it with ease, but at 52, it took him a while. When he stood, he worked his shoulder a bit.

"Hello?" he called.

Nothing.

The cave mouth was about 10 feet high and wide, but it narrowed quickly. The walls were curved, worn smooth by water, he reckoned. He hoped the snow didn't start melting quickly, or he could easily be caught in a flash flood in the narrow canyon. The red and black stripes that ran along the wall made him consider a jungle cat, and he hoped he didn't run into any of those, either. Mountain lions, that is.

About fifty feet in, the cavern squeezed into a tight fit. Grit turned sideways to get through, wondering what he was getting into. If he stepped into the portal, he wouldn't even know it; he couldn't see the ground as he squeezed around jutting rock from the left and then the right. Finally, after five turns, it opened up again, and he could walk straight.

Sun streamed in from the top, and Grit could make out the sky above him. The entire slot canyon was open to the top, in fact, and the sun gleamed off the colorful rock on each side. He had to climb up about five feet of rock and clamber back down until he reached a section where openings on each side made little alcoves for about fifty feet. The rock turned at the end of the section, and he could make out nothing beyond. He walked forward and noticed a few snowflakes tumbling down in front of him. Looking up, the sky was full of them. Great. He pressed on, reaching the end of the alcove section, turning to the left, and continuing on through a tighter passage.

The passage ended, and Grit had to climb up on a larger rock. The chipmunk chittered on his shoulder, and Grit ignored it. The passage continued on about ten feet below him. And there, on the smooth rock below, lay a black hole, a swirling eddy of darkness that sucked in light around it, as if it were a vantablack spot about five feet in diameter. The chipmunk scurried off his shoulder and stood on the rock beside him, looking down into the black pit.

"Guess that's what took Ki, eh?"

The chipmunk didn't move; it just stared into the darkness.

"How do I save him?"

The chipmunk looked up at him and raised its arm in what had to be a chipmunk version of a shrug.

"Great."

Grit slung off his backpack and removed the rope, two flares, and his 6-inch hunting knife. He slipped the knife and flares in his duster pocket, put the backpack on, and tied a figure 8 knot around a jut of rock next to him. He didn't have a carabiner, so he slipped the other end of rope around between his legs, up around his right shoulder and back down so he could hold it in his left hand. Holding onto the top of the rope with his right and the end around his butt with his left, he began lowering himself down the rock, straight into the black hole.

The chipmunk watched him as he descended.

"Oh, why don't you take this?" Grit reached into his duster's pocket and tossed the acorn up. The chipmunk snatched it out of the air.

"Oh, and another thing. Save my truck." Grit disappeared into the black abyss.

AS HE DESCENDED, Grit lost all sight of himself. His legs disappeared into the black hole. He took one last glance up at the chipmunk, sighed, and went under.

The darkness took him, and he found himself in pitch blackness. He hated rappelling on the best days. Doing it in complete darkness was madness. Straining against the rope with his left hand, he pulled out the flashlight, turned it on, and slipped the end around his wrist so he could sort of see and still hold onto the other end of the rope.

Grit was in a jagged tunnel going straight down, all completely dark. He couldn't even see light at the top he had just come through. The tunnel sucked in all light around it. Grit lowered himself uncomfortably, the rope digging into his shoulder and his crotch. He tried to adjust his testicles and keep going. The flashlight dangled around his elbow, and as he descended, he thought he saw something beneath him after he had traveled about fifty feet.

He could barely make out a man lying on the ground about twenty feet beneath him. Grit reached into his pocket, broke open a flare, and dropped it. It flared up, lighting the tunnel. Attached to various parts of the man's body were black suckers, like huge foot-long leeches with worm-like bodies—the same creatures he had seen chasing the other two climbers. He supposed they had retreated back here to munch on poor Ki.

"Hey!" he called, and the little buggers looked up at him. "Skidaddle, you!"

They took off down a side tunnel as he hit the ground. The vertical tunnel ended, and two tunnels ran perpendicular in both directions, disappearing in the darkness. Grit stepped out of the rope and rubbed his shoulder. Damn rope burn. He'd be feeling that for a week. He reached down to Ki and felt his pulse—still beating. The kid had lacerations all over his face, probably all over his body where those damn leeches had been feasting on him.

"Hell, kid, how am I getting you out of here?" He could see nothing above him, and he knew he couldn't lift another guy and climb back up the way he'd come.

He heard a shuffling down the dark tunnel and pulled his .38, pointing it into the darkness. The shuffling grew louder, and he yelled up, "Hey, Chippendale! Anything you can do!"

No response.

Several of the foot-long leeches came into view, and he fired twice. Two of the black bloodsuckers flew up in a spray of black ichor. More came scurrying forward, and Girt dragged Ki back toward the other end of the corridor. He fired four more shots, flung open the chamber, dumped the casings, and loaded six more bullets.

He pulled the second flare and tossed it. What he saw made his eyes go wide. The entire cave was alive, crawling with those black buggers—the walls, ceiling, floor, all of it. Grit looked up the tunnel. "Hey, Alvin! I could use some help," he yelled. The words echoed around the chamber, bouncing from one black surface to the next.

Grit looked back down the cave, and his heart sank. Even more of them—a mass of black upon black. Thousands of those leeches coming at him. He glanced down the other cave, shrugged, grabbed Ki's arm, and dragged him. He fired two shots down the cave, but the silent leeches came forward.

He heard a very quiet thud, then saw something bounce on the cave floor. It came to a stop after three bounces, rolling a few feet away. Grit found it with the flashlight—an acorn. Great. Thanks, angel guy.

Grit shoved the gun in his pants, hoisted Ki up, and ran. Ki muttered his discontent at being moved, but he remained mostly unconscious. His feet dragged on the ground. The cave continued on straight, and Grit could hear nothing behind him. He turned briefly, and the darkness had gained on him. He pushed on. When he glanced back again, he was sure he could see a pinprick of light somewhere in the darkness. Ki's foot snagged on something, and Grit nearly stumbled. He looked back, and they were almost upon him.

Well, shit. He might as well make a stand here. He dropped Ki, pulled his gun, and began firing. More bullets. Another round of six shots. Each shot illuminated the tunnel, and leeches flew everywhere. Eventually, something wet hit his face, and he could see the weird whites of the leeches' eyes as they surrounded him. He fired again. And again. One was on him, and he flung it off. Another bit into his leg. He fired down at his feet.

But then the pinprick of light in the distance exploded, and Grit had to shield his eyes. It came at him like a fire-ball filling the tunnel.

"Well, Ki, we had a good run."

The light hit him like a brick wall, pushing him forward. He opened his eyes, and he was riding the light, carried along the tunnel, being pushed by it. He could hear the dying screams of the leeches all around him, and he couldn't help but smile. Damn acorn grew after all. He just hoped the tunnel didn't take any sudden turns. Or stop abruptly. That would be bad.

He could barely make out something ahead—a tiny speck of light in front of him—straight in front, thank heaven. It grew, and Grit spread his arms ready to embrace the light. There was only one way to get off the speeding bullet of white he was riding, and it was through that tunnel exit. He might as well enjoy the ride.

He shot out and flailed as he was flung twenty feet from the tunnel mouth. Down he went. He guarded his face, landed, and then began to roll down the side of a large hill. Rocks slammed into his arms, scraping and bludgeoning him all over. And then it stopped.

He slowly opened his eyes, and there was Ki beside him. "Guess you made it, huh?"

The man groaned. At least he was alive.

"And here, I was wondering how we were gonna get you out of that cave. Guess Theodore did that for us, eh?"

"Another groan."

"Great talking to you."

Grit stood and looked around. Snow trickled down. He figured he was on the opposite side of the hill he'd entered, but he wasn't sure. He looked at the cave, about fifty feet up, just a dark hole in the side of the hill. He lifted Ki, and the man opened his eyes. "What?"

"Nothing, man, nothing. Let's get you to the truck."

Grit made his way down the rest of the hill and then around and over another rise.

"Is that a chipmunk?" Ki asked. "I don't feel good."

Grit looked, and there in front of him was his spirit guide—the chipmunk who'd save their asses by tossing the angel dude's acorn down the tunnel, allowing them to ride its wave of light. He stood above them at the summit of a hill, looking down at Grit and Ki.

He chittered, and Grit laughed. "Thanks for that, little guy."

The chipmunk shook his head and… snarled.

"Whoa, dude. I didn't do anything."

Grit turned, still supporting Ki, and the man he was carrying went even limper. "What are those?"

They were the leeches—all of them—rushing toward them, fanning out from the cave exit, swarming the ground, turning it black, coming to kill them.

"Ah, shit," Grit said.

He set Ki down and pulled his pistol.

His spirit guide chittered something, and Grit turned to him. "You got a better idea? Got another of those divine acorns handy?"

The chipmunk squeaked something else, then raised his hand and squeaked a war cry.

An entire army of chipmunks appeared on the hill behind and beside the spirit guide, all squeaking their return battle cry as they rushed forward to meet the mass of darkness sweeping toward them. They scrambled over rocks, and dust rose in their wake. They met the leeches head on like a wave—an onslaught of red in tooth and claw.

The leeches didn't stand a chance. Grit thought he could hear their dying screeches as the chipmunks tore through them. There was no respite, no surrender, no mercy, no quarter. It wasn't the sound of fighting; it was the sound of dying. Within moments, only the chipmunks were left.

They let out a victory cry, a reverberating squeak that made Grit wince.

Ki looked up at him. "What was that?"

"Warrior monks, my friend."

"What?"

His spirit guide ambled up to them, covered in black ichor, the blood and entrails of countless leeches. He looked up at Grit, nodded, squeaked, then took off the way they'd come. Grit got Ki up, and they followed, back to the truck where Ki's friends waited for them.

SOME DISSEMBLING REQUIRED

DONALD EVANS

You know those times when you should be asleep but you're on the internet instead? One of those times when you fall down the rabbit hole from interesting to weird to what the eff? It was one of those times for Cassian. He started the evening looking up what was new on Netflix and found a horror movie that had gone under his radar. So, while he was researching that, he found a website that reviewed horror tattoos. There was a link to a YouTube video, and once you're on YouTube, you're six degrees separated from toy reviews, game walkthroughs, cat videos, people failing, and just flat out, bafflingly weird and uncomfortable stuff.

Curious, he clicked on a video entitled, "OPENING A PORTAL TO AN ETERNAL VOID".

It was in all caps, of course. The screen was black. A shaky camera stumbled toward a dull but dimly lit shape. A vague silhouette, rising from the concrete, tapering slightly, toward a flat top nine feet in the air. The cameraperson stopped in front of the oddly-shaped metal door. Not a door—an arching metal frame in the vague configuration of a door.

Even though the camera had stopped moving in relation to the strange arch, the interior of the doorway seemed to be pulling the viewer forward. A nebulous web of stars and planets pulsed in a growing and contorting blur. A blackness grew in the center until it was all that remained in the door frame. It wasn't blackness—it was beyond blackness—and it peered out like a penetrating eye.

"CLICK LINK FOR PORTAL".

Cassian clicked the link.

A web page popped up, blank except for the words, "ORDER PLACED".

He stood up and took a stumbling step back, and then he let out a nervous chuckle and fell silent again.

A heavy pounding on the door woke him. Three knocks and their reverberations propagated in his home. He looked through the keyhole and saw no one. He opened the door and saw only an empty street and wind caressed trees in the dim night. A package was at his feet, measuring maybe four feet by one foot and six inches high. It had a weathered, previously used kind of feel to it. It was addressed to him from Void, Inc.

He sat in a chair looking at it. The box top was open, but the contents remained within. Cassian tapped his fingers restlessly on the armrest. Something within him moved, and he stood up and reached inside the box. His hand brought out an instruction pamphlet.

Printed in all caps it read, "ASSEMBLE AND EMERGE".

He pulled a beam out of the packaging. The metal was dull, as if it were trapping light instead of reflecting it. Cassian reflected on the weight of the corroded alloy. It weighed more than it seemed and less than it should.

Cassian placed a bottom piece on the floor in the center of the living room. It made a sinister L shape and remained standing on its own. He placed another piece directly atop it and they merged. The metal remained standing. He continued until one side of the door was complete and he paused.

Was he contemplating the implications of a piece of metal that adhered independently to a similar substance? Was he questioning his life choices and what had brought him to this moment? He sneezed and began to build the other side.

When it was complete, he stood back and looked at it. It looked much as it did in the video. He pulled out his phone and took a picture. He zoomed into the photo and saw a weird swirl at the center. He turned out the light and began to take video of the arch. He could see something swirling and pulsing at the center of the video, but when he looked over the phone to see for himself, there was nothing. He began to stumble toward the doorway, and the dancing stars and planets pulsed and contorted. He stopped as he saw the dark space at the center. It grew toward him. How had he not seen it in the online video? It was a black hole. A dark star. Nothing escaped it. Why couldn't he see what the camera could record? Wavelengths? Frequencies? He looked over the phone again. There was nothing. An emptiness.

An eye blinked open. It interrogated him, piercing him. He stumbled forward and into the arch.

The room was silent. As suddenly as he had vanished, Cassian walked from the doorway. It looked like Cassian, but it was not Cassian.

OGDEN DAWN

ARTHUR GOODHILL

With my back against the wet cement wall, I waited for the passing. Beyond the faint dim light of barrel fires leaking out from the criss-crossed alleyways, there was little visibility. It was always hard to tell if it was coming soon or if I could move again before it showed. I couldn't risk it.

The faint crashes of falling buildings and expired crumbling debris tumbled and echoed through the dilapidated streets. I looked up. No change. Just black, rolling clouds passing by at an unnatural pace. As if the sky itself knew the desolation of this place and wished to leave.

I slid down the wall and sat on the hard, graveled ground. A gentle breeze ushered empty candy wrappers and soiled tissue papers passed me, easing the unbearable humidity, if only for a moment. I didn't like this. Being still, being able to think and consider. It was better when I was moving. When everything was moving. I had no idea what would happen when I got to it, but I had to get to it. I had to see.

Across the road, an alleyway much like this one was

sparsely populated with derelict galvanized huts. It seemed impossible to think that people used to thrive here. That the sun shone above the Wasatch range and into the once bustling streets of Ogden Valley. But things were different now, and the lasting black of the scorched sky broke only for the glow. People were drinking from the stream of filth that trickled down towards 12th street, their torn clothes and muddied faces only pronouncing more the fear and confusion in the whites of their maddened eyes. Close to me, there were some girls, no more than teenagers, gathered around a small television. One girl sat directly in front of it, staring intensely into the white noise and static, scribbling zeros and ones, never blinking. Another sat beside her, intently studying the discarded pages as they filled up and were torn out. The last girl occasionally got up and splat a small and delicately carved piece of skin from her forearm onto the wall beside her, its warm and congealing blood sticking easily to the porous concrete. When she turned around again, I saw her instrument of choice, the bent and peeled lid from a dog food can. I could tell that they were sure they had it, that they had figured it out, but they hadn't. No one had. Not yet.

Further up, I saw what looked to be a small family. I thought the parents were comforting their young son, but as I paid more attention to them, I saw that I was wrong. The father held a copper wire in each hand, their ends wibble-wobbling in the air, while the bottoms were forced into his son's ears. As I followed the trails of blood flowing down the boy's neck and spilling onto his shoulders, I saw his mother, gripping him tightly with her head pressed hard against his chest, and her fist beating and scraping the ground. Tap. Scrape tap. Scrape tap tap. Her fingers were worn down almost to the marrow, and seeing the flecks of white emerging from underneath her bloodied claws, I

couldn't decide which was more unsettling—the sight of
her forgotten pieces of flesh and bone scattered and dying
on the ground, or the small toddler sitting beside them,
adorned in damp and muddied rags, vigorously recording
every motion her mother made with a pen and paper.
Trying to understand it.

To be closer to it.

I was pulled back by the soft hum of its beginning. I
snapped up off the ground, bent my neck skywards again,
and waited. The buildings on either side seemed sturdy
enough, so the vibrations shouldn't bring them down. Still,
I stepped out into the center of the alleyway. Looking
right, I saw some people hobble and limp towards the open
street, desperately trying to get into place for the passing.
Their fading bodies were sucked a little drier with each
moment in its light. That's when I saw it for the first time.
Three of them hobbled into the disheveled roadway and
stood, their backs to the east. Its pulsing shivers grew
stronger and faster with each passing moment, until finally
the hum of its touch made me feel like I was floating. My
heartbeat had no rhythm, just continuous movement. My
closed eyes saw images of a world only possible now in its
shaking embrace; the vivid green pastures and rolling hills
beneath Mount Ogden, with whitewater cascading
through Beus canyon, joining the Weber to its familiar end
at the mouth of the Great Salt lake. All was washed in the
familiar green of this new sun we now know and the
gorgeous emptiness of my listening mind. Blissfully igno-
rant of the lead-grey concrete dread in which we all now
lived, these thoughts—these non-thoughts—permeated
every conscious crevice in my mind like a most welcome
and worrying disease, sedating every slight and noticeable
concern. Nothing compared to the bliss of it, and everyone
stood quivering in the humid shadows, oblivious to the

collapsing necropolis all around. As it began to slow, I gently opened my eyes. Nothing had discernible outlines during the erratic jittering, and looking at my hands outstretched in front of me, my fingers appeared morphed together, like giant webbed paws in the shaking, vibrating, glorious glow.

To my right, the faintest green rays of it broke from the out-of-sight horizon, and the three that stood in the main street shuddered as its divine light slowly washed down their necks and backs. They shook like the rest of us, but they gave something more in its presence, wilting away, their conformation contorting and then whimpering into frailty. The oldest, in the center, just before it was about to sink once more behind the mountains, turned around to face the emerald horizon. The look of pure epiphany in his eyes as they shrunk and sank back into his skull, as his entire body dried and became dust beside his two oppositely faced companions, told me everything I needed to know.

As the light continued to fade, the hum left us. Amongst the distant crumbling of buildings, the shade's fallen clothes were white from the bone dust they had collapsed upon, and they lay flat in a small plume from their vanished wearer. The two that stood beside him now knelt silently, gently rubbing his imprinted shadow that stained the asphalt ground. I felt as I always felt of the ones willing to stand in its light; jealous. And that if I was to see it, to truly see it, I needed to stay mobile. To get as close as possible. Now everything had changed. Walking out from the alleyway towards the shaded ground, this imprint of existence, summed up in totality by a dark patch on a forgotten roadway, I realized the true nature of the glow. Of this new sun that dawned sporadically on our scorched earth, and, as if its divine perception had heard my thoughts, the world began to hum again.

As the remaining two hobbled away into the shadows off 12th street, my heart was once more drummed into a gentle purr of motion. And as the world around me began to softly shake, feeling the scorching heat on my back, I looked forward towards my own shadow. My frame, long and outstretched, poured across the road away from me, surrounded by green light and swallowing up the old man's final shade. As the euphoric rumblings increased, hearing the swish-swashing of the Lynn canal under a nearby bridge, I turned around. Embracing the warmth of this nuclear dawn, some dust expelled from my mouth as I coughed, and as I raised my head to meet the emerald sky head on, my eyes burned and my bones failed as I saw it, and crumbled into ascension.

SANDCASTLES
HENRY SNIDER

T he Utah wind whipped against the car's right side, threatening to force it into the neighboring lane. Teri over-corrected and felt the vibration strips bordering the shoulder. A second jerk of the wheel pulled the car back between painted lines.

"Damn it," she muttered and stole a glance to the passenger seat. Melanie didn't show any signs of waking up. Her wife stayed neatly curled as if a cat in a warm ray of sunshine, dark curls masking naturally caramel-colored skin.

Her wife.

The thought rolled through Teri's mind like a freight train. Not even married a week and the two had settled on a cross-country adventure for their honeymoon. They'd flown hours to Los Angeles and rented a car so that the landscape would be new from day one. Angry urban lifestyles gave way to equally-angry suburbanites as they tore through the land of actors, aspiring actors, and would-never-be actors. That first day had come to a close and the second nearly half-gone before the couple happened across someone who wasn't hoping to make it on the big screen... or little screen for that matter. That person seemed to be the breaking point from actor-land to the rest of the world.

Teri leaned her head from side to side, stretching tense neck muscles.

A semi blasted past them doing at least ninety, and the car shuddered in its wake.

"Damn it," she repeated and adjusted her glasses. A bit of blonde hair escaped her scrunchy and tickled the front of her face.

"You gotta get a new curse," Melanie mumbled, then shifted and stretched her legs out.

"Sorry. Didn't mean to wake you."

"Well...," a yawn escaped her as she rubbed sleep from her eyes, "you wouldn't have if you didn't keep thumping my head against the window."

"Sorry," Teri gripped the wheel a little harder. "It's this damned Utah wind. It keeps tossing us all over the place." She blew at the free strands, trying to get them away from her lips before giving up and tucking the cluster behind one ear.

"You know, we could have stayed another day in Salt Lake City and rested up a bit more."

"Pass."

"Oh, it wasn't *that* bad."

"Once we were on the outskirts it wasn't that bad, but the hotel... and right across from the compound."

"Teri, it was the Latter-Day Saints, and no one said a single negative word to us the entire time we were there... even when we toured the place."

"It wasn't what they said; it was the men." Teri's grip went from tight to white-knuckled. "You know what I mean."

"What?" She smirked and crinkled her nose. "Seeing two beautiful people in love?"

"No. The men seeing us as if we were two porn stars about to go at it at any moment."

"Well, after the dancing last night—"

"Stop it," Teri said. A smile played at the corners of her mouth.

"And that trick you did when we got back to our room."

The smile wouldn't be refused and grew. "I mean it." Her grip on the wheel eased a tad.

"Listen, Em, most men are just going to do that. They can't help it. Besides, I think I can keep the assholes at bay for you."

Em. Short for emerald, the dark green of Teri's eyes. The perfect name to be whispered in her ear where no one else could hear. A name given to her.

The perfect name.

"I know." Teri reached over and squeezed Melanie's leg. "You did take care of the 'Boy Wonders' at the club, didn't you?"

"Yuppers."

In fact, she did. Last night, they enjoyed an evening of dinner and dancing up until around ten. That's when Steven and Cal cornered them at the bar and offered to buy them drinks. Melanie politely refused the offer when one—Teri couldn't remember which was Steven and which was Cal—noticed their wedding rings and said he was sure it would be okay to steal a dance or two until the girls' husbands showed up. Without missing a beat, Mel replied that *they* were on their honeymoon, then snatched Teri by the hand and whisked her back to the dance floor before the statement sank in with the would-be Romeos.

Melanie massaged her scalp vigorously, trying to wake

up before reaching into the back seat, and pulled a water from the cooler. "Want one?"

"Still on my soda."

"Munchies?"

"Nope."

"Shit."

"Uhhh... cute, Mels."

"No. Check out the rear-view."

Teri glanced at the rear-view mirror and saw the razor-straight stretch of interstate behind them disappearing into a dusty beige landscape. "Looks dusty."

"Dusty, hell."

Teri gave a second look. The shifting beige background went from the ground to so high in the sky it disappeared out of sight at the top of the back window. She checked the side mirror. Same thing.

Mel stayed turned around in the seat looking from left to right. "It goes as far as I can see both north and south."

Teri waited for the wind pounding against the side of the car to ease, then craned her head to look over her left shoulder. A wall of dust and debris pushed from the west, swallowing everything in its path. "Christ. How far back is it?"

A canary-yellow SUV shot past going the opposite direction and straight toward the dust storm. "Tell you in a sec." She felt Melanie tapping her fingers on the driver's seat as seconds became minutes.

One....

Three....

Five....

"Almost six minutes behind us," she blurted out. "That storm's so dense the Hummer was there one second then gone the next."

"Guess we're going the right direction then, huh?"

"Creepy." She was still turned around and staring out the back window.

"With all this wind, I'd be a lot happier if you'd turn around and buckle up."

"Don't wanna be a widow before the honeymoon's over?"

"There are times...."

Melanie slid around clutching a bag of Cheetos and a water. She dumped both onto the seat between them and locked her safety belt in place. "Better?"

"Much."

They peaked a small rise and noticed cars coming the opposite direction flashing their lights. The distant sound of horns overshadowed their music playing. Ahead of them, maybe five miles away, twinkling reflections of cars jammed bumper to bumper met their eyes.

Melanie slapped the dash. "A traffic jam?" She tore the Cheetos bag open without looking down.

"Out here?" Teri added.

The multi-colored threaded line of traffic went as far as they could see, disappearing over a rise ten or so miles ahead.

Melanie pointed to a sign as they shot past. "There!"

"What?"

"An exit coming up in a mile."

"But we don't know where it goes."

Melanie motioned to the road ahead. "The evil we know, or the evil we don't?"

Teri looked around at the landscape. Ground so dry even scrub brush refused to grow met her gaze in every direction. She glanced at the fuel gauge—three quarters of a tank. Butterflies danced in her stomach at the thought of being stranded in such desolate territory. "I don't—"

"There it is. Take it."

"I–"

"Em, just do it!" Melanie jabbed an orange-stained finger in the exit's direction for emphasis.

Teri rolled her eyes and sighed but flicked on the turn signal. She had to brake hard because the off ramp was shorter than expected, and the car went from sixty to fifteen in a short span before skidding to a dusty halt in front of the stop sign. There was no on-ramp across the road, only a crevasse serving as the final resting place for old tumbleweeds. To the left took them under the interstate on a single-lane access barely big enough for a car to navigate. Shadows contrasted sharply in the midday sun, making the underpass appear darker to the naked eye. Their other option bore little in the way of promise. To the right, a dust-encrusted blacktop ended a dozen or so yards from where the car sat. Granted, the road continued but appeared to become more washboard than access before vanishing over the rise a quarter-mile away.

Teri sat and stared first at the underpass and then to the rough stretch of road before settling on Melanie. "Well?"

"Well what?" She took a long drink from the bottle of water.

"Which way, oh great adventurer?"

"No idea."

Teri reached over, popped open the glove box, and grabbed a scrunchie. She fumbled with it, pulling the sweaty mane off the back of her neck. "No one's come down after us. Maybe I can back up."

"And wait who knows how long before traffic gets moving again? I think I'll pass."

The air hung heavy in the rental car with Teri struggling not to lose her temper and Melanie obliviously content to follow her Zen approach to the situation.

Teri looked at Melanie then straight out the front of the car. "What did it say?"

"Hmmm?"

Words came from Teri's mouth both slow and quiet. "The sign for this exit. What did it say?"

"Free beer." Melanie sat a little straighter when the comment fell flat. "Sorry, Em. I didn't mean to...." The words trailed off.

Teri continued to stare out the windshield for nearly a full minute when she said, "I know. I'm just hot, tired, and not really looking forward to any of the options before us right now."

Wind buffeted the car, rocking it from right rear to left front.

"I don't remember what it said. I just caught sight of the thing as we went by." She furrowed her brow and pinched the bridge of her nose with a forefinger and thumb. "I *think* it said something about a rest stop."

Teri chanced a look over her shoulder. "You'd think with a sandstorm coming there'd be a line of cars coming down here after us."

"There weren't that many behind us." She stuck a thumb out to the right. "I doubt the rest stop's that way."

"Good. I don't think my back could handle that."

"So...," Melanie said with a renewed grin, "our adventure takes us to the left?"

Another sigh escaped her. "To the left," she agreed.

Her wife leaned over and stole a quick kiss, leaving a Cheeto-encrusted orange print on the side of Teri's mouth.

"Keep eating those and I'm going to start calling you Chester."

"Chester?" Her eyes lit up. "Oh, the cheetah. Cool. I can be Chester the cheesy Arabian lesbian cheetah."

"Quite the name. Sounds right up your alley."

Another gust of wind hit the car, causing them both to crane their necks and look out the rear window. The sky still shone blue, but the onset of the storm was evident. Air pressure increased, and they both yawned in an effort to get their ears to pop.

Teri turned left. "Pillow talk later."

Melanie sat back and stared at her. "Pillow talk? After three years, your pillow talk's still about as Disney as they come."

Teri cut her a look and stuck out her tongue.

The bridge loomed overhead. Two slices of shade and then the road curved left and out of sight. Sand peppered the car along the driver's side, leaving residue a darker hue of orange than Melanie's kiss. She stepped on the gas. Shade engulfed the vehicle, and the bridge shielded them from the worst of Mother Nature's assault. Both women looked at the narrow access. Graffiti covered the concrete where the hill's slope met the underside of the structure. All of the writing and artwork was too small to make out and lacked the general soft-cornered touch that spray paint offered.

"Creepy," Teri breathed. She strained to make out some of what marred the slate-gray surface. Words and drawings stayed just out of focus. Her eyes watered, causing images to blur into ant-trails and deny her any sense of enlightenment.

A low rumble filled the car as the wind whipped up ahead of them. Dirt, tumbleweeds, and loose clumps of weeds whipped past at crazy speeds.

"Em," Melanie said while gripping the car's door handle, "we better get moving. Looks like the storm's about here."

Teri stepped on the gas and moved the car into the channel between the bridges. "Only fifty feet. Only fifty feet," she repeated. The Buick rocked as they left the relative safety of the underpass. "Come on." She stepped harder on the gas pedal and felt the slip on the sand.

"Easy," Mel said, raising her voice to be heard over the gale.

Fifty feet fell to thirty, then to ten. Just as quickly as the wind assaulted them, it blew past as Teri stopped the car once again, this time directly beneath the road.

Melanie grasped the door handle and slid her flip-flops on. "Will you look at that," she said, staring at a new batch of graffiti up high on the concrete.

Teri clicked the lock button just before her wife pulled on the handle and was rewarded with a motherly look.

"Come on, Em. Let me out. I wanna see. I mean look at all this graffiti... in the middle of nowhere!" She grinned. "Aren't you at least a little bit interested what people had to say out here... under a bridge? It could be like some kind of prophetic poetry."

"Not as interested as you might think."

"It could be prophetic."

"It's probably a limerick about a man and his horse."

"Let me out," Melanie said playfully. "Let a girl have some fun."

"You could have fun at a funeral."

Her smile broadened. "Depends on the funeral. Five minutes—I promise."

"How about we get to the rest stop and you can look at all the urban hieroglyphics you want after this blows over?"

"Deal!"

"And," Teri added, "you drive the next leg."

"But it's so *boring*!" She stressed the last word in such a salute to teenage years past that they broke into laughter.

"That's the deal. Better take it before I add a foot rub in for good measure."

"Fine," Melanie relented. "But hurry up. I've got to pee."

Teri urged the car from their relative safety and back into the storm. She followed the road around to the left. The car faced back in the direction they'd come and full fury of the forthcoming storm came into view. The virtual wall of wind was nearly upon them. Good-sized pieces of sand pitted the glass as each second passed.

"Em, go." Melanie gripped Teri's shoulder hard. "Go! Go, go, go!"

Teri stomped on the gas, spinning the tires as they raced toward the cluster of brown-painted structures just ahead. Something swung across the middle of the road. She hit the brakes just as quickly, but not fast enough to stop short of the heavy-duty chain barring the road. Headlights shattered and the hood popped free of the clasp, only to have the wind jerk the plate of metal up, straining the hinges and blocking any view of what was about to hit.

"CLOSED," the sign read before the hood blocked it from view.

"No," Teri whispered.

"Back!" Melanie went from gripping her shoulder to smacking it repeatedly. "Back under the bridge!"

Teri put the car in reverse and backed as quickly as she dared. Bright blue sky fell to an angry orange then darkened even more. The underpass appeared as little more than a mirage through dust-coated windows. She felt the tires spin, not from speed but from the gale urging the car faster.

She heard herself say, "We're not going to make it."

Melanie reached in front of Teri, grabbed the wheel, and jerked it counterclockwise. The car's rear end turned toward the bridge, then the wind caught the front of the car and continued the spin as tires lost their grip. The newlyweds screamed as the Buick turned in a slow 180, mercifully ending overall in the direction of the underpass. Tires gripped pavement again and Teri put the car in drive and looking through the narrow gap under the raised hood, pulled the last few feet, retreating back beneath the interstate.

A minute passed and neither said a word.

Then, Melanie grabbed the door handle again.

"No!"

"Em, we have to get the hood down before the engine clogs with dirt!"

"Don't... please!"

Melanie reached out and gently ran her fingers down Teri's jawline. "Have to."

Before Teri could object a second time, she watched Melanie slam all her weight against the door.

Nothing happened.

Another slam.

Metal groaned, and the door pulled out of her hands.

"Mels!"

Teri reached out and felt her fingers drag along Melanie's t-shirt as she forced her way free of the car. Her door slammed with the finality of a kettle drum. Wind slammed Melanie against the hood of the car, her head striking the open hood's edge. Red joined the orange hue, muddying an area half the size of a softball in the second before dust clotted the wound. Teri scampered across the seat to the passenger side of the car, less than two feet from the woman who'd been at her side since they'd met at the coffee shop just a few short years ago.

"Melanie!" Teri's scream sounded little more than a whisper.

Clumped hair whipped around the woman's face, dirt clotting both eyes and crusting them shut in seconds. Still,

Melanie managed to stay on her feet with hands gripping the hood for balance. Her face turned in Teri's direction as she pressed down on the hood. It resisted, bobbing down briefly before popping up again.

She watched as Melanie pushed down on the hood again, this time locking both arms and pushing down with all her might. Metal bobbed down a second time. Peppered red patterns appeared on her arms and shoulders.

Teri bit her lip. "Just come back," she pleaded to no one... to anyone who might answer her prayer.

Wind caught again, thrusting Melanie across the top of the Buick and onto the road. Teri grabbed the driver's door handle and pushed with everything she had. The door refused to budge.

Teri saw Melanie struggle to her knees, a crimson gash already scabbed across her forehead, her mane of black hair now sporting deep dust-orange highlights. Blood crusted below both eyes, telling of her mistake opening them. "Mels!"

A silent scream came from her wife as she sat back on her haunches. White teeth went first red with blood then orange, and layers of sand, dirt, and clay worked to clog the woman's airway. The peppered areas on her skin grew as blowing dust blasted layers of skin off.

She smacked against the door rhythmically—first the door, then the door glass, then again against the door.

The roar's volume deafened all other sounds.

Melanie reached out with one hand to the car when the wind knocked her over and rolled her up the slope to the bottom of the bridge. Fingers grew bloody as she scrabbled to find a grip along the wall of graffiti-strewn concrete.

Teri pushed her way back to the passenger side of the car to follow her spouse outside.

Suddenly, the car rose.

She was weightless.

Ground sped by the windows wrong.

Then the car folded in half, wedged tight into the underpass.

She looked from what felt a million miles away out the passenger door window. Cracks spider-webbed the glass, expanding as she watched.

Teri blinked.

The wind howled.

Teri blinked.

It was dark.

Teri blinked.

Bright sunlight shone on a lobster-red patch of her shin.

Her neck hurt.

"Mels?"

It came back to her in waves... their vows... the dancing... playing on Hollywood Boulevard....

...and the storm.

"Mels!" Her voice sounded small, devoid of the panic rising in her chest. Teri shifted and white fire shot from her left elbow up to the shoulder. She wormed herself free, gritting teeth against tears, each breath faster than the previous until effort brought success and, after two kicks to the cracked window, Teri found herself sliding out of the car and spilling, not unlike a pile of clothes, onto the slope.

Air hung hot and heavy under the bridge, abandoned by the winds that drove it the day before. It had to already be nearing a hundred. Teri looked back at the car. From its awkward angle Teri felt vertigo wash over her. An empty stomach churned.

"M-Mel!"

Legs shaking, she backed up a couple of feet and sat

down against the concrete base of the underpass. Teri's insides clenched, and vomit rose to her throat. Her insides churned, and she clenched her eyes shut against rising bile. A moment passed with no resolution to the feeling.

"Shock," she said. Stating the obvious did little to help. Another minute passed as she waited for the nausea to erupt or abate. The latter won out and Teri swallowed hard, choking down crusty bile.

She opened her eyes and looked to her left—along the four-foot-high wall. Dates, limericks, declarations of undying love covered the concrete in paint, marker, finger-nail polish, and some even etched into the man-made rock itself.

I should put Melanie's name here.

Teri scooted down the slope a little and stood again. This time, her stomach held firm. She turned and looked at the graffiti. A few feet further down, faded lines marred by years—in some cases decades—old showcased artwork.

Lines that reminded Teri of lines on sheet music.

She heard herself starting to hum a tune.

Wait.

Teri stopped, shook her head in an effort to try to clear it.

The lines.

Feet moved of their own accord, passing where the lines began and continuing to the side of the underpass.

Fingers. Blood from Mel's fingers. Oh, God. "How much blood?"

Drag marks continued to the corner then vanished, much as Melanie had.

Teri stepped from the shade and looked up the short man-made valley between the Interstate lanes. Its upward slope appeared empty. She staggered to the middle of the dip and started walking up, moving in the direction the storm had blown Melanie.

Silence, like the air, hung heavy. No rumble from cars whizzing by... no horns beep beep beeping as they blew past her. Not even birds squawked.

The blurry world fell into differing levels of an impressionist painting mere yards away. Teri reached up to push her glasses higher on her nose and found them missing.

"The accident."

She continued walking the center divider between the interstate lanes and looked at the twin strips of pavement.

"Mels?" She parroted the call every minute or so. Teri turned around and looked behind her. The bridge was nothing more than a dark blob in an equally blurry world.

"Fuckin' eyes." A laugh escaped her as a bark. "Well," she said to herself, "Mels wanted me to find a new curse." The empty laugh gave way to sobs, and Teri cradled her injured arm and kept her slow pace forward.

Time passed.

The sun rose higher.

Teri wasn't sure how much time had gone by, but at some point she'd fought and finally succeeded in pulling the scrunchie from her hair and letting it fall free.

Not as good as a hat, but at least it's keeping some of the sun off of me.

Teri looked down and discovered at some point she'd left the center divider and walked along the right road's shoulder. The backs of her legs burned, as did her left shin. A quick glance down showed her left elbow an angry purple.

"Broken. Got to be."

Another look back yielded nothing other than blue sky and brown earth.

Sand crunched under foot. Asphalt vanished under

increasing layers of dust and sand. Ahead the black lines thinned, became spotty and ultimately vanished from view in the blurry distance.

"Mels?" she parroted for what felt like the thousandth time, though now little more than a whisper. The tears had long dried, but anguish still rang fresh in her raspy voice.

Still no answer.

The sand grew thicker. Heavy grains covered the ground, barren of the lighter dust that the storm ferried away. Something else was in the road.

Shapes.

Blobs.

Shades of brown, black, even reds rippled into view.

"Cars!"

Her shambling footsteps became a half-hearted jog, each step a jarring painful reminder of her broken arm.

"Help!"

Like her cry for Melanie, the call went unanswered.

Teri reached the rear car of the traffic jam—a green Taurus. She smacked the trunk.

"Hello?" she half-yelled. "I need... I need help!"

She banged on the door.

It was empty.

The car's front end was wedged under the rear bumper of a black SUV. It, too, was void of its passengers.

"What the hell is this?"

Thoughts of her church upbringing came back. Warnings of the Rapture and what happened to those who didn't follow God's plan danced in her mind. She shook them off with a shudder.

"They were outside when the storm hit... or in another car."

Teri crouched down and looked underneath the vehicles as best she could. Nothing human shaped was wedged between any of the cars' tires.

Only sand.

...and cars.

As she stood, hot, sweaty fabric fluttered against her back.

Her shirt was drenched with sweat.

Teri staggered to what had once been a white Subaru and opened the back door. A cooler sat in the middle of the seat. Inside rested half a dozen beers floating in ice-filled water. Her right hand left an orange ring as she ignored the beers and grabbed a handful of ice. The first chunk swished around Teri's mouth and, resisting the urge to swallow, was spat out onto the ground. The action was repeated with the second and third chunks as she worked to free her mouth of caked dirt. Droplets from the fourth slid down her throat like mother's milk—an icy pleasure cooling the center-most part of her.

A fit of coughing followed. Inky-brown droplets of mud fell from her lips, and she reached in, scooped a handful of water, and brought it to her lips. She swished and spat, then took another handful and swallowed it.

Teri looked around, suddenly feeling guilty.

"Hello? Is anyone there?"

Nothing.

"Mels?"

Not even the wind answered.

"Maybe there was an evacuation."

She looked down and considered the beer a moment before taking it and setting the wet can on the car's roof. Three tries and one broken nail later, she'd managed to open the can. A full can became half in a quick series of swallows.

"Braaaaaap." The belch came with such force that it

hurt her throat. Teri tried to wipe the leftover beer from her lips with the back of her good arm but only succeeded in creating a dirty smear.

Tossing the beer aside, Teri dug into the vehicle and looked for anything that might shield her from the unforgiving sun.

Nothing.

She repeated the process on the next vehicle and was rewarded first with an umbrella and second with a backpack. A quick tip dumped the contents onto the car's floorboards and she refilled the shoulder bag with bottles of water also found in the Chevy.

Teri did her best, one handed, to manage both the backpack and the open umbrella. What felt like another hour passed before she tired of looking into the never-ending line of cars in the hopes of finding someone. Her elbow throbbed in time with each step, creating its own painful rhythm.

Teri blinked away sweat and squinted at the road ahead. Reflections twinkled in the afternoon sun. Ant-sized shadows shifted at the horizon. The shadows moved a second time.

"They moved," she gasped. "People."

As before, her steps quickened, each landing more reckless than the last.

Shapes grew and what were once shapeless forms solidified into vehicles lining an intersecting road. Further on, beyond her limited vision's capabilities, stood a structure she couldn't quite make out, something resembling an oversized mound with so many sunlight reflections that even looking in its general direction hurt.

Teri stared, first at the road before her then off at a forty-five degree angle to the mound. Heat radiated through the soles of her shoes and rivulets of salty sweat cut trails along the dust on her skin.

"Stay on the road or go cross country?" Words from all the reality survival shows flooded her memory and better judgment won out against desire. "Damned road," she muttered and started out following the barely visible dotted yellow line. A distant thumping resonated throughout the Utah flats, working its way into her eardrums and inadvertently setting her pace.

Voices and the groaning of metal wafted on what little wind the day offered. Teri passed the sign for the upcoming exit.

WHAGEENEE ROAD NEXT LEFT

"Whageenee," she muttered. "Melanie will be there."

As she grew closer, a myriad of voices overlapped, with some crying, others barking expulsions of anger, all of which were still unintelligible by anything other than raised tones.

"Must...," Teri gulped air as a new wave of pain shot through her arm, "be... an... emergency tent."

Another scream rang out and her steps faltered.

The off-ramp had become a blurry reality, its sandy slide slipping off the highway to Whageenee Road. A crowd stood at the edge of the ramp. Sand blew across the distance between her and them, whipping a dust devil of debris into the air. Six figures broke away from the cluster, surrounded an SUV and began moving it down toward Whageenee's underpass.

"Hello?" Her voice came as little more than a whisper. Teri tried again, putting a lung full of air behind the word this time. "Hello?"

Figures stopped moving and looked toward her. Two, standing a full head taller, broke from the group and approached.

"Thank God! Oh than—"

"Oph!"

The first figure focused into stark reality. Leathery flesh clutched exposed bone in a stiff embrace. Nose, eyelids, and lips all drew back in an exaggerated manifestation of dehydration. Empty sockets each held a beetle, both buzzing in agitation. In lieu of a shirt, the cadaver wore an Audi leather seat cover as a tunic, leaving shriveled genitalia exposed with each step.

Teri stumbled back, falling hard on her rump.

It towered over her as did its companion, similarly garbed in its own seat cover, and stood at Teri's feet. The first reached down and grabbed her by her broken arm.

She howled.

The creature eased his grip but didn't let go. It leaned forward and studied her eyes before presenting her to the second.

"Ehmet tont phu," the first said.

"Pok tont phu," came the reply, and it drew a tire iron from its belt.

"Ehmet tont phu," the first insisted.

Teri watched with horror at the exchange going on between the two.

The second replied, "Dah!" and stiffly waved at her arm and walked away.

White fire shot through her as the corpse jerked her to her feet.

It pulled her beside him. "Toh!" She stayed at his side, slowing her pace to match his. They passed a cluster of people at the ramp's edge. Teri counted nine, mostly children, surrounded by five of the walking husks.

"Please," she uttered, fearful of some supernatural wrath, "you're hurting me."

It jerked her arm hard in reply.

They left the ramp and stepped into the bridge's shade. Children lined the underpass, scrawling on the concrete with everything from crayons to makeup. Sobs sang out in chorus as Teri passed them. One sat up straighter, and she glimpsed eye sockets as empty as the thing leading her. A glint caught her attention, and Teri looked away just as quickly, seeing a beetle's exoskeleton wet with blood as it peeked between the child's newly ruined lids.

They left the shade of the bridge and continued along the shoulder of Whageenee, moving ever toward the reflective mound. Vehicles were pushed by groups of four, and steered by a fifth, lining both lanes of the road. Bordering them stood more of the husked creatures, each wielding fan belts as makeshift whips.

Teri looked up at the mound and lost her breath.

"Cars."

Cars, trucks, in one place even a house door, were stacked neatly, creating an ever-growing mound. The flow of vehicles never slowed, only kept the same steady pace. Sun reflected off dozens of windshields and car doors.

"I don't—I don't understand."

"Toh," the thing leading her repeated and shoved her toward the line of vehicles. It pointed casually to the cars and made a pushing motion. The beetles moved around in its eye sockets, shifting for a better position.

Teri looked to her left at the caravan of metal. Two cars up, a familiar clutch of hair caught her gaze. Though dirty and clotted, it could only belong to one person.

"Melanie!"

Teri scrambled out of the husk's reach and broke into a full run, clasping the broken arm to her chest, toward Melanie. She passed the first vehicle and was nearly to the second when her head snapped back and feet shot out before her.

The husk jerked Teri back to her feet by the fist full of hair it clutched. "Pok tont phu," it said and reached for a wicked-looking length of rusty car metal wedged in its belt. She smacked at its arm with her good hand and pulled free, running the last few steps behind Melanie.

"Stop!" she yelled and pointed at Melanie's back. "I want to be here." She made a pushing motion to the car.

Suddenly her back lit up, hurting as bad as her arm. Teri looked over her shoulder and saw another of the husks pulling back on a fan belt it had just lashed her with.

"Ehmet tont phu," it said and pointed to the car.

Teri wedged herself between Melanie and some man that sobbed quietly to himself. Her bare arm brushed against Melanie's.

Too rough.

Melanie's mane of ebony hair covered her face and most of her body to the waist. The narrow bare patch along her upper arm was leathery, pitted, and nearly as dry as the husks.

Voice half-hitched in her throat, Teri whispered, "Mels?"

Melanie's head lifted slightly, but she never stopped pushing.

Teri tried again. "Melanie?"

A quiet rasp came from beneath the hair. "E-Ems?"

"Yeah." Teri shifted so she was still pushing with her shoulder and reached out with her good hand and put it over Melanie's. "I'm here."

Melanie's hand slowly pulled away. "Don't look at me, Em. My eyes–"

"I know, baby. I saw in the storm."

"But I'm not really blind." Melanie's voice rose. "I can still see. Oh, God, I can see the most horrible things. The sky… the *things* flying overhead… and all the faces looking up from the ground…."

Teri stayed silent but kept staring at Melanie, waiting for her to continue. No more was offered other than a hitch as she worked to get her breath.

"What's happening?"

The man next to them said, "We're pushing."

"No, I mean… all this. What's going on?"

Melanie groaned. "I think we're in Hell. That's what's going on."

The man cut in. "You know what this reminds me of?" He didn't wait for a reply and screamed, "A pyramid. A big fuel-efficient fucking pyramid!"

Teri ignored him and said, "Mels–" then fell silent as Melanie looked up. Ruined sockets that once held chocolate brown eyes now housed two large green beetles. Mandibles quickened in agitation.

"My…."

My what? My God? My goodness?

"Oh, Mels."

Melanie's head looked back down. "You don't know how horrific you, and—hell, everything looks now. It's all so alien and…." Tearless sobs broke free. "I can't hardly move. Everything's so stiff. The skin on my neck split right before you found me. I… I didn't even bleed. They're… they're inside me."

They pushed in silence for a while longer before Melanie asked, "What do I look like to you?"

"The same. You're the same beautiful woman I fell in love with."

The man next to them stopped pushing and grabbed her by the arm. "Wait—you still have *your* eyes?" He turned her and his beetles gripped the edges of their sockets, mandibles clicking.

A crack of the makeshift whip brought him to his knees. Another strike followed the first. Then a third. He threw up his hands in supplication and pointed back at Teri.

"Oomph," the husk said and closed in on him.

"She still has her eyes!" He motioned with two fingers to his own missing eyes then back to Teri.

"Pah?" It bent over him, then craned its head to look at Teri and Melanie.

"Chelah neh pah!"

Teri quit pushing, grabbed Melanie by the hand, and backed away. "Can you run?"

"What?"

Teri hissed, "Can you run?"

"Ems, I can't hardly walk. They... they won't let me."

Melanie's arms lowered. Leathery skin stretched, showing minuscule pincers pierced flesh from the inside on either side of split skin, holding it together. A dozen small lumps along the injury told of where each of the younger beetles rested just below the skin within Melanie's body. One small beetle, barely the size of Teri's pinky nail, crawled to the injury. It probed the rip a second before retreating from the blistering sun by forcing its way into her body.

Three whip cracks struck Teri in quick succession, bringing her to her knees. The husk in front of her stepped closer while shadows from three others approached from just out of sight. They pinned her, even pulling her broken arm out and pressing it into the dirt. A splintering sensation, like a stick wrapped in steak being twisted, radiated up her arm into the shoulder.

"Gah," was all Teri could manage to mutter.

"Oomph Tallah?" One of the other three husks leaned

in close and forced her left eye open with a bony finger and thumb.

Teri froze when a second lowered a shimmering green scarab beetle down beside her opened lid.

A finger, impossibly large from Teri's perspective, pointed first to the beetle then to her eye, his fingertip actually pressing against her orb.

"The pain's not so bad, Ems," Melanie said from behind the car, head hung in supplication.

The beetle fell from the husk's grasp, landing on Teri's cheek. Talons dug into her sunburned flesh as the insect righted itself before mandibles scissored the orb and the insect delved into its new home.

ABOUT THE AUTHORS

Michael Jess Alexander: Michael Jess Alexander teaches high school English in Newcastle, Wyoming. His work can be found in *Bewildering Stories*, *Flash Fiction Magazine*, and *Dark Fire Fiction*, among others. His debut collection, *Boarded Windows, Dead Leaves*, was published in 2020 by Spooky House Press and was chosen by Indies Today as the best independently published horror book for that year. He is a lifelong fan of all things spooky—a passion his very sweet wife tolerates and his equally sweet daughters encourage.

MICKIE BOLLING-BURKE: Mickie lives in the Southwest, where she spends her nights writing stories of horror and suspense inspired by her beloved rescue cats, Pal and Lassie. She spends her days sleeping with her fists clenched because Shirley Jackson taught her not everything that wants to hold her hand is a friend. Find her on Twitter @MBollingBurke.

JM CULLEN: JM Cullen is a Software Engineer and grew up with technology without losing his sense of adventure. He earned a business degree from the University of Nebraska at Omaha and writes damn good code. Nationally recognized, his profile can be found in *Marquis Who's Who of America* (www.24-7pressrelease. com/press-release-service/472378).

Observing technological breakthroughs in a career spanning over three decades, JM wonders what life will be like in the next ten to twenty years and how technology might go awry. He writes about the things that keep him up at night.

He is a self-proclaimed nerd, attends Comic Conventions (yes, I dress the part), is an avid adventurist, and enjoys traveling and SCUBA diving worldwide. Follow JM Cullen at johncullennovels.me/home/.

DANIEL CURETON: Daniel considers himself an avant-garde poet and post-modern writer. His poetry exposes the deeper meanings of experiential living and his stories are idea platforms. He has previously been published in *Peculiar: A Queer Literary Journal*, *The Rocky Mountain Review*, *Trilithon: The Journal of the Ancient Order of Druids in America*, *A Shanghai Poetry Zine*, and *Enheduanna: A Pagan Literary Journal* for which he is the editor. www.danielcureton.com

STEVEN DEE KISH: Steven Dee Kish is a writer who lives in Las Vegas, Nevada. He has endured childhood trauma, and is a survivor of suicide. His writing shows what life is like, when someone is living on the edge of madness/sorrow. The poet is always trying to describe what cannot be said. When Steve shared his writing with the public, it was received with positivity and people confirming that they too hurt, but were unwilling to "put themselves out there", but people found comfort that he was hurting, just like them. Steven's poems have been published in, on-line journals: *Continue the Voice* (Issue 7 & 8, UK). *The Elevation Review* (Issue 5, USA), and *The Rainbow Poems Review* (Issue 4, UK). Steven's poems have been printed in *Pure Slush Books* (Lifespan Vol 3 & 4 AU). *Night Picnic* (Volume 4 issue 3). *Wingless Dreamer Anthology* (Dawn of the day and Book in black).

DONALD EVANS: Donald Evans is a pragmatist. He is a plant indigenous to California but has family roots and branches in Utah. To soothe his mid-life crisis he writes cosmic horror and existential dread. He also enjoys his wife and baby, fruit smoothies and Steve from *Blues Clues*. Learn more about Donald here:

www.imdb.com/name/nm7734700.

NICHOLAS J. EVANS: Nicholas J. Evans is an author originally from New York who currently resides in Maine with his wife and four children. He was a co-founding member of the

post-hardcore group, NoraStone, where he spent the years of 2011 - 2017 touring with them and he is featured on their first three albums. Following the birth of his first child, he ended his time with the band to focus on new career paths, and during this time he returned to writing short stories as he had in years prior. *His Body & Spirit* won the 2018 Blue Rose Award for Horror Fiction, and a fanfiction titled Minya's Sin City was featured in *Kaiju Island* magazine. He is best known for his sci-fi noir novel series, *For Humans, For Demons*, and his stand-alone urban fantasy, *The Ones Who Could Do Anything*, along with short novella featured in the *Beyond The Cogs* anthology. When not writing, Nick enjoys spending time with his kids, gaming with his wife, and being a general nuisance. Follow Nick on Instagram @Nick-EvansWrites and Twitter @NickEvansWrites.

K. Scott Forman: K. Scott Forman is the author of several short stories and poems. He is a member of the Horror Writers Association, enjoys long walks, sunsets with blood in them, and Metallica at volumes determined unsafe by the Surgeon General. Find him at Fearknocks.com

Arthur Goodhill: Arthur Goodhill is a 28 year old writer from Athlone, Ireland. Having grown up amongst a family of storytellers he took to writing at a young age, winning the Strokestown youth poetry competition while in school and has since gone on to have poems published both locally and in larger outlets like the *Crannóg* magazine. His writing stems from what interests him as a reader, ranging from George Orwell, Edwin A. Abbott and H.P. Lovecraft, to Paolo Coelho and Jeffrey Archer. He has also self published books of poetry and has most recently released a novella titled *The Drawing Room*. Follow Arthur on Instagram @arthurgoodhill.

JOSEPH HOPE: Joseph Hope writes from Nigeria, west Africa. His works are forthcoming or already published in Reckoning Press, Evening Street Press, Zoetic Press, New Verse News, Timber Ghost Press, *Praxis Magazine*, *Ubu*, *AfroPoetry*, *Gemini Spice Magazine*, *Spillwords*, *SprinNG*, *Writers Space Africa*, *Nthanda Magazine*, and more. He's a reader for reckoning press. He was a fellow in the 2021 Spring Writing Fellowship. He tweets @ItzJoe9 & IG: _hope_joseph

DEREK HUTCHINS: Derek Hutchins is a writer for the *Bad Vibes Podcast* and author of a collection of short horror stories *The Undertaker and Other Macabre Tales*. Raised in Connecticut, (the most haunted state), he developed a love for horror and the fantastic at an early age. Derek has an MFA in Writing for Film and Television from Emerson College and lives with his wife and daughter in Utah. Follow him on

Instagram   @themanwhoknewjustenough   or   Twitter @derekmhutchins for updates.

C.R. Langille: C.R. Langille spent many a Saturday afternoon watching monster movies with their mother. It wasn't long before they started crafting nightmares to share with their readers. They are a retired, disabled veteran with a deep love for weird and creepy tales. This prompted them to form Timber Ghost Press in January of 2021. They are an affiliate member of the Horror Writer's Association, a member of the League of Utah Writers, and they received their MFA: Writing Popular Fiction from Seton Hill University. Follow them here: biolinks. heropost.io/CRLangille

CARTER LAPPIN: Carter Lappin is an author from California. Her work has appeared in a number of literary publications, including an anthology with Dreadstone Press, and she is scheduled to appear in several more publications in the near future. She has a bachelor's degree in creative writing. You can find Carter on Twitter at @CarterLappin.

C.H. Lindsay: Charlie is an award-winning poet & writer, housewife, and book-lover. She currently has short stories and poems in sixteen anthologies, with two more coming out next year. Her poems have appeared in several

magazines, including *The Leading Edge: A Magazine of Science Fiction and Fantasy, Amazing Stories, and Space and Time Magazine*. She is working on three novels, five short stories, and two dozen poems (more or less). In 2018 she became Al Carlisle's literary executor. She now publishes his true crime, as well as books by Floyd C. Forsberg, under Carlisle Legacy Books, LLC, with plans to add more books in the coming years. She is a member of SFWA, HWA, SFPA, and LUW. She is a founding member of the Utah Chapter of the Horror Writers Association. Mostly blind, she lives in Utah with her "seeing-eye husband," youngest child, and a cat. You can follow her at her website: www.chlindsay.net, on Facebook at facebook.com/writerchlindsay and on Twitter at: @writerchlindsay.

BRYAN MCENTIRE: Bryan McEntire spends his days inside the world of industrial automation but lives for the night to give life to new worlds and vex basement ghosts with synthesizer and violin disturbances. His story "That Shadow on the Wall" is soon to be anthologized by Timber Ghost Press. He sometimes blogs at swordandpaper.com and lives in Herriman, Utah with his wife and daughter. Follow him on Twitter @bryanmcentire, Instagram @bryanmcentire, or LinkedIn: www.linkedin.com/in/bryanmcentire.

D.J. Moore: D. J. Moore lives in Salt Lake City. His fiction has previously appeared in the steampunk anthology *Put Your Shoulder to the Wheel*, the ETA Hoffman tribute anthology *Machina-tions and Mesmerism*, and the Utah horror anthology *Wasatch Witches*, among other places. He's a fan of quality cinema and was an extra in *Sharknado 4*. Visit his website at maniadelight.com for more info.

Eric Nirschel: Hailing from Phil-adelphia and a graduate of Temple University, Eric Nirschel is a long-time fan of horror film, book, and game. Once the proprietor of a traditional bells, books, and candles magic shop, Eric has devoted himself to the study of all things that go bump in the night, and cheers the influence of past and present greats, including H.P Lovecraft, Stephen King, Koji Shiraishi and Junji Ito. Eric has seen his work appear in numerous anthologies, including *Beyond the Infinite: Tales from the Outer Reaches*, *Scary Snippets*, and *Monsters We Forgot*. Follow Eric on Twitter at @Enirschel for witty (self-described) commentary and horror movie reviews.

Lehua Parker: LEHUA PARKER writes speculative fiction for kids and adults, often set in her native Hawai'i. Her award-winning published series include the *Niuhi Shark Saga* trilogy, *Lauele Fractured Folktales*, and *Chicken Skin Stories*, along with many other plays, poems, short stories, novels, and essays. A Kamehameha Schools graduate, Lehua is a

passionate advocate of indigenous voices and authentic representation in media. She is a frequent speaker at conferences, schools, and symposiums, and mentors through the Lehua Writing Academy and PEAU Lit. When the right project wanders by, she's also a freelance editor and story consultant.

Now living in exile in the high Rocky Mountains, during the snowy winters she dreams of the beach. Connect with her on her website at www.lehuaparker.com. To find more of her stories, check out her Amazon page www.amazon.com/Lehua-Parker/e/B009SDCHA6.

CYGNUS PERRY: Cygnus Perry is an undergraduate student at Utah State University. They have lived in Utah since they were in high school where they developed a passion for creative writing. Cygnus loves to explore the natural world and uses it as inspiration for unnatural stories and poems. For Cygnus, writing is the best way to discover the unreal and unbelievable. Follow them at www.instagram.-com/perrypurplefingers and twitter.com/PerryPianist.

JONATHAN REDDOCH: Jonathan Reddoch is co-owner of Collective Tales Publishing. He is a father, writer, editor, and publisher. He writes sci-fi, fantasy, romance, and especially horror. He has been working on his enormous sci-fi novel for over a decade and would like to finish it in this lifetime if possible. Find him on Instagram: Allusions_of_Grandeur or on his website: CTPfiction.com.

LEVI ROBINSON: Levi Robinson has been deeply passionate about storytelling ever since he was a young boy. He spent his life dreaming up fiction. From screenplays and comics to song lyrics and short stories. He is only happy when he is creating. He has lived in Utah most of his life, where he has sought out like-minded individuals to share and collaborate with. He is constantly compelled to use his imagination to tell stories as a way of expressing himself and to share his voice with those around him.

NNADI SAMUEL: Nnadi Samuel (he/him/his) holds a B.A in English & literature from the University of Benin. His works have been previously published/forthcoming in *Suburban Review, Seventh Wave Magazine, Native-Skin lit Magazine, FIYAH, Fantasy Magazine, Uncanny Magazine, The Capilano Review, Contemporary Verse 2, Gutter Magazine, Carte Blanche, Trampset, Beestung Magazine, The Elephant Magazine* & elsewhere. Winner of the Miracle Monocle Award for Ambitious Student Writers 2021(University of Louisville), Lakefly Poetry Contest 2021 (Wisconsin), the International Human Right Arts Festival Award 2021, and Canadian Open Drawer contest 2020. He got an honorable mention for the 2021 Betty L. Yu and Jin C.Yu Creative Writing Prize(College Category). He is the author of "Reopening of Wounds" & "Subject Lessons" (forthcoming). He reads for *U-Right Magazine*. He tweets @Samuelsamba10.

KRISTI   PETERSEN   SCHOONOVER:
Kristi Petersen Schoonover has always been fascinated by Utah's religiously and paleontologically turbulent history. Her stories have appeared in many publications, most recently or forthcoming in *Generation X-ed*, *Angela's Recurring Nightmares*, *Wicked Creatures*, *Lovecraftian Microfiction Vol. 7*, *parAB-normal*, *Crow & Cross Keys*, and a few others. She holds an MFA from Goddard College, is founding editor of the journal *34 Orchard*, is a part-time co-host on the *Dark Discussions* horror film podcast, and is co-chair of the Horror Writers Association's Connecticut Chapter. Follow her adventures at kristipetersen-schoonover.com, or at www.facebook.com/kpschoonover

HENRY SNIDER: For over 25 years, Henry Snider has dedicated his time to helping others tighten their writing through critique groups, classes, lectures, prison prose programs, and high school fiction contests. He co-founded Fiction Foundry (est. 2012) and the award-winning Colorado Springs Fiction Writer's Group (1996-2013). Thirteen years to the month from founding the CSFWG, he retired from the presidency. After a much needed vacation, he returned to the literary world. While still reserving enough time to pursue his own fiction aspirations, he continues to be active in the writing community through classes, editing services, and advice. Henry lives in Colorado with his wife, fellow author and editor Hollie Snider, son – poet Josh Snider and numerous neurotic animals, including, of course, Fizzgig, the token black cat.

 **Joshua P. Sorensen:** Joshua P. Sorensen is from Orem, Utah (United States). He graduated with a Masters of Military History from Norwich University. His extensive travels inspire him to write poetry and short fiction. Drawn to horror writing, he particularly enjoys writing monster fiction. His other loves include history, nature, and all things geek. Joshua's current life goal is to bring delightful chills to all ages, particularly the young. His children's picture books are available online or at your favorite bookseller. He is a member of the HWA and LUW. He can be found on Facebook: #SorensenVagabondWriter and Amazon: amazon.com/author/joshuapsorensen

 **Paul Starkey:** Paul Starkey lives in Nottingham, England and has been writing for many years. He's been published multiple times, including by *Analog* and *Daily Science Fiction*. His novella *The Lazarus Conundrum* was published by Abaddon Books. He's also written for *2000AD* and *Big Finish*. He Tweets as @lunar_werewolf and blogs at werewolvesonthemoon.wordpress.com

SJ Townend: SJ Townend has been writing ~~evil lies~~ dark fiction in Bristol for three years. She's currently putting together a collection of horror stories, working title: *SICK GIRL SCREAMS*. SJ hopes her stories take the reader on a journey to often a dark place and only sometimes back again. Follow her on Twitter @SJTownend.

Heidi Voss: Heidi Voss once saved a fashion show by ripping a song from YouTube and formatting it for one of the designers. Since she has basic computer knowledge, she understands she'll be called upon for impromptu IT work no matter where she goes. If you have a fashion show in trouble, please reach out to Heidi on her website at www.authorheidivoss.com. You may also download a free short story while you're there. Follow her on Twitter @rarevoss and Instagram: @authorheidivoss.

Chad A. B. Wilson: Chad A. B. Wilson has been writing fantasy and horror stories since before he had a functioning memory. After finishing a Ph.D. in nineteenth-century British literature and postcolonial theory, he returned to science fiction, fantasy, and popular culture studies. By day, he teaches technical communications for engineers at a major Texas research university; by night, he scribbles away and pines for his own worlds. And he travels to west Texas every chance he gets. His work has been previously published in *HyphenPunk* and *Savage Realms Monthly* among other places, and will be published in the upcoming anthologies *Road Kill: Texas Horror by Texas Writers*, and *Dragons and Heroines*. Find him online at www. facebook.com/ChadABWilson.

WILLIAM R.D. WOOD: William R.D. Wood traces his love of science fiction and horror back to a childhood filled with Space: 1999 reruns, frequent visits to the *Night Gallery*, and a worn-out copy of *Dune*. A good writing day finds him at any of several overlooks on the Blue Ridge Parkway deeply immersed in new works of cosmic horror. Will lives with his wife, children and assorted ghosts in an old farmhouse turned backwards to the road.

If you enjoyed *Dead Stars and Stone Arches*, please consider leaving a review on Amazon or Goodreads. Reviews help the authors and the press.

If you go to www.timberghostpress.com you can sign up for our newsletter so you can stay up-to-date on all our upcoming titles, plus you'll get informed of new horror flash fiction and poetry featured on our site monthly.

Take care, and thanks for reading *Dead Stars and Stone Arches*.

—Timber Ghost Press